CHILDREN AWARD
jA
Hunt Ire

Hunt, Irene
Up a road slowly

W9-BCI-297

DISCARDED
Mead Public Library

9000532808

9000532808

DO NOT REMOVE CARD FROM POCKET

C

Children's Room OK

Mead Public Library
Sheboygan, Wisconsin

Each borrower is held responsible for all library
materials drawn on his card and for all fines
accruing on same.

INDEXED

DEMCO

Up
A Road Slowly

Up
A Road Slowly

IRENE HUNT

Cover painting by Don Bolognese

FOLLETT PUBLISHING COMPANY
Chicago

The lines from Edna St. Vincent Millay's poems
"Renascence" and "God's World" are from *Collected
Poems,* Harper & Row. Copyright 1912, 1913,
1940, 1948, by Edna St. Vincent Millay. Reprinted
by permission of Norma Millay Ellis. "I Shall Not
Care" is from *Collected Poems,* by Sara Teasdale,
Macmillan copyright © 1915; copyright renewed 1943
by Mamie Wheless. Used by permission of the publisher.

Copyright © 1966, by Irene Hunt. All rights reserved.
No portion of this book may be reproduced in any form
without written permission from the publisher. Man-
ufactured in the United States of America.

Library of Congress Card Number: 66-16937

ISBN 0-695-49009-5 Titan Binding
ISBN 0-695-89009-3 Trade Binding

15161718/8281807978

c. 3

532808

To Beulah, Shirley, and Freda

I

Three children stood outside our gate in the bright October sunlight, silent and still as figurines in a gift shop window, watching each step I took as I came slowly down the flagstone walk across the lawn. I was still weak from the same sickness that had stricken my mother, and it had been many days since I had played with any of the neighborhood children. There was a strong breeze that afternoon, and I remember how a brown oak leaf floated down and rested upon the red hair of the only boy in the group. It was funny; that shining leaf looked like a girl's hair-bow on a boy's head. For a few seconds I almost forgot the feeling of bewilderment and

7

desolation within me, and I wanted to laugh at the silly look of a boy with a huge, flat hair-bow on his red head. I didn't, though; I remembered quickly that it was not a day for laughter.

We stared at one another in the blank manner of young children confronted by uncertainty. As late as the hot, dry days of August we had played with one another, but now they saw me touched with a sorrow unknown to them, and I was suddenly a stranger. Their solemn faces reflected the warning of their mothers: "You must be very kind to Julie — very kind —"

The smallest of the three finally spoke. She was a child of five or so; she had a high, piping voice, and there was a look of determination about her as if she had suddenly decided to get at the bottom of a piece of mysterious gossip. "You're not going to live here anymore, are you?" It was actually more nearly a statement than a question. "We hear that you're going to live with your aunt in the country."

That is when I began to scream. I knew that there was something terribly wrong inside our house, but I hadn't known that something was about to drive me from my home. There had been many people in the house for the past two days; my aunt Cordelia was there, our own family doctor and another strange one, many neighbors, all of them with grave, white faces. "Adam hasn't said a word," I heard someone whisper. "He only sits and stares." That was Father they were talking about. There had been another whisper. "The doctor says that Julie is near hysteria; you must watch over your little sister carefully, Laura."

8

There was a stillness all through the house in spite of the activity. I had sat for a long time in Mother's little sewing room that afternoon, and had watched the wind whip great wrinkles in the white sheets that hung on the line. The wrinkles had come to look strange to me as I watched them; they grinned at me, malicious, hateful grins.

The child who had spoken to me was frightened. I hated her because I feared that what she said might be true, and so I screamed and would have struck her if I had been able to get beyond the gate. She grasped the hands of the two on either side of her and they scuttled away, frightened and outraged.

Then my brother, Christopher, who had followed me out to the gate called loudly for Laura, who was quickly beside me, speaking to me, lifting me in her arms. Laura was seventeen, beautiful, and my idol. It was she, rather than our frail mother or our father, a preoccupied and overworked professor, who was able to control a stubborn, somewhat overindulged little sister; many of my tantrums had been short-lived because of Laura. I would risk losing favor with almost anyone, but not with my sister.

She carried me up to her room overlooking the flower garden. The windows were open and the dry, bitter scents of autumn were in the air that stirred a curtain near the bed where Laura laid me. I vaguely wished that I could control the screaming that distressed Laura, but I was completely helpless.

The doctor came in after a while, I remember, and forced me to swallow a small pill with a little water. After that I went to sleep and while I slept, the prediction of little five-year-old-at-the-gate came true, for when I awoke the next morning, I was, indeed, at my aunt's house in the country, five miles out of the small college town where I had lived my first years. All the forebodings seemed to be coming true, and the bottom was surely falling out of my world.

Aunt Cordelia was not at home that morning, but a gentle, plump woman in blue gingham with a white apron tied at her waist was sitting beside the bed when I opened my eyes. I knew her slightly; she was Mrs. Peters, and I knew that she and her husband had for many years managed the farm which Aunt Cordelia and Uncle Haskell owned jointly. She was a kind woman, but in my anxiety, her mannerisms irritated me; she smiled too continuously, and she avoided the pronoun "I" as if it were taboo.

"Now Mrs. Peters has a good breakfast ready for our little girl. Let's get dressed nicely and when our Julie has had a bite to eat she can go outside and play with the children Mrs. Peters has asked up here for the day. That will be lots of fun, now won't it?"

"I don't want to play," I said stonily, "and I don't want to eat breakfast."

Mrs. Peters did not comment upon that, but she clucked a great deal and made vague little remarks as she helped me to dress. "Now, our little socks and shoes," she said, "and now our pretty petticoat."

The drug in the doctor's pill had left me limp and somewhat out of touch with reality. I felt unreasonably critical of Mrs. Peters, but too tired for any further pro-

10

tests. We walked together down the curving staircase to the living room, through the dining room and out to Aunt Cordelia's kitchen where, again, there were children facing me with wide solemn eyes, children who knew something I didn't quite know, or wouldn't quite admit.

The boy was Danny Trevort, and the girl was Carlotta Berry. I liked Danny better, even that morning, although I had little reason for it beyond the fact that he talked less than the little girl.

"You're coming to our school, aren't you?" she asked after a breathless little speech of welcome which I now realize was learned by rote. "My mama says you'll be in my class because you're seven same as me —"

Then the woman was back, clucking softly again. "Now, now," she said, "let's think about a game we can play after we have our breakfast. Couldn't we play hide-and-seek, Danny? Wouldn't that be a fine game?"

The boy nodded gravely. "Sure, if the new girl wants to play," he said.

"No," I answered, and turning my back to them, I walked out of the kitchen, silently daring them to follow me. I had a feeling that the three of them watched me, uncertain of what to do next.

Aunt Cordelia's house was familiar, but at that time still awesome and forbidding to me. It was a large old house, set well back from the road in a grove of oak and white pine and stately elm; its twelve rooms were spacious and airy, a delight in summer and a monumental heating problem in winter. There was a wide veranda across the front of the house with tall white columns and a half dozen steps leading to a brick paved walk which curved in and out among the trees until it reached the big gate at the road.

There were evidences of prosperous years and tight ones, pressed shoulder to shoulder throughout the house. There were wide marble-topped fireplaces in the library, living room, and dining room, even in some of the bed-rooms upstairs, but there was no central heating and in winter the beauty of the rooms downstairs was marred by great coal-burning stoves that too often belched black smoke when a damper was inadequately adjusted. There was a grand piano in the living room, an instrument bought with much sacrifice by my grandmother, who had fancied that her eldest son, my Uncle Haskell, was des-tined for the world of music. The great, gleaming piano deserved a Persian rug or at least a parquet floor beneath it; instead, it stood upon a rag carpet made on a country loom, as simple a bit of tapestry as might have been found in any country home in the years of Aunt Cordelia's youth. It was my aunt's grim, reality-facing answer to her mother's wastefulness.

The rooms upstairs held fear for me during my early childhood. Half of Aunt Cordelia's life had been spent in caring for her aged mother and two spinster aunts, and one of these latter, a tiny gray wisp of a woman, I had encountered once when I had wandered upstairs on a tour of exploration. I had opened a door tentatively in order to peek inside, when a woman turned in her chair and smiled toothlessly at me.

"Whose little girl are you?" she quavered, and I stood there for a few seconds, numb with fear and saying nothing. Then as I fled down the hall I heard a dreadful little cackle of laughter following me, and I nearly fell headlong as my feet raced down the stairs. It was a long time before the small gray presence was exorcised from the otherwise pleasant rooms of Aunt Cordelia's second floor.

Uncle Haskell lived in a renovated carriage house out back. There were a number of reasons why he preferred the privacy of his own establishment, one of which may have been the desire to save himself the distress of seeing his sister carry the load of responsibility which he had no intention of sharing. He liked drinking in private, too; it was easier to maintain the myth of a cultivated taste for an occasional glass of fine wine or some exotic beverage from a foreign port, since he did not relish the image of himself as a common drunkard. He once told my brother, Chris, and me that the bottles we found on the shelves of his kitchen held rare wines from the sunny vineyards of France, and we were impressed until Chris, who was able to read, pointed out that the labels bore the blunt English words, "Old Crow." Naturally, said Uncle Haskell. The French are a very obliging people. They placed the English translation of *Le Vieux Corbeau* on bottles destined for America.

He was a handsome man, this uncle who was both an alcoholic and a pathological liar. His face at fifty-five was unlined, and his skin instead of showing the ravages of alcohol, was youthfully fresh and clear. His blue eyes, large and heavily lashed, were full of innocent good humor, a kind of bland assurance that all the world loved him and believed in him. He had a thick growth of wavy,

13

golden hair which he wore rather longer than did the men who were our neighbors, and he kept it immaculate and shining at all times. He was slender and supple; when he walked it was as if he heard an inner music that delighted him down to his heels.

Uncle Haskell had had reason to be furious with Chris and me once in our very early years, and at that time he had borne himself with a magnaminity which somehow impressed me. We had found in Aunt Cordelia's basement a box containing twelve large bottles of a beautifully colored red-gold liquid bearing the English translation of *Le Vieux Corbeau,* although at that time we were too young to read it. The size and shape of the bottles had suggested bowling pins to me. Chris, to his credit, had said no to the game which I suggested, but after I had kicked a couple of bottles from an inverted washtub onto the concrete floor and we had waded in triumph through pools of richly fragrant liquid and had splashed one another lightly, he could not resist joining me in the demolition of another bottle. By the time we were apprehended, five of Uncle Haskell's bottles lay broken on the basement floor.

Mother had been appalled and chagrined. She apologized stiffly to Uncle Haskell, for she was torn between shame at the destructiveness of her children and a conviction that at least a sizable amount of her brother's whiskey was where it belonged.

Uncle Haskell, leaning gracefully in the doorway, turned a look of mingled pain and amusement upon the two culprits and then placed a comforting arm around Mother's shoulders.

14

"Don't fret your pretty head for another minute, little Ethel," he said, knowing well that Father would repay him for his loss. "No doubt we should feel a certain measure of gratitude at being able to contribute to the innocent pleasures of childhood." He patted her gently and then added, looking me full in the eye, "Next time, let's leash your brats, shall we?"

All that was long ago and far away from the October morning when I first came to live with Aunt Cordelia. The memories came back in little pieces as I walked through the large, high-ceilinged rooms, hurrying through them with only one purpose: to get away from Mrs. Peters and the two children. There was a place I remembered, the closet under the stairs that led from the attic to the second floor. Chris and I had played there once, half afraid, half fascinated by the dimly lighted cavern in which the ceiling followed the line of the descending stairs, becoming so low toward the back that even a young child had not room to sit upright. I found the entrance and hesitated; the place looked grim and forbidding, but for all that, it offered security to a small bewildered animal wanting to lick its wounds in solitude. I got down on my hands and knees and crawled as far back into the musty smelling shadows as my height would permit. There I rested against a pile of neatly packaged bedding, finding little comfort in loneliness, but preferring it to the company of the other children.

Mrs. Peters discovered me before long and she stood at the door, pleading, cajoling and finally threatening a little.

"Now, let's be a good girl, Julie; come out and let the

15

sun shine on you for a while. Mrs. Peters won't insist that you play if you don't want to — just come out and get a breath of good fresh air. This place will give our Julie a bad headache."

But I wouldn't budge, not even when she bribed me with chocolate cake. And when she finally started to crawl into the closet in order to pull me out by force, I screamed in such a way that she must have been frightened. Finally she placed some food at the entrance of the closet and left me for the rest of the morning and early afternoon.

I lay there in the darkness for hour after hour with no clear-cut understanding of what my sorrow was; there was a sense of helplessness as to what was going to happen to me, a sense of bewilderment, and the aching memory of yesterday's white faces, the whispers, and the little girl who said, "You're not going to live here anymore, are you?"

I must have slept at last and when I wakened there were voices outside my hiding place and shadows of long legs, sweeping dresses. After a while they moved away, and only two were left, two whom I recognized by their voices. They were Mrs. Peters and Aunt Cordelia.

"I tried half the morning, Cordelia," I heard Mrs. Peters saying earnestly, and it struck me that she did, after all, know how to use the word "I." "I coaxed and begged and once I started in to get her, but my lands, she screamed like a child gone daft. I tell you the truth, I was afraid she might go into a spasm. I hope you don't think I've done wrong."

Then Aunt Cordelia's voice, low and very calm. "No,

Cora, you did right. I am grateful to you for staying with her, very grateful." She paused and then got down on her knees preparatory to crawling back into the closet toward me. "I'll see to her. You can go fix coffee for the others if you will be so kind."

I was afraid of Aunt Cordelia Bishop, not that she had ever been unkind, but there was an aloofness about her that had always made her keep a considerable distance between us. Chris liked her, and he was obviously her favorite, a fact which didn't interest me especially, for with me Aunt Cordelia simply didn't count. I had once overheard Father telling someone that "Cordelia and the little one bristle at one another in almost exactly the same manner." Perhaps we did. I hadn't been aware of it, but on that October afternoon she was the last person in the world I wanted to see crawling toward me in the depths of the dark closet.

When she was near me she spoke the name by which she, alone, called me. I had been baptized "Julie," but Aunt Cordelia felt that certain feminine names ending in "ie" or "y" indicated a frivolity of which she disapproved. Thus, among her pupils, a small Elsie became "Elsa," and a Betty had to answer to a stern "Elizabeth." She had told Mother that "Julie" was simply a sloppy pronunciation of that fine old Roman name which their paternal grandmother had borne. And so Aunt Cordelia called me "Julia."

"Yes, Aunt Cordelia," I answered, just a little above a whisper. Mother had seen to it that I was always polite to Aunt Cordelia whether I liked her or not.

She came a little nearer to me, and leaning forward,

17

put her arms around me and drew me to her lap. My head was against her cheek, and when I sobbed, I could feel the trembling of Aunt Cordelia's body, and I knew that her face was wet with tears as mine was.

That was the one time I have ever known her to cry, and it was the first time I remember her holding me in her arms. We sat in the dark closet together for a long time; then when there were no more tears left, we crawled out and began our decade together.

2

To be suddenly catapulted into a new way of life at seven is very hard. I envied Laura; she, at least, had our old home, her own rose and cream-colored room, the closets full of Mother's dresses. She had Father, too, and the good smell of his cigar in his study; she ate her meals in the same old dining room with him, went to school with the young people she had always known. I thought that life was much kinder to Laura than to Christopher and me.

What I didn't realize was that at seventeen, Laura did not have the adaptability, the readiness to forget, that Christopher and I had at seven and nine. We thought of

19

Mother often in the early days of our new life; sometimes we cried when we were homesick for times that were gone, for the old sense of security within our family. But the days slipped by and the memory of Mother grew fainter, the rooms of the old house that had once been awesome and fearful became familiar and pleasant; school had its compensations, Uncle Haskell was a huge joke, and Aunt Cordelia was a challenge.

Aunt Cordelia was our teacher as well as our guardian. At the small white schoolhouse where she had taught since she was a young girl, she was *only* our teacher; she gave no sign of knowing us any better than the other children. We called her "Miss Cordelia" as the others did, and when she stood behind her desk, slender and erect in her plain tailored suit with her rich brown and gray hair coiled in braids about her head, we looked at her with the proper respect she expected of us. She demanded obedience, but she was not a grim teacher; if we read a gay story that brought laughter to us, we could count on Aunt Cordelia's appreciation too. She read aloud to us on Friday afternoons, and she read beautifully; I came very close to loving Aunt Cordelia during those long afternoons when I rested my arms upon the desk in front of me and became acquainted with Jim Hawkins and Huck Finn, with little David and Goliath, with Robinson Crusoe on his island, and with the foolish gods and their kinfolk somewhere above the clouds on Mount Olympus. She could be very stern about some misdemeanor in the classroom, but when her point had been made, she seemed to forget the matter entirely and became a pleasant, forgiving friend. Sometimes it was a gambling matter to predict Aunt Cordelia's reactions.

Ordinarily, Chris and I walked the mile and a half to school with our aunt, shoulders pushed well back, every breath employing the use of our diaphragms, our minds fixed, at Aunt Cordelia's suggestion, on the beauty of Nature and the glory of the firmament. On especially inclement mornings, Aunt Cordelia would drive her precious car, which was almost as shining and beautiful as it had been ten years earlier. We loved driving to school in style, but our pleasure soon became dimmed a little by the fact that we knew we must spend an hour or so that evening in washing and polishing the car before it was put away for Sunday and holiday driving.

Aunt Cordelia didn't really have to teach for a livelihood; the income from the farm was sufficient for her needs, and the modest salary she received for each month of the school year was not the incentive which brought her back to her desk year after year. Her reason for teaching was actually the belief that no one else would do the work quite so well, would understand the backgrounds of these children whose parents she had taught when she was young. There was never a doubt in Aunt Cordelia's mind but that *her* teaching was the best to be had, and she would have felt that she was denying something beyond price to the handful of country children who sat in her classroom, if she allowed a younger or a less dedicated woman to take over.

And so she went back year after year, teaching from nine until four o'clock, then sweeping and dusting the

21

room after school, carrying in great buckets of coal to bank the fire for the night, arriving at school an hour early on Monday mornings during the winter months in order to get the fire started and the room warm before the children arrived.

Twice a year, in the fall and again in spring, we got a half holiday during which time we helped Aunt Cordelia wash and polish the windows, scrub the floor, wash and wax the desks. By the time Danny Trevort and Chris were ten, they had, of their own accord, taken over the task of carrying in the coal of an evening. Often the three of us stayed after school and did the sweeping and dusting for her, I with a big apron protecting my school dress and one of Aunt Cordelia's round dust caps protecting my hair. She never failed to thank us for our help, and now and then, as a special treat, Danny would be asked to spend the evening with us and there would be a wiener roast or a fried chicken dinner in payment for our janitorial service.

Aunt Cordelia did pretty well at treating all her pupils with the same impersonal detachment, but sometimes she was hard put to hide a particular warmth which she felt toward both Danny Trevort and my brother, Chris. They were both rosy, smooth-cheeked little boys, mischievous at times, but frank and honest, sharing a respect for Aunt Cordelia which I did not always feel. Sometimes at night, when Chris was bent over his homework, Aunt Cordelia would let her hand rest for a second on his head and when he looked up, they would smile at one another. I felt very alone and lost when they did that; sometimes I felt very angry too. As for Danny,

he was the one child in school whom Aunt Cordelia ad-
dressed by his diminutive name. It is true that he had
been baptized "Daniel," and Aunt Cordelia had as little
patience with pet names as she had for most feminine
names ending in "ie" or "y"; still, for some unaccountable
reason she broke with her principles in his case: he was
always "Danny" Trevort.

Most of us carried our lunches in tin pails. Carlotta
Berry had a basket with daisies painted all over the lid,
which set her apart socially. We ate out under the trees
when it was at all possible; in all the years I never
became quite reconciled to eating inside with the smell
of dust and winter garments and many kinds of food.

The problem of eating lunch with Aggie Kilpin was
one of sharp annoyance to me for a long time, but by the
end of my first year in the new school, I had found the
solution.

Aggie was a mistreated, undernourished and retarded
girl, the youngest child of a shiftless, vicious father and
a mother who had been beaten down by the cruelties of
her life. Aggie must have been ten or eleven the first
winter that I knew her and even then, she hardly recognized a dozen words in the primer from which Aunt
Cordelia tried to teach her. She would stand beside my
aunt's desk floundering through a page that the youngest
child in the room could have read with ease, and after
each mistake, looking around the room to grin and smirk
as if her failures were evidences of some bit of clever-
ness on her part. It was dreadful to watch her; I averted
my eyes from Aggie whenever possible.

But it was not Aggie's retardedness that made her a

23

pariah among us; it was the fact that she stank to high Heaven. Aunt Cordelia had pled with the girl for years to treat herself to an occasional tub of soapy water, to shampoo her hair, to wash just once in a while the shabby dress which she wore every day of the year. Aggie would grimace and mouth some half-intelligible garble, but she never lost any of her over-ripe fragrance. Aunt Cordelia stopped trying to do anything about it after a while; as a matter of fact, she thought it quite possible that Aggie's family might have turned upon her if the girl had shown any disposition to be different.

I loathed poor Aggie, who seemed to have a perfect gift for making herself repulsive. She stood at the blackboard one day, I remember, and before the entire school used a word that all of us had been brought up to consider dirty. It was a slip of the tongue with poor Aggie, but I was shocked. Some of the big boys laughed. Danny didn't, and neither did my brother; they sat side by side studying the pages of their geography with frowning intensity and very red faces. None of the girls laughed except Carlotta, who didn't want to, but became hysterical and had to go outside to the pump and wash her face until she got hold of herself.

Then Aunt Cordelia demanded "Silence," whereupon silence descended upon the room. Everybody was ashamed except Aggie; she was not accustomed to being the center of attention, and she threw sly glances at the boys who had laughed, preening herself a little at the success of something she had done, a something of which she was completely unconscious.

I used this incident to convince Aunt Cordelia that

Aggie was no proper companion for the rest of us, who were considerably younger, that we had every right to shun her company. But Aunt Cordelia was not convinced. She saw to it that Aggie was included in all of our games, and what was hardest for us to bear, that Aggie was invited to join our little circle at lunchtime. Sometimes we would try sneaking away hurriedly at noon; inevitably we would hear a stern, "Julia — Elsa — Carlotta, I believe that you girls have forgotten to invite Agnes to go with you."

And so we would have to ask her, and Aggie would come galloping eagerly, usually to *my* side because I was Aunt Cordelia's niece, and she seemed to know that I was under special pressure to be a decently behaving classmate. She called me "kid," and she would throw her arm around my neck until I learned to dodge. Then when we were seated under the trees she would take out unappetizing-looking food which usually smelled strongly of onion, and would eat noisily, laughing at everything that was said and inching nearer to my side each time I inched away from hers.

Finally I organized a seating arrangement and did not hesitate to use my prestige as Aunt Cordelia's niece in enforcing the rules.

"We will sit in a big circle," I explained, "and the Queen will sit in the middle. Aggie is the oldest so she gets to be the Queen. The rest of us are subjects, and we are not allowed to look at the Queen while she eats, so of course, we will have to sit with our backs to her. Do you know, Aggie, that you could have us beheaded if we dared to look at you while you were eating?"

Aggie *didn't* know, and she didn't much enjoy her royal role after the first day or two. She wanted Lottie or Elsie to be the Queen — *not* Julie, because she wanted to be a peasant at Julie's side. But we were adamant. "You are the oldest, Aggie. It wouldn't be right for one of us to be the Queen." And again, "Shame on you, Aggie; you ought to be proud that we are letting you be our Queen."

The circle of peasants grew wider and wider as the days went by until our poor unlovely Queen sat in splendid isolation where she could not offend her subjects.

Aunt Cordelia discovered our game one day. We explained it to her with the same wide-eyed innocence that we had feigned when we explained it to Aggie. For a minute I was unsure; I thought I saw a storm approaching. But Aunt Cordelia was silent. She stood looking at us for a little while and, although I was pretty young, I detected amusement, sadness, and a kind of baffled uncertainty in her look. Finally she turned away without saying anything.

In the months before Danny and Chris and I were old enough to help Aunt Cordelia with her janitorial work, the three of us walked with Carlotta, Elsie Devers, and Jimmy Ferris down the road from school each evening. We ranged in age from seven to ten; Elsie and Jimmy were the two oldest and a little superior in their attitude because they knew about the intricacies of decimal fractions; Lottie was the prettiest, Chris was the tallest, I was the youngest and toughest, and Danny was the sweetest. I loved Danny secretly, or thought I did, but for all my love I didn't hesitate to hurt him one evening, an act that hurt *me* to remember for many years.

It started with Jimmy betting a million that Danny wouldn't dare kiss me, and Danny betting a million that he would, too, dare, all of which led to Chris and Jimmy pinning my arms behind me and Danny giving me a triumphant if unenthusiastic kiss. I was furious at all three of them, not so much because of the kiss as at the indignity of being thus kissed. It was Danny, however, who, as soon as my arms were loosed, got the impact of a small hard fist that I had learned to use effectively as Chris could have testified. Danny's eye was swollen shut and rimmed with green and purple by the time we reached the big house in the grove and found Aunt Cordelia in her kitchen.

She bathed the eye of her favorite in cold water and held a silver spoon against the swollen flesh while she listened to the story of what happened. She said nothing at first, but after a while she quietly gave us her private opinion that a small boy's kiss was hardly in as poor taste as a small girl's physical violence. That, at least, was the gist of her remarks; after that she ignored me and asked Chris to go the rest of the way home with Danny and to apologize for his sister's behavior.

I slunk out to the surrounding woods, disgraced, heavyhearted and resentful. Public opinion was against me as I could see by the prim looks which Carlotta and Elsie bent upon me. I had hurt someone who was gentle and good, someone I loved, and that brought a heaviness to my throat. Aunt Cordelia, however, had blamed me and not any of the three boys; I resented that so much that it almost overcame my remorse.

There was a cluster of slender birches just beyond a thicket of blackberry vines, four silver-barked trees arranged in a rough semicircle with intertwining branches forming a leafy roof. I called this cluster of trees my cathedral, and I came there often when life's problems became particularly heavy. It was in this retreat that I found shelter on that spring evening after I punched Danny.

I knelt in what would have been true penitence if Aunt Cordelia's rebuff had not kindled so much rage, and I gave the Divine Presence all the details. I asked Him to consider the fact that three boys, all bigger than I was, were the ones who had started the trouble, and that a lady who pretended to be so dedicated to fair play had behaved in a way that no one, certainly not He, could call fair.

"Why is it," I demanded, "that Thou lettest these things always happen to *me*? Why dost Thou always let me be the one to get into trouble? I'd hate to think that Thou wert as unfair as Aunt Cordelia but it begins to look as if —"

I heard a slight stirring then, from behind one of the trees, and opening my eyes, saw Uncle Haskell, golf bag over his shoulder, leaning nonchalantly against one of the trees, laughter spread all over his face.

"You're snooping," I told him angrily. "I was trying to pray, and you have no right to snoop when someone is praying."

"I am *not* snooping, my darling niece, nor do I have the slightest interest in your prayers." He laid the golf

28

bag aside and sat down in front of me. "As a matter of fact, however, you weren't actually praying, you know. You were giving Jehovah a penny lecture."

I felt too depressed for an argument. When he asked me what the trouble was, I went through the story once again. "Aunt Cordelia isn't fair," I said finally. "She likes boys better than girls; it's as plain as anything. She likes Chris and Danny and even Jimmy Ferris better than she likes me."

Uncle Haskell laughed lightly. "The very trait she most resented in Mama. Ah, Cordelia!"

"You mean that my grandmother liked you better than Aunt Cordelia?"

"Naturally! I was male, beautiful, and brilliant; Cordelia was female, only so-so as to looks, bright enough, but certainly not scintillating."

"What about my mother?"

"Oh, Ethel was a rather charming child, but by the time she came along, Mama was so wrapped up in me that she was happy to leave Ethel's upbringing to Cordelia."

I sat for a time, tongue-tied with resentment. When I was finally able to speak at all, my protest was, even to my own ears, weak and inane.

"And do you really think that was right?" I asked, trying to put my anger into each syllable.

"My dear child, I couldn't care less as to whether it was right or not. All that concerns me is that I got the best of the bargain." He looked out at the shadowy woods, his clear blue eyes shining with what appeared to be perfect content. Then his brows suddenly shot up in sharp V-shapes. "Or did I?" he asked, still smiling, but somewhat more subdued. "I suppose that's debatable. Well, you'll have to ask your Aunt Cordelia. Or your father, the impeccable Adam."

"What do you mean — 'impeccable'?" I demanded, getting ready to defend Father.

"Without defect. Faultless. Don't worry; Adam is so charmed by middle class values that he will accept 'impeccable' as a proper tribute. At least, I think so. And if he doesn't —" Uncle Haskell spread his beautiful, well-kept hands before him and took time to admire for a second the shining ovals of his nails. "It's strange," he added after a little, "that both of my sisters should have fallen in love with high-minded, irreproachable gentlemen, so different from their brother — and so immeasurably more pedestrian."

"Did Aunt Cordelia actually fall in love at one time?" I asked incredulously.

"My dear child, do you mean that a generation is growing up without having heard of Jonathan Eltwing? Certainly, your Aunt Cordelia fell in love — I am not sure that she has ever pulled herself out of it."

Jonathan Eltwing held no interest for me, nor did Aunt Cordelia's love life; however, new words held a fascination for me, and I was drawn to the word "impeccable." It had a good sound; moreover it meant without defect. Well, good. I did a quick bit of generalization based upon what I had heard of Uncle Haskell's heavy drinking and the ultimate ravages it was bound to bring to his system.

"Is your liver impeccable?" I asked pointedly.

30

Another man with his weakness might have been angered, but not Uncle Haskell. His laughter rang through the woods.

"My liver is in an enviable state of health and well-being, dear niece," he chortled. "Much to the consternation of all the prophets, my general health, including the condition of my liver is — yes, impeccable."

I felt that I had, perhaps, been a little rude. "I'm glad," I told him politely. "I hoped that your liver was impeccable."

"I'll just bet you did." He looked at me good-humoredly. "You evidently weren't as solicitous about young Trevort's health an hour ago as you are about mine. Are you quite sure that you didn't knock some teeth out?"

"I don't think so. Just his eye. Not out, but I made it black."

Uncle Haskell shook his head. "What Mama would have done to any brat who might have messed me up like that." He smiled to himself. "Dear Mama," he said, "dear, dear Mama."

I got the impression that he wasn't nearly as fond of Grandmother as the many "dears" might have indicated.

"If I ever have a boy, I'm going to see that he gets the blame for the things he does just as much as the girls do," I said.

"You're never going to get the chance to have a boy if you don't do something about that truculent little chin of yours." He got to his feet, hoisted the golf bag to his shoulder, and stooped to tweak my nose. "Accept the fact that this is a man's world and learn how to play the game gracefully, my sweet."

31

I watched him as he strode off with his characteristically buoyant step into the shadows. It occurred to me that there was no golf course within five miles, and that if there were, it would be too dark at that hour for a game; moreover, I suddenly realized that there were no clubs in the brown bag over Uncle Haskell's shoulder.

When I went back to the house at twilight, Aunt Cordelia looked at me thoughtfully, and her voice was kinder than it had been when she passed judgment on me earlier.

"The boys certainly have their share of blame for this unfortunate episode, Julia," she said. "I feel that I erred when I placed all the blame on you this afternoon."

My heart warmed to her in a sudden rush of love. I wondered if she had remembered how her mother always favored Uncle Haskell; I had a feeling that she would not have wanted to be like her mother if she could help it. Whatever it was, she had made me happy.

"That's all right, Aunt Cordelia," I said, smiling at her. "I forgive you."

3

Christopher and I discovered the secret of Uncle Haskell's nocturnal golfing before the summer was over. About once a month we would see him step buoyantly into the shadowy woods some fine evening, often with a beret set jauntily upon his head, a golf bag without visible clubs slung over his shoulder.

One night we trailed him with what we thought was perfect stealth, keeping clumps of trees and underbrush between us and him, moving slow step by step until the three of us were at the banks of a creek that flowed between the woods and one of the wide fields that Mr. Peters cultivated for our aunt and uncle.

Down at the creek, Uncle Haskell crossed the bridge to the south bank, where the growth of underbrush was heavier, and removed a spade from his golf bag. My heart flopped in sudden terror. A grave, I thought; Uncle Haskell was a monster who dug graves in the moist soil under the bushes, and buried, Heaven knew what, in the grim depths. Chris took my hand, and I could see the same horror in his face that must have been in mine.

I don't know whether it was our gasps that betrayed us or whether Uncle Haskell had been playing a cat-and-mouse game all along; at any rate when he removed the spade, he stuck it in the ground, leaned upon it a moment, and then chuckled as at some private joke.

"Scat, you little devils," he said pleasantly enough, and we did not wait for further words. We ran breathlessly back through the woods and spent the rest of the evening speculating.

When Uncle Haskell drove into town the next day, presumably for a replenishment of *Le Vieux Corbeau*, we took advantage of his absence to do some further sleuthing.

We got Danny to join us that afternoon, and the three of us raced down to the creek to find what Uncle Haskell had been up to. It didn't take long. The "graves" were quite shallow — Uncle Haskell would not be one to expend a great deal of energy in digging — and we were not long in unearthing what he had buried: empty bottles of *Le Vieux Corbeau*.

It didn't seem sad to us that day. The boys lay on the ground kicking their heels and shrieking, and I joined them, kicking almost as high and shrieking quite as lustily.

34

During the months of vacation Aunt Cordelia, somewhat against her principles, allowed me to wear my brother's outgrown blue jeans in order to save wear and tear upon my school dresses. I loved that. There was a freedom in blue jeans that delighted me and brought me into closer relationship with Chris and Danny. Now I could straddle a horse with the same ease that the boys did when we rode over the country roads together. The three of us climbed trees and ran races and helped Mr. Peters cut weeds out of the corn. Mr. Peters called us his "three boys," and I couldn't understand how any girl would want a frilly dress when the joy of blue jeans was available. And so that afternoon when we discovered Uncle Haskell's secret, I was able to kick and roll in the grass with the same abandon enjoyed by Chris and Danny.

But Chris didn't approve of my behavior. He had always felt a certain responsibility toward me, and on that afternoon he suddenly stopped laughing and looked at me sternly.

"You oughtn't to roll on the grass and kick like a boy, Julie; Laura wouldn't like for you to act like that."

"Oh, slurp, slurp," I answered airily, but I sat up all the same, partly because of the reference to Laura, partly because I had a feeling that Danny agreed with my brother.

But I had Chris to look after me for only a few weeks longer that summer. We had told Father about Uncle Haskell's cemetery of empty bottles, and I think that our obvious delight in our find set Father to thinking about the advisability of sending Chris away to boarding school. Aunt Cordelia reluctantly seconded the proposal, agreeing with Father that Uncle Haskell was hardly the proper father-figure for a growing boy. And so Chris had to leave for boarding school that fall and both of us were desolate for many weeks. I begged Father to take me home with him after Chris left, but Aunt Cordelia intervened. I was too young, she told Father, too undisciplined to be on my own in town where both Father and Laura were away from home most of the day. I overheard her use the words "strong-willed" and "adventurous" in talking about me. She persuaded Father that I should remain with her until I was ready for high school.

Once again, both Chris and I were manipulated like small puppets in our world of adults. We didn't like it, and we suffered, but the tall ones around us said that we would soon get over our sadness, that we would "adapt" in a matter of weeks.

Poor Chris had only strangers around him, which made his life hard that autumn; I still had Danny and the big horse, Peter the Great, that I claimed as my own. I still had the woods with my cathedral hidden in them and I had Aunt Cordelia, who in her reserved way, was especially kind to me during the days of my sharpest loneliness. And strangely enough, I found that I had a source of comfort in Uncle Haskell. He came up to the house to eat with us a bit oftener that fall, and Aunt Cordelia, true to her mother's upbringing, made these meals very special ones with the best silver and Grandmother's china laid out upon the table. Uncle Haskell was always a gracious guest, gay and serene in his belief that he was doing us an honor in dining with us, but an honor which he was bestowing cheerfully.

There were times when it was good to escape from the quiet austerity of Aunt Cordelia to the gay, never-never land of Uncle Haskell. I was always welcomed to his neat, well-kept living room with its many wall shelves filled about equally with books and bottles. In spite of the fact that I knew the truth wasn't in him, I gave myself up to the delight of listening to accounts of the mythical years when he had roamed the capitals of Europe, loved and courted by the intelligentsia for his wit, for the books he had written (unfortunately all out of print by my day), for his never-failing charm and erudition. He had been quite a man, had Uncle Haskell, and he was about to emerge into a second blooming when his new book appeared, his magnum opus which was carefully kept out of sight in his rooms. It seemed strange, I thought, that I never happened to call on Uncle Haskell when there was a sheet of paper in his typewriter, but I wouldn't have considered it polite to mention the matter. I heard about long distance telephone calls from his publishers, patient gentlemen it seemed, who urged him to take his time; a magnum opus, they agreed, does not spring into being overnight.

For all my quite justifiable suspicions of his integrity, I liked Uncle Haskell, and he recognized that fact.

"It is no credit either to your discrimination or to your character, my dear child," he told me lightly. "Adam and your sister will have you carted off to a nunnery if you're not very careful to disown me."

It was true that neither Father nor Laura cared for Uncle Haskell. They came out quite often to see me or to take me into town for a holiday in my old home, but on such occasions they did not go back to Uncle Haskell's quarters at all, or if they chanced to meet him, they were pointedly cool. Father was fond of Aunt Cordelia and felt that she had suffered unduly at the hands of an egotistical parasite; Laura mirrored Father's feelings as she had all the years of her life.

How I loved Laura! It was a time of perfect happiness when she came out for the weekend, when we rode together or hiked or swam or skated; most particularly was it perfect for me when we slept together in my room upstairs that had been Mother's when she was a child.

It was Laura who helped me to rid myself of the memory of the gray old woman and the cackling laugh that had frightened me in one of those rooms upstairs; it was also Laura who pointed out the beauty of the changing scene outside my bedroom window, the green and gold and crimson of the woods from spring through autumn, the soft white stillness of winter with the trunks of half a hundred trees standing in penciled darkness against a pale sky.

I would lie close to her, and she would tell me stories or repeat poetry until I went to sleep with the heavenly security of being with someone who was almost Mother.

"You really love me, don't you, Laura?" I asked her.

"I do, indeed, Julie. Very much."

"And we'll always be like this together. You'll never change, will you?"

"Never, Julie," she promised, a little rashly, for she was still quite young.

She did change though. Not much. She still loved me after she was wearing Bill Strohmer's ring, but her eyes were full of dreams, and sometimes she would say, "Let's not talk now, Julie; let's just lie quietly and think for a while."

There was a little change in Laura, but it was still not great enough to alarm me. Sometimes when her eyes were closed, I would prop myself on my elbow to look at the thick lashes against her cheek, at the waves of bright hair that fell back from her forehead. I loved beauty, and I ached with the consciousness that I would never have the blonde beauty of my sister. I was dark, more like Father, or as some people said, like my mother's dour, dark father who had married a golden flibbertigibbit.

Laura and Bill were married the summer I was ten. Chris was home for the wedding, very straight and tall; both he and I were in the wedding party and so excited over the swarm of activities that I had no time to brood over the fact that life was again making a big change for me.

Uncle Haskell sent Laura a silver coffee server which was charged to Aunt Cordelia's account at one of the local stores, but he was not able to attend the wedding. He sent her a note explaining that a deadline set by one of his publishers prevented his being with his beloved niece on the day of her great happiness. Laura was not crushed.

One very special guest at the wedding was Alicia Allison, one of Laura's high school teachers, of whom she was very fond. Miss Allison was a very attractive woman, I thought, crisp and slender in her coral linen dress, very youthful looking in spite of her thirty-eight or forty years and the few lines of glistening white in her dark hair. Father was especially attentive to Miss Allison, I noticed;

he smiled at me when I very carefully served her wedding cake and hurried away to bring her fresh coffee.

I liked Miss Allison, and I thought her name was lovely. I was beginning to write stories in the privacy of my room at that time, and for the next several weeks after Laura's wedding my heroines, most of them characters who bloomed on paper for several pages and then faded suddenly, were named "Alicia."

I had a nice note from Laura when she was on her honeymoon and a line or two from Bill at the bottom of the sheet. They wanted me to visit them in their new home, but not for a while, not until all the new curtains were hung and all the new furniture was in place. When all that was done, the three of us would have a wonderful time together. They were both looking forward to it. Eagerly.

It was a year, however, before I got to visit them. I missed Laura sharply for a long time, and my daydreams were all centered around her, how happy she would be to see me, how we would lie in bed and talk until dawn, how she would perhaps say that I should come to live with her and Bill instead of staying with Aunt Cordelia until I was ready for high school. Bill, I had rather forgotten. He was a pleasant young man, friendly and kind, but of no particular consequence so far as I was concerned. I had something of Uncle Haskell's way of dismissing all persons for whom I felt no personal need.

Then during the summer of my eleventh year the three-hundred-mile train ride was behind me, and Bill was there at the station ready to drive me to their home and Laura.

She was so terribly changed; she didn't look like my Laura at all, and for a minute I was dismayed. I had known that she was going to have a baby; Father had told me that, but I was not prepared to see her swollen grotesquely, her bright hair a little dulled, all the fresh radiance changed to a kind of pallid weariness. But I was reassured when she kissed me and joined Bill in laughing at my look of disbelief.

"Don't be shocked, darling; babies do this to their mamas, you know. Two months from now when you're Aunt Julie, you'll have a slender sister again — at least, I hope so," she added with a wry smile at Bill.

"You'll be svelte and the most elegant young mother in town," Bill assured her. "Won't she, Julie?" he added, smiling at me.

Then I kissed her again and followed them around as they showed me all the details of their pretty cottage, told me of the picnic they had planned for the next day, spoke of some girls they had invited over to entertain me on the days when Laura would be busy with some work she was doing for Bill. He was completing his doctorate that summer, and Laura was typing his thesis as well as doing some spots of last minute research and an occasional bit of rewriting. They were both deeply involved in his work, very close and happy, very much like two people welded into a single unit. I didn't quite like it; I felt a nameless fear beginning to grow inside me.

My fear did not become a reality, however, until about ten that evening when Bill ruffled my hair and said, "Well, Laura, hadn't we better let Aunt Julie get her beauty sleep now? She must be a little tired after her long train ride." And Laura said, "Yes, darling, come along. I'll show you the room you're to have."

She would show me the room *I* was to have, not the one *we* would share. There was a single bed in that room with a blue dust ruffle around it and a lacy white spread on top. It was a very pretty room and a pretty bed, but it was not a room to be shared by two sisters, not a bed where they could lie close together, where they could talk girl-talk until their eyes grew heavy and they drifted off to sleep, almost as secure as in the days when a mother had been alive.

Laura wouldn't look at me. I tried to force her to look into my eyes. If she would do that, I knew she would see there my agony and she would say, "Yes, Julie, I'm going to stay here with you. That Bill doesn't much matter." But she wouldn't look at me; she kept chattering about the paper they had picked out with me in mind, about how I could sleep as long as I pleased the next morning, and would I like for her to make blueberry muffins for our breakfast. But she wouldn't look at me, and when she kissed me good-night, there was still the pretense that she didn't know I was sick with disappointment.

I cried on the white pillow that night and, switching on the bedside lamp, I was impressed by the sad stain my tears had made. Then I thought how Laura would never notice and would send the slip out to some laundry and impersonal hands would wash away the marks of grief, never knowing, never caring that part of a little girl had died with those tears. Then I cried again at that thought, and I felt the great loneliness I had felt that day of Mother's funeral. But this time my loneliness was mixed with resentment and an unreasoning jealousy.

Things were better the next morning. Both Laura and Bill were very gay and obviously determined to see that I was happy. We ate in the sunny kitchen from the gay breakfast service that Alicia Allison had given Laura for a wedding gift, and breakfast was delicious: fruit and muffins, bacon, strawberry preserves, and coffee blended with hot milk. Bill teased me a little, wondering if I had blacked any more little boys' eyes for the reason that I had blacked Danny's; Laura thought that my new blue robe was very becoming, and she and Bill agreed over my head that I was really growing up to be a very pretty girl. Everything was delightful and it should have remained that way except that the dark streak within me refused to be propitiated.

When Bill had gone off to the university and Laura and I had finished the dishes, she gave me a new book, bought especially for me, and suggested that I read while she looked up some references that Bill needed for his thesis. It was then that I wondered, not in so many words, but quite pointedly, if Bill had not sufficient academic aptitude to do his own research.

That brought the first flare to my sister's eyes and she assured me of Bill's brilliance and of her own gratitude that she was able in a small way to help him in an effort that meant so much to both of them. She said something about the fact that Father had considered Bill the ablest student he had known in years, and seeing that she was angry already, I dug my claws in deeper and told her that Uncle Haskell said that Father was a man of "middle class values."

Then she really did throw out sparks. "You tell Uncle Haskell," she said angrily, "that if by 'middle class values' he means a sense of integrity, a willingness to contribute to society rather than to be a leech, then Father is, indeed, a man of 'middle class values.' Uncle Haskell should talk of values — if he has any at all, they are of the shoddiest sort. I think it's high time," she added furiously, "that Father marries Alicia and gets you away from Uncle Haskell's influence."

It had never occurred to me that there was a remote possibility of Father's marrying Alicia. Father was married to Mother and that was the way things were and should always be, world without end, and I thought that Laura should be heartily ashamed of herself for the remark she had just made.

"If Father marries Alicia — if Father marries any woman in this world, I'll never go home again; never, as long as I live. I should think that you would love Mother enough to feel that way too," I added accusingly.

If I had known how tired and unwell Laura was feeling at that time, I surely would have been kinder. But I had no interest in anyone's feelings save my own, and for the first time, I deliberately tried to hurt the feelings of the person I loved above all others.

Laura grew almost hysterical with tears and anger as she defended her own love for Mother and her wish to see Father with a companion of whom Mother would have approved. "I don't know what has happened to you, Julie," she sobbed, wiping her eyes. "You have always been such a darling child. What has got into you?"

I was miserable by that time, ashamed and sorry. "I don't know," I wailed, "unless it's because I'm standing where the brook and river meet."

Then Laura said, "Oh, good Heavens," in a tone that suggested I had said something completely idiotic, and she laughed at the same time she was crying in such a way that I was at first deeply offended and then frightened. It was an unhappy morning.

We smoothed each other's feelings, of course, and the visit was not quite spoiled. But it was a disappointment, a dreary, heartbreaking disappointment, and when we kissed one another good-bye the morning I left, we were both heavy with the certainty that we had lost something precious.

Bill took me to the station that morning, a very grave young man and unusually kind. He explained that if Laura had seemed a little sharp, a little unlike herself, it was because she was not well, that she was nervous and perhaps a little anxious in her first pregnancy. He told me that she loved me very much, that she was going to name the baby "Julie" if it was a girl, that the three of us would back Aunt Cordelia into a corner and persuade her that the French "Julie" was quite as legal as the Roman "Julia." There wasn't a word about my share of the blame for which I had no excuse except a childish jealousy. My sense of guilt was very deep when I boarded the train for my journey home.

I sat beside a window on the green mohair seat and stared out at the countryside, all but lost in a gray mist of rain. I thought of Laura having a baby, and I wondered if it hurt dreadfully and considered the possibility that she might die. And how, I thought, could I live the rest of my life remembering how she had tried to make me happy in all the little ways she could, and how I had repaid her with snide and cruel remarks that had possibly destroyed all the love she had felt for me. Finally I covered my face with my hands and shook with the misery pent up inside me.

A gray-haired, blue-uniformed conductor had looked at me kindly when he took my ticket, and after a while he came back, bringing me a chocolate bar bulging with almonds. He sat down in the seat beside me when I thanked him tearfully, and he patted my shoulder.

"Maybe it would help to talk about it," he said gently. "I've raised five little girls to womanhood; like as not I'll be able to understand."

To my surprise, I told him all about it, this stranger whom I would probably never see again. I had to tell someone, and I knew that it would shame me terribly to tell either Father or Aunt Cordelia. And so I talked and talked, sometimes between sobs, and although it didn't bring me peace of mind, it somehow helped for me to put my guilt feelings into words.

The conductor nodded often during my story and when I was through, he was silent for a long time. He pursed his lips thoughtfully and tapped the fingers of his left hand against the arm of the seat.

Finally he spoke, almost as if to himself. "It happens the world over — we love ourselves more than we do the one we say we love. We all want to be Number One; we've got to be Number One or nothing! We can't see that we could make ourselves loved and needed in the Number Two, or Three, or Four spot. No sir, we've got to be Number One, and if we can't make it, we'll rip and tear at the loved one till we've ruined every smidgin of love that was ever there." He sighed. "I don't know what to tell you, little lady."

He had to leave me then to go about his duties, and he didn't return to my seat until it was almost time for the train to pull into the station where Father would be waiting for me. Then he leaned down and spoke to me almost in a whisper. "I believe that, was I you, I'd try growing up a little and giving some thought about what I could do for my big sister from the Number Three or Four spot."

The last days of that summer were troubled ones for me. I wondered if I had ripped and torn at Laura as the conductor had said people did, the world over, if I had destroyed all her love for me because of my anger at being somewhere other than in the "Number One Spot." I recalled all the brattish things I had said, though I wanted to forget them. The little Cathedral of Four Silver Birches became my hideaway during those troubled days, and the tears I shed were those of the true penitent.

Aunt Cordelia noticed my preoccupation, and she was unusually kind. "Laura is young and healthy and under good medical care, Julia. I don't think that we need to be fearful. In a few weeks she will be as happy as your mother used to be after each of you was born."

I nodded, but the dreariness inside me was undiminished. Even when Father called us early one morning in September to tell us that Laura and Bill had a little daughter, that Laura was well and happy, that the baby was healthy and beautiful — even then, I crawled off to my cathedral and wept because I didn't believe that Laura could ever really love me again.

A new year of school had begun and each day Aunt Cordelia and I marched off to the white schoolhouse, sometimes joined by Danny and Carlotta, all of us employing our diaphragms in deep breathing and obediently fixing our thoughts upon the beauty of September skies and the glory of wild asters and goldenrod — sometimes with sly grins at one another. Once again I lost my identity as Aunt Cordelia's niece, put my mind upon the tasks she set for me, avoided Aggie Kilpin, became a devoted friend and then an avowed enemy of Carlotta Berry. But this year was different; I missed Chris sharply when I looked at the empty seat beside Danny, and I grieved, even as I learned to find the area and circumference of a circle, for my big sister's love which I was sure that I had lost forever.

Another telephone call came on the sixth of September. I shall never forget the date for it was the day of my return to happiness. Aunt Cordelia answered the telephone. I heard her address someone as "William" — that would be Bill, of course — heard her ask about Laura and the baby, heard her say thoughtfully that yes, she thought it could be arranged; no, the schoolwork could be made up easily; yes, she felt that it would be a good thing for both girls. Then she called me to the telephone and Bill's voice, now grown very dear to me, told me that the baby's name was "Julie," that Laura

48

was home from the hospital, that he had wanted to hire a woman to help her with the baby, but that Laura had said no, she wanted her sister with her for the next few days. He asked me if I would come, and I began to cry and told him between hiccoughs that, yes, I would be there.

Aunt Cordelia found one of my old dolls that evening, and she showed me how to protect an infant's head and back; she told me what an extra pillow could mean in a new mother's chair and how a flower on a luncheon tray could make a plain bowl of soup something of a treat for a convalescent.

When I went to my room that night the world was a better and brighter place, and I was controlled by a new discipline which I imposed sternly upon myself.

"Bill is in the Number One Spot, and don't forget it, Julie Trelling. And the baby is in the Number Two Spot." I hesitated at that point, and then drew the haircloth shirt a little tighter. Father was in the Number Three Spot, one had just as well admit it. But when I thought of Chris preceding me as Number Four, I balked. Chris could share that place, I supposed, but that was all. There was a limit to my humility.

When I burrowed down between my white sheets that night, I breathed deeply of happiness. I wished that I could tell the old conductor how wise I had grown; I thought of how much more than an almond chocolate bar he had given me.

4

My twelfth year, we supposed, would be my last one with Aunt Cordelia, since I would be entering high school the next year and be going into town to live with Father; therefore Aunt Cordelia agreed that I might have a birthday party that spring and the talk among the girls at school centered for a period of several weeks upon the social event of the season. Word of it got to Aggie Kilpin, who still sat in the center of a wide circle of peasants during the noon hour; Aggie gleefully told me that yes, kid, she would be coming to my party too. I didn't think she would.

Alicia Allison sent me a box of tiny pink notes and

matching envelopes on which I could write, "Miss Julie Trelling requests the pleasure," and so on. I spent a happy and satisfying hour in preparing these notes and addressing each tiny envelope. Aunt Cordelia had said, "Boys and girls, or just girls?" when I had suggested the party, and I had decided in favor of just girls, including some of the girls from town. Since she hadn't demurred at the exclusion of boys, I rather hoped that she would not notice one other omission. She did, of course. Ruffling through the little pile of envelopes, she said quietly, "Julia, you have forgotten to include Agnes."

"Oh, Aunt Cordelia, I can't. I simply can't have Aggie. She would spoil the whole party. You know that."

"She knows about your party, Julia, and it has been something she's looked forward to for weeks. You can't do this to another child; it would be too cruel."

"I can't invite her. I simply can't have the town girls thinking that she is my friend. I'm sorry for Aggie, awfully sorry, but let's face it, Aunt Cordelia: Aggie smells."

Aunt Cordelia sighed. "Julia, that child has been in my classroom since she was five; that means she's been there almost ten years, and she has stood at my desk, learning nothing, but giving off a more unbearable stench each year. I know Agnes very well; I know that she's smelly as you say, but I also know that if you stab her, she feels pain. I can't encourage cruelty on your part."

I shook my head. "I'd rather not have a party if I have to ask her," I said shortly.

"That's up to you, Julia; think it over," Aunt Cordelia answered.

I made my decision. The little pink envelopes went

into the wastebasket, and I had to tell all the girls at school that there would be no party. There was general indignation directed toward Aunt Cordelia, indignation coming from my closest friends, from some of their mothers, even from Aggie, who muttered that Miss Cordelia was mean to Julie, never once suspecting that she herself was the cause of all our broken plans.

Aunt Cordelia maintained her usual calm. No one of us was fool enough to believe that she would change her mind though the whole school should rise in mutiny. Her only nod to our disappointment was a casual remark that, although the party had been cancelled, there would be birthday cake for everyone, a remark that delighted the boys, who had not been especially pained at the disappointment of the girls in the first place.

Father never interfered with Aunt Cordelia's disciplinary measures, but I think that he felt a little sorry for me at this time. He came out and took me for a long drive the night before my birthday, and he brought me a silver pen and a quire of good white paper in a leather box, material for the stories I wanted to write. Alicia sent me a gift too, a beautifully bound volume of Edna St. Vincent Millay's poems. In a little note Alicia said, "There is something about you, Julie, that reminds me of Millay's early poems; read them now and save the darker ones for later years." She had placed her note in the book so that it opened to the lines:

"God, I can push the grass apart
And lay my finger on Your heart!"

And turning a few pages, I found lines that mirrored an ache and longing I had so often felt when the beauty around my woods cathedral was too intense, when the need to grasp and keep loveliness left me with a sense of desolate frustration.

> "Thy winds, thy wide gray skies!
> Thy mists that roll and rise!
> Thy woods, this autumn day, that ache and sag
> And all but cry with color! That gaunt crag
> To crush! To lift the lean of that black bluff!
> World, world, I cannot get thee close enough!"

When I was through, my eyes were wet and I loved not only Millay but Alicia and Laura and Aunt Cordelia — almost everyone in the world except poor little Aggie Kilpin.

Compassion was not yet aroused within me, and the better nature that loved poetry and beauty was completely overshadowed the day of my twelfth birthday. Aunt Cordelia drove her car to school that morning because she was taking the two huge angel-food cakes that she had baked and iced the night before. I was invited to cut the cakes at noon and after sliding each piece on a napkin, to place my birthday offering on each pupil's desk. It was a poor substitute for a party, and most of the girls felt as downcast and low spirited that noon as I did.

But not Aggie. She grinned in delight when I placed the cake before her, and she clambered out of her seat when she saw the rest of us preparing to go outside.

"I won't be queen today, kid," she garbled eagerly. "I'm goin' to set by you 'cause it's your birthday. I'm goin' to be your best friend."

And then I did it, a thing one does not forget. I turned on an innocent human being in fury, and I threw Aggie's love for me back into her simple, uncomprehending face.

"Don't you dare follow me, Aggie; don't you dare come near me," I told her, and I didn't care in the least what measures of discipline Aunt Cordelia might think up for me. I flashed a hostile look toward her as I strode past her desk, and I noticed that she looked quite tired and a little drawn. She said nothing to me, but she held out her hand to Aggie.

"Would you like to go with the little children and me, Agnes? We're going out to the woods and get a bunch of wild flowers for Julia's birthday."

Aggie seemed to be afraid of me after that. She would grin timidly at me and nod her head as if encouraging me to be kind. Sometimes in shame, I returned her smile, but it was always a weak thing, and Aggie was never reassured. I did not read Edna St. Vincent Millay's poems during those last few weeks of school; belatedly, I had a miserable feeling that the gentle young poet would not have liked me.

It was a hot, dry summer that year, and in early August, when the heat seemed almost unbearable, we heard that Agnes Kilpin was very ill with a fever resulting from the infection of a cut foot for which she had received no medical attention. Aunt Cordelia immediately drove up to the Kilpins', taking ice and cool fruit drinks with her. That evening she told me something of the condition in

54

which she had found Aggie and of the futility of trying to help her.

"I wanted to bathe the poor child and put clean sheets on her bed, but Mrs. Kilpin wouldn't allow me to touch her — said she wasn't going to have her girl catch pneumonia by having a bath." Aunt Cordelia closed her eyes briefly in exasperation. "Afraid of pneumonia, but not of filth and the agony of heat and fever. I wanted to tie that woman up outside the room and see to it that Agnes was cared for properly — for just once in her life."

A few days later on a hot Sunday when tempers were shorter than usual, Aunt Cordelia and I had one of our not infrequent clashes. She had given my room a quick inspection after church that morning, and had found its condition unsatisfactory.

"You will put your books and clothing in their proper places, Julia, and you will dust the room, including — especially including — the windowsills, which I find absolutely white with dust. And understand this, Julia: no lady has a right to that title unless she is not only clean of body and clothing, but is equally clean in her surroundings. Never let it be said that you have grown up in my home and have been so remiss as to throw your discarded underclothing under the bed — which is exactly where I found yours just now."

Her wrath was formidable; mine was rather intense too, for I felt that I might have been instructed to clean my room with considerably less sermonizing. Our clash was brief and bitter, and Aunt Cordelia was the victor. I spent the next hour converting the energy of rage into a zest for cleaning which resulted in an immaculate state that would have satisfied any top-sergeant.

Aunt Cordelia inspected my work and nodded approvingly. "I should think now that after a shower and a brief apology for your impertinence you might feel very much better, Julia."

"I am very sorry that I was impertinent, Aunt Cordelia," I managed to say, and then fled for the bathroom and a shower. I wished as I stood under the cooling, cleansing flood of water that I were as fortunate as Uncle Haskell, living apart in the old carriage house, working on a magnum opus and communicating with Aunt Cordelia only infrequently.

That was the afternoon that Carlotta Berry called, asking me to go driving with her. To receive an invitation to go driving with Lottie that summer was a coveted honor. Being an only child of unusually indulgent parents, Lottie had a great deal more in the way of clothes and expensive toys than most of us, and for her birthday that year she had received a gift that was the envy of all her classmates. The gift was a pony, a snowy, dainty-hoofed little creature, a wonderful gift in itself, but this one was harnessed to a wicker and patent leather cart. Carlotta had power in the possession of that pony cart: those who pleased her might share it, but there were no rides for those who did not.

I supposed no favors would be granted me that afternoon, but Aunt Cordelia was a much fairer person than I sometimes believed her to be.

"I see no reason why you shouldn't go," she said pleasantly. "You have fulfilled your duties and are entitled to some recreation."

56

"I can go!" I told Lottie joyfully, and when she arrived, cool and pretty in blue and white organdy, Aunt Cordelia looked at me thoughtfully and suggested that I might wear the dress from Laura's wardrobe which she had altered to fit me, a fine white linen embroidered with tiny wreaths of rosy flowers and tied with a gay sash. It was plain that Aunt Cordelia wanted me to look no less well-dressed than the darling of the Berry household.

Our gladiolas were in full bloom that week and while I dressed, Aunt Cordelia cut a great armful of the bright flowers and then sat in the porch swing waiting for Carlotta and me to come downstairs.

"Since you're going to be driving all around the neighborhood, I think it would be nice of you girls to take this bouquet to Agnes. You won't mind doing that, will you?" she asked.

Aunt Cordelia was too much the voice of authority for either Carlotta or me to resist her suggestion. We didn't want to think of Aggie, much less to visit her, but a sense of decency prodded by the determination which we knew was back of my aunt's quiet suggestion, led us to accept the errand.

"Isn't it just like her?" Carlotta sputtered when we were out of hearing. "She spoils your party on account of Aggie, and now, she spoils our afternoon by making us stop at the dirty Kilpins'. Sometimes I can't *stand* Miss Cordelia; I mean it — I just can't *stand* her."

I had been annoyed too, but at that speech I turned loyal niece and remarked that if Lottie didn't like my aunt, she might well have invited someone other than a relative of Aunt Cordelia's to go riding with her, and Lottie replied that since the pony and cart were hers, she might rescind her invitation.

I wanted the ride enough to tolerate Carlotta's airs. Both of us were conscious that we made a pretty picture on the country road, our gay dresses and the bright flowers filling the little cart with color, Lottie's blonde hair and my black shining as brightly as the pony's silver coat. Uncle Haskell took off his hat and made us a sweeping bow when we met him driving home from town, and a mile or so farther on, Danny Trevort and Jimmy Ferris chased us on their bicycles, scorning our elegance although we were pretty sure that they secretly envied us.

"O, ki-tinka, ka-tonka," they shrilled in pained mockery. Then, riding close to the cart and holding on to the sides, they gave us the benefit of their supreme contempt. "Slurp, slurp," they added as if the sight of us was a little more than either of them could bear.

Their behavior bothered me a little. Danny was still as close to me as in the days when he and Chris and I rode and swam and skated together. Danny was often at Aunt Cordelia's, and I was just as often at his home where gentle Mrs. Trevort always made me welcome. Now, in the presence of Carlotta and Jimmy, he was scornful of me, and I found myself acting as haughtily toward him as if we were foes of long standing.

There is something wrong with this world, I thought. And then, a few minutes later, I found a world in which there was a greater wrong than I had ever known.

Carlotta refused to go inside when we reached the Kilpin house.

"I don't have to mind Miss Cordelia while it's summer vacation, Julie," she said, and I had to respect her point of view. "I guess you'll just have to take the flowers in yourself — since you can't help being her niece." She glanced back down the road, obviously hoping the boys would soon appear again.

I climbed out of the elegant cart and crossed the road in some trepidation. I had heard stories of the Kilpins; they were trash, and vicious trash at that. The cluttered dooryard and the sagging front steps added to the ominous look of the place; I rather hoped that no one would hear my light knock on the half-open screen door.

But Mrs. Kilpin had seen my approach, and she came to the door as soon as I knocked. She was a withered, bent woman with a narrow strip of forehead wrinkling above close-set, sullen eyes. She motioned me to come in, but she didn't speak; when I offered her the flowers and told her they were for Aggie, she nodded toward a table where I laid them, pretty sure that they wouldn't be touched until they were thrown away.

Aggie was lying on a bed in the corner of the room. It was a filthy bed, sheetless and sagging in the middle, and Aggie rolled restlessly upon it, her mouth parched with fever and her eyes glazed and unseeing. The heat, the stench, and the closeness of death made the place so unbearable that I wanted nothing so much as to break away and run from it. Somehow, however, I managed to walk closer to the bed and speak to the girl who lay there.

I really think that I half expected to see Aggie grin again, to hear her call me "Kid" and declare that we were friends. But Aggie was another person that day; she was a part of the dignity of a solemn drama, no longer the phony "queen" seated in the center of a mocking circle of her subjects. Aggie was as indifferent to my presence as if I'd been one of the houseflies crawling along the edge of a spoon that lay on the table beside a bottle of medicine.

I was awed and unsure of what I should do. "Is she going to get well?" I finally whispered to the shadowy woman who stood beside me.

"No, she ain't a-goin' to git well. She's a-goin' to die," the woman said without emotion.

"I'm sorry," I said, and Mrs. Kilpin answered in the same dead voice.

"No, you ain't. You ain't sorry. Nobody's sorry that my girl's a-goin' to die. Not even her pa's sorry. Nobody."

I couldn't answer that. "I guess I must go, Mrs. Kilpin," I said miserably. "I guess I'll have to go."

"Yes, you go," she said, and I saw her eyes studying me from head to foot. "Them clothes is too fine for this place. You go 'long."

I turned toward the bed with agony in my throat. If I could have kept Aggie from dying by ignoring the stench and the ugliness, it would have been such an easy thing to do; it would have been a privilege to put my cheek next to hers and to tell her that yes, I was her friend. But Aggie would not look at me, and her mother's look held only sullen hatred for me.

"I know that sometimes I've been mean to Aggie. I'm sorry, Mrs. Kilpin; I wish that you'd believe me. I'm really sorry."

"I said that you'd best be gittin' on," Mrs. Kilpin said,

without looking at me. She pointed toward the door.

When I was out of the house, I ran to the cart where Carlotta was waiting. "Hurry, Julie," she said, her doll-like face pink with anticipation. "We're going to go north at the corner. The boys just went that way, and I almost know they're hiding to surprise us. We won't even speak to them," she added, the instincts of the born coquette asserting themselves more strongly by the minute.

"Take me home, Lottie," I said desperately, as I climbed into the seat beside her. "Please. Just take me home — then you can do whatever you like."

"Don't be silly, Julie. For goodness sake, was it *that* bad? I didn't know you liked Aggie so much."

"Will you take me home?" I asked her once again, my voice sharp because of the tumult inside me.

"No, I won't. Your old aunt had to spoil things by making us come up here. My mother didn't say that I had to come and see Aggie, but I just brought you up here because I supposed that Miss Cordelia would have a fit if I didn't. Now, I'm going to go wherever I please, and I just don't please to take you home."

It wasn't the first time we had quarreled. Lottie and I were at swords' points as often as we were bound together in friendship. And beside the fact that our friendship was not very deep, the day was ghastly hot and beyond the discomfort of heat I was sickened by the glimpse I'd had of "something terribly wrong in this world." I jumped from the seat into the dusty road.

"Go right ahead," I told her. "I'll walk."

"Very well, Miss Trelling," Carlotta said loftily, and

61

off she drove, her pony and cart, her blonde curls and organdy dress as beautiful as a picture.

There were two miles before me, and I was already tired. The thick yellow dust felt hot through my thin slippers, and the half-burned weeds stung when they swished about my bare ankles. It would have been a long and wretched walk if Danny hadn't rescued me, but he did, and there wasn't a trace of the taunts he had yelled at Carlotta and me hardly a half hour earlier.

"What's the matter, Julie?" he asked as he stopped his bicycle at my side. "What did Lottie do to you?"

"Nothing. She just won't take me home." I looked at Danny bleakly. "I think Aggie is going to die, Danny, and her mother almost hates me. I can't ride around the country in a pony cart after I've seen Aggie and her mother."

Danny looked down at the ground. Somehow the subject of death embarrassed us both. I wondered about it later.

I rode for the remainder of the two miles home on the handlebars of Danny's bicycle. We didn't talk much, and Aunt Cordelia didn't say much either when I told her briefly what had happened. Some grease from the spokes of a wheel had soiled my white dress, but she didn't scold; she made cold lemonade for Danny and me and the three of us sat together on the wide porch, all of us grave and thoughtful.

Mrs. Kilpin had been right; we heard of Aggie's death the next morning, and Aunt Cordelia again drove up to the bare, wretched home where she and Mrs. Trevort and Mrs. Peters got Aggie ready for a decent burial.

The three women looked pale and tired when they came back from the Kilpins that night. Aunt Cordelia and I sat together in the high-ceilinged library where a cross-current of air made the room cool and pleasant.

"She's clean, at last, poor little creature." Aunt Cordelia shuddered involuntarily when she spoke. "I washed her hair. It was a task the like of which I hope never to have to do again. But do you know, Julia, the child had pretty hair. When it was clean I was able to press two big waves in it above her forehead, and when it dried it was a deep brown color with bright lights in it."

Aggie's hair clean. Not only clean, but pretty. It seemed impossible, but I knew that it was true or Aunt Cordelia would not have said so. I wished that Aggie could have known. It seemed such a terrible waste — ugliness all one's life, and something pretty discovered only after one was dead.

I had never attended a funeral; Aunt Cordelia had always excused me from going with her for one reason or another. But four of us, Elsie Devers, Margaret Moore, Carlotta and I, were pressed into attending Aggie's funeral. We carried big armfuls of flowers and followed Aggie's casket to the altar of the little country church.

When I looked at Aggie lying in her coffin that afternoon, I was filled with wonder as I saw that she was gently, almost gracefully pretty in death. She was clean, so beautifully clean in the soft ivory-colored dress that my aunt and other neighbors had bought for her, a dress that would have sent Aggie into ecstacies if she could have had it while she lived. I noticed that her hair was, indeed, bright with copper lights in it, lights that sparkled

63

when the afternoon sunlight, channeled in through the church windows, touched Aggie's head and face. It had been the filth and the stench and the silly grimaces, the garbled speech and the stupid responses that had made Aggie revolting. And now she was pretty.

But it was a prettiness touched with a cold aloofness that reproached and tormented me. I knew with a terrible certainty that I might beg her forgiveness until I was exhausted, that I might kneel before her as we had done in mockery when we first made her queen of the lunch hour, and that she would remain as coldly indifferent to me as I had once been to her.

There was a poem of Sara Teasdale's which I had heard Aunt Cordelia read many times. It hadn't meant much to me until that afternoon when, I found to my surprise, that I was able to recall every word of it. I whispered the lines to myself:

"When I am dead and over me bright April
  Shakes out her rain-drenched hair,
  Though you should lean above me broken-hearted
  I shall not care.

  I shall have peace, as lofty trees are peaceful
  When rain bends down the bough;
  And I shall be more silent and cold-hearted
  Than you are now."

When we walked home after the funeral, Carlotta said, "You were saying poetry to yourself in the church, Julie. I think that's very bad manners, with poor Aggie lying there dead — and all that."

At twilight that evening I wandered out to the carriage house, where Uncle Haskell sat on his porch enjoying the light breeze that stirred the leaves of our surrounding wooded acres. He laughed lightly as I seated myself on the steps at his feet.

"Your face, my treasure, has a funereal aspect this evening. Are you responding to our popular stereotype — the proper mourner who must tense his muscles for the correct number of days before he can cheerfully thank Heaven that it was the other fellow and not he, who had succumbed?"

I didn't answer immediately. Sometimes Uncle Haskell seemed like a bad-mannered child, someone who deserved to be ignored.

"Do you know what it means to feel guilty, Uncle Haskell?" I asked after a minute.

"No. I thank whatever gods may be that no such emotion has ever disrupted my equanimity." He toyed for a while with the pipe which he always carried but never smoked. "Now, why should you feel guilty, my little Julie? You know very well that if this Kilpin girl could approach you again, as moronic and distasteful as she was a month ago, that you'd feel the same revulsion for her. You couldn't help it."

He was right, of course. I thought how awkward it would be to have to say, "Oh, Aggie, you were so nice when you were dead, and now here you are — the same old mess again." That wouldn't do, naturally; one couldn't say *that*, even to Aggie.

Uncle Haskell was speaking again. "Hadn't you rather

thank Heaven that she has escaped what life had to offer her? And isn't it a blessing that society escaped a multiplication of her kind? Come, Julie, death may be the great equalizer; let's not give in to the hypocrisy that it is the great glorifier."

We sat in silence after that, and I listened to the sounds of night around us. Uncle Haskell's words beat in upon me as I sat there; I knew that he expressed something that was true, but I knew as well that he was missing something. In Aggie's life and death there was something more than a distasteful little unfortunate's few barren years and her fever-driven death. But what it was I could not put into words; it was strange that I should have sought out a cynic such as Uncle Haskell with the hope of finding an answer.

Finally I rose, the need for action of some sort strong within me. "I think I'll saddle Peter the Great and ride for a while," I said.

Then, for some reason, I suddenly felt very sorry for Uncle Haskell. Obeying an impulse which I did not understand, I mounted the five steps up to the porch, and standing beside his chair, I bent and kissed him on his forehead. It was the first time in my life that I had ever done anything of the kind.

He didn't move. He muttered, "Don't ride too far," and that was all. I ran out to the barn, saddled the big old horse who was much gentler than his namesake, and rode away through the woods, pondering for the first time over the mysteries of life and death.

Uncle Haskell's light was on when I returned, and I could see that he was working at his typewriter. That was unusual. His writings never seemed to reach his typewriter; one supposed, innocently at first and then in mocking derision, that his magnum opus was being done in longhand.

I slept rather late the next morning and when I opened my eyes, I saw the folded white paper which had been slipped underneath my door. I jumped out of bed to pick it up and then propped myself comfortably against the pillows in order to enjoy whatever it was that I was about to read.

The letter read as follows:

Dear Julie:

What you were seeking tonight was a good, gray uncle, full of wisdom, and you came to an uncle who is neither good nor gray nor very wise.

I am annoyed with you, my sweet. I do not like stepping out of character even for a little niece who kisses me good-night, and by that token, makes a vapid old fool of me. But I'll be for a few minutes your good, gray uncle, full of wisdom. I'll say to my sad-faced little Julie: Guilt feelings will do nothing for either you or the Kilpin child. But your compassion as you grow into womanhood may well become immortality for the girl you call "Aggie."

Uncle Haskell

I read his letter several times and then secreted it in the little leather box where I hid other treasures. Hopefully, I half expected to find a changed Uncle Haskell that morning, a man who had given up lying and drinking and had awakened to his responsibilities to society. But he hadn't changed; he did not show by a single glance that he remembered the note he had written to me.

5

Uncle Haskell had mentioned the name of Jonathan Eltwing once or twice; Mrs. Peters had also spoken of him
in a mysterious way as if she didn't want Aunt Cordelia
to overhear her. Once I had grown bold enough to say
quite casually, "Do you know a man named Jonathan Eltwing, Aunt Cordelia?"

She hadn't blinked an eye. She said very smoothly,
"I knew him a number of years ago, Julia. Why do you
ask?"

I was embarrassed then and ill at ease. "I just wondered," I said.

"Then it was an idle question, wasn't it?"

"Yes, ma'am," I answered and resolved never to get myself out on such a limb again.

But when I went to help Laura out the fall little Julie was born, I remembered to ask her what she knew about this character, Jonathan Eltwing. Mother had long ago told Laura all about the man who, she suspected, had once been Aunt Cordelia's sweetheart. I listened, agog with interest, as Laura repeated the story to me.

Jonathan Eltwing was about Aunt Cordelia's age, which meant that he must have been eighteen the fall she commenced teaching in the country school. She was still teaching in the same school thirty-five years later, when Chris and I with all the others sat at the wooden desks and watched her firm hand write out instructions and examples on the blackboard.

He had come to school that fall, this awkward, earnest boy who towered above the young teacher, and he confided in her the hope that some day he might be able to go to college, although the hope was dim for he had neither money nor the prerequisite high school training. The father of the Eltwing children had little use for higher learning, and was unwilling either to pay for their schooling or to allow himself to be deprived of the benefits of their labor on his farm. However, he had made one foolish mistake: he had married a woman who had a hunger for learning, and every one of their six children was born with her intelligence and was later stimulated by her to seek an education. Jonathan was the first; encouraged by his mother and Aunt Cordelia, he broke with his father and started the climb which was to lead to the finest universities of the country and to the highest aca-

70

demic honors. The other five, one by one, followed him.

Aunt Cordelia had been immediately fired by anger against the father and sympathy for the son. She had family problems of her own, even at eighteen, but she turned them aside that winter and gave herself up fully to the project of getting Jonathan Eltwing ready for his college entrance examinations.

She had only a high school education herself, but she had been an excellent student, and she was a natural teacher. She carried loads of her own books to school, and she and young Eltwing mapped out a course of study that would have overwhelmed two youngsters of less enthusiasm and determination.

It was soon apparent to Aunt Cordelia that she had excellent material with which to work. Jonathan Eltwing had high intelligence and a motivation that drove him to attack with fury the piles of work she laid out for him. She was delighted when he soon overtook her in mathematics and the natural sciences; she guided his reading in history, in American and English literature, and in spite of an occasional groan from him, she made him learn a little Latin and considerable English grammar and rhetoric.

They worked together early of a morning before school, and then during the day while Aunt Cordelia taught younger pupils, Jonathan Eltwing sat at a desk in the back of the room and labored at the pile of work his young teacher had assigned to him. In the late afternoon, following the dismissal of the other children, they worked again, sometimes until the winter twilight drove them home.

Of course, tongues began to wag in hopeful suspicion that youthful immorality was afoot in the small schoolhouse, and one evening Aunt Cordelia had word that the directors of the school planned to visit her the following morning.

My grandfather seems to have had perfect confidence in his daughter and pride in what she was doing for Jonathan Eltwing. Grim, tight-lipped old Amos Bishop went with Aunt Cordelia to school that morning, and while she and Jonathan stood on either side of him, gave the school fathers a stern dressing-down. However, after that scene, Aunt Cordelia always kept my mother, a child of eight or ten, with her after school hours. Laura told me the story of how Mother would sit reading in the back of the room from four until five or later, a patient little chaperone guarding the good name of her sister.

Whether the two had fallen in love that winter, no one ever quite knew. Laura said that Mother thought they did. She remembered looks that passed between them, and clasped hands that were quickly unclasped; she remembered too, that on the night before Jonathan left for college she had seen two shadowy figures standing close together in the dusky woods beyond her window. She remembered that many letters came for a while, that finally they came much more rarely, that Aunt Cordelia became less pretty, with a tightened mouth and a stiffer air. She never had another "beau" and by the time she was twenty, people were speaking of her as "the old-maid school teacher."

Jonathan Eltwing took advanced degrees, performed

brilliantly in the various universities he attended, became an authority on Russian literature, and married a delicate girl with large, brilliant eyes and a passion for music.

Through the years he had never returned to the community until the autumn which I remember. His mother had joined him as soon as he was able to support her; the father had died, never seeing or even asking about his oldest son until a few days before his death when he had inquired of a neighbor if the man knew what "this Phi Beta Kappa business was all about." He had read in the local paper that it was something that had happened to Jonathan.

One day in the fall of my twelfth year, Father called Aunt Cordelia, and I remember that her face flushed and then grew pale as she stood at the old-fashioned telephone anchored against the dining room wall. I heard her say, "Why, of course, Adam; I'd like very much to see Jonathan again and to meet Mrs. Eltwing. Why don't you bring them out Saturday, say, at three in the afternoon?"

She was quite calm and matter-of-fact when she turned away from the telephone. "Your father tells me that Dr. Jonathan Eltwing is buying the old Merridan place and is moving out here for the winter while he finishes his latest book." She corrected the height of a window shade and ran her finger across the sill at which gesture I trembled, but she smiled at me in a very friendly way. "You really are becoming very careful, Julia; your dusting is much more thorough than it used to be."

I decided to try once again. "Who is Dr. Jonathan Eltwing, Aunt Cordelia?" I asked, betting to myself that she would never get into the romantic angle involving the distinguished professor.

She didn't. She raised her brows ever so slightly and adjusted another shade. "He is a noted lecturer and writer," she said, "an authority on nineteenth century Russian literature. I knew him rather well when we were young; it will be very nice to see him again — and his wife, of course." She hesitated, frowning thoughtfully. "I have heard that Mrs. Eltwing's mind is a little deranged; if she should seem — different, we must be very tactful."

We commenced right away to get the house in order for the Eltwing visit. "There will be a lot to do, Julia; I think we had better get Mrs. Peters to help us if she has the time." She stroked her chin in concentration. "I wonder if we should serve tea; Mrs. Eltwing is English, I believe. No, I think in spite of that, we'll serve coffee. Jonathan used to enjoy coffee and a special kind of cinnamon roll my mother made for him. Mama was very fond of Jonathan until he outshone — someone very dear to her."

Uncle Haskell, I thought. Grandmother's fair-haired darling. I guessed that there was no love lost between Jonathan Eltwing and Uncle Haskell.

There was a pleasurable excitement in the air that week as we made our preparations. My grandmother's china had to be taken from the closet and each piece washed carefully and wiped. I was not allowed to breathe upon it, much less to touch it and so, with proper humility, I helped Mrs. Peters wax floors and wash windows, tasks in which my lack of coordination could

74

do no particular damage. I didn't mind at all since I enjoyed working with Mrs. Peters; she was a chatty little woman, and a very good source of information regarding Aunt Cordelia and Jonathan Eltwing.

"Oh, they were in love, all right. She herself once admitted as much to me when we were young together," Mrs. Peters told me in a low voice as we washed the outside of the living room windows and kept on the lookout for any sudden appearance of Aunt Cordelia. "But after he left, the months went by, and she would have to say no to Jonathan's urging that she come to him — there was always sickness or debt or another worn-out old woman to be cared for. One couldn't blame Jonathan — he waited and hoped for a long time, and after a while I suppose that if the memory of her hurt, there were other women to soothe that hurt. I suppose I haven't any right to say this, Julie, but I'll say it anyway — if your grandfather had lived, things would have turned out differently around here. He would have seen to it that a certain person who shall be nameless would have carried his share of the burdens that fell upon this household. But not old Mrs. Bishop. Oh, no! According to her way of thinking, Cordelia was created to carry on for the rest of the family." Mrs. Peters paused for a few seconds and polished a pane of glass with a flash of energy out of all proportion to the need of her task. "I've said to Jim Peters many a time," she continued, "and he's always agreed with me, that old Mrs. Bishop was lacking in the qualities that make a good mother. And saying it that way makes her sound a good deal better than she really was."

By the week's end the whole house shone with the effects of ammonia and wax and furniture polish. On Saturday morning Aunt Cordelia allowed me to arrange several bowls of flowers for the piano and the mantel of the living room fireplace. "You show very good taste at that task, Julia," she said of my flower arrangements. There was an unmistakable air of graciousness about Aunt Cordelia that morning.

Fortunately it was chilly enough to warrant a fire in both fireplaces, and so we laid the kindling and wood, all ready to be lighted a half hour before our guests were expected. I polished the silver coffee service and set it on a low table in front of the fire, and Aunt Cordelia brought out a collection of little cakes and rolls which she had baked at ten that morning in order that they be oven-fresh.

The fires were crackling brightly at two-thirty, and the reflection of flame was deep in the polished mahogany lid of Uncle Haskell's grand piano, in the old wine decanter and the silver coffee service. Outside, the day was perfect with bright skies and the gay colors of our wooded surroundings. If Jonathan Eltwing had ever loved this old place, it must have wakened memories for him that afternoon.

Father drove up with Dr. and Mrs. Eltwing precisely at three o'clock; he knew Aunt Cordelia well enough to respect her passion for punctuality. I watched them walk up the brick-paved path to the porch where Aunt Cordelia stood waiting to greet them: Jonathan Eltwing so tall and huge as to dwarf my handsome and rather tall father; Mrs. Eltwing, a tiny, graceful woman wearing a pale gray velvet suit with a frilly blouse and a heavy gold pin at her throat. She had great, strangely brilliant eyes that dominated her tiny face and a mass of half-blonde, half-gray hair that she drew back smoothly from her forehead and wore in a great bun close to her neck. She was a lovely little creature with an air of childlike sweetness and innocence; she stood smiling and looking off into our bright woods as Jonathan Eltwing took Aunt Cordelia's hand in both his own and stood looking at her as if he were searching for the girl he had once known. I was proud of Aunt Cordelia; she looked slim and elegant standing there in the autumn sunlight, not once losing her cool composure as she greeted Jonathan Eltwing and his wife. I noticed that Father kissed her with special tenderness as if he understood that it was a difficult moment for her.

Then we were all in the living room in front of the fire. I sat close to Father, and watched the faces of those around me with keen interest.

Dr. Eltwing gave all of his attention at first to Aunt Cordelia, asking her many questions, the two of them exchanging memories. Mrs. Eltwing seemed to pay no attention to any of us; she gave a little exclamation of pleasure over a plate of tidbits, and seating herself near it, picked up one piece after another, placing them quickly in her mouth and sucking off the grains of sugar or specks of frosting that clung to her fingers. There was somehow nothing greedy in her actions; each bit of food was held daintily, was bitten into with what seemed more like gay satisfaction than greed. Even the little gesture of removing the sugar from her fingers was done lightly

77

and with a kind of merry charm. But the eating continued steadily until Dr. Eltwing held out his hands to her.

"Come and sit here beside me, Katy," he said gently. "I want to be sure that you understand who Miss Bishop is. Do you remember that I have often told you about the girl who tutored me when we were young, the one who helped me day after day until I was ready for my entrance examinations?"

Mrs. Eltwing uttered an amazed little "O-h-h" and turned to Aunt Cordelia in what seemed to be complete surprise. "O-h-h, I want to thank you — many, many times. You have been so good to my Jonathan." She hardly glanced at Aunt Cordelia as she spoke, but took the chair at her husband's side and looked up into his face as if to ask if she had said the right words.

Dr. Eltwing was very nice to me, once he got around to noticing that I was there. He was interested that I had read Tolstoi's *Anna Karenina*, and that I had tried to read Dostoievski's *Crime and Punishment*, but hadn't been able to get much out of it. He smiled a little at that admission.

"I think Dostoievski is pretty heavy fare for a young lady of your age," he said. "Aren't you pushing her a little, Cordelia?"

"I haven't pushed her at all, Jonathan," Aunt Cordelia answered, "but I don't forbid her to browse either. She soon knows when she is beyond her depth."

"She pushed me, Julie; she really pushed me without mercy. And I've loved her for it — all these many years," he said quietly, and he was no longer smiling.

78

Aunt Cordelia's face was flushed, but she turned pleasantly to Mrs. Eltwing. "I know that you are a composer and a musician, Mrs. Eltwing. Do you feel like playing for us this afternoon? We've just had the piano tuned; I think you'll find it in good condition."

Mrs. Eltwing just smiled at Aunt Cordelia without answering until her husband bent down to her again. "Cordelia has asked if you will play for us, Katy. Do you feel up to it?"

She jumped eagerly to her feet as if he had interpreted a pleasant message in some foreign tongue. "Oh, yes, I'll play, Jonathan. Of course. Of course."

She walked lightly over to the piano bench, seated herself, and pushed back the cuffs of her velvet suit. It was then that I noticed the ruffle that extended from the sleeve of her blouse beyond the velvet cuff. It was torn and hung loosely; it was also a little soiled. A sad sign of her illness, I thought. No normal woman having the taste to groom herself so carefully in all other details would have overlooked that dangling ruffle.

In another minute, though, I had forgotten everything about me as Mrs. Eltwing poised her hands above the keys and then struck them as if in a wild fury. Waves of music crashed throughout the rooms of the old house, mountains began to shake and comets to fall under her hands while I could imagine tidal waves rolling in and the wind uprooting trees and sending ships spinning to the bottom of the sea. Then as my heart seemed almost ready to burst with the tumult, her music suddenly subsided and the sky became bright; the storm was over. The melody had become quiet, but it was not happy;

it seemed to cry as if some lonely soul walked over the earth and mourned the ravages that Nature had committed.

There was something eerie about Mrs. Eltwing as she played. Her frail body swayed a little with the music, her eyes that had looked so blue as she smiled at us in greeting, were now quite black and brilliant with light. She looked strange, and I felt for a moment that I would be afraid to be alone with her.

Then it was over, and Mrs. Eltwing dropped her hands into her lap. I was too moved to applaud, but from the doorway between the library and living room came a cry of "Bravo! Bravo!" and standing there was Uncle Haskell, slender and graceful, clapping his hands and smiling at Mrs. Eltwing.

I had never seen him look so handsome or so outlandishly affected. He was wearing the black velvet smoking jacket which he kept folded in layers of tissue paper, and under that, a white silk shirt. His skin was clear and firm, and his thick blonde hair waved back from a brow unmarked by either time or anxiety. He looked a little like a foolish mannikin suddenly animated; he also looked a little like a Greek god. I couldn't quite decide which description best fitted him.

Mrs. Eltwing stood up at the sound of his cheering, and she gave a little gasp as she looked at him. She reminded me of a small girl who has suddenly discovered an unbelievably beautiful toy; her eyes never left him as he came forward, took her hand lightly and kissed it.

"Thank you for that music, dear Mrs. Eltwing, thank you a million times. You have given me something precious just now, something infinitely precious."

Father looked strained as he always did when Uncle
Haskell put in an appearance; Jonathan Eltwing's eyes
had a preoccupied, brooding look; Aunt Cordelia did not
move a muscle. Only Mrs. Eltwing looked pleased, even
radiant. She did not say a word, but she looked at Uncle
Haskell as if she had never seen a person so beautiful
or so charming. When he turned to greet Dr. Eltwing,
she continued to look at him, her eyes shining.

Uncle Haskell greeted Mr. Eltwing brusquely. "So
good, Jonathan," he said, and our guest replied with a
brusque greeting that matched the one he had received.
Father and Uncle Haskell shook hands, nodded, and
murmured something, nothing very cordial; then Aunt
Cordelia invited her brother to sit down with us.

"Sorry, Cordelia, darling, I think I must get back to
work. Deadline to meet by next week," he said, smiling
at Mrs. Eltwing. "I'll have to be in New York for a
conference with my publishers at the end of the week
— events are crowding in on me a bit."

"Your book is coming out soon then?" Jonathan Eltwing asked politely.

"By spring, we hope," Uncle Haskell said airily. I
was amazed at him. He knew that Father, Aunt Cordelia and I knew positively that he was lying, that Jonathan Eltwing was pretty well convinced of it, but these
facts seemed not to affect him in the least. He had an
audience of one person who believed him; sometimes I
wondered if he didn't vaguely believe himself. He was
not in the least embarrassed, but the rest of us were. I
wondered how Aunt Cordelia had managed to stand it

all through the years. I had had much less of Uncle Haskell than she had, and even I felt a little sick as I watched him.

"You will be staying in New York for some time, I suppose?" Jonathan Eltwing asked, mostly, I think, because it seemed necessary to say something when the silence became awkward.

"Only a week or ten days — at least I hope not any longer. I can't leave my girls alone too long, you know." He rumpled my hair, and I grinned inwardly. Aunt Cordelia and I could have been robbed, stabbed, drawn and quartered and Uncle Haskell would have known nothing about it. I wasn't too sure that he would have been greatly concerned, if he had known.

He went back to Mrs. Eltwing. "Thank you, thank you for a moment of pure delight, dear lady," he murmured. Then he bowed slightly to Dr. Eltwing. "So good, Jonathan," he said again. "Adam," he nodded at Father. "Until this evening, Cordelia — Julie, my sweetheart." Then he was gone, a flash of glory we were all relieved to see ended.

All but Mrs. Eltwing. She stood beside the piano looking after him, her face full of bewilderment and disappointment.

"Who was that man, Jonathan?" she asked her husband in a low voice, and we were all chagrined. Uncle Haskell's dramatic entrance had made us forget an introduction.

"That was Cordelia's brother, darling. Haskell Bishop."

"So beautiful," she said as if she were alone. "Such a beautiful and good man."

82

"Yes, Katy," Dr. Eltwing said gently. Then he turned to us, speaking quietly of other things.

The next hour was one of pleasant conversation in which everyone joined except Mrs. Eltwing. She sat close to her husband, leaning lightly against his shoulder, smiling a little to herself. I loved her somehow, and I really hadn't intended to, because she was the woman who had married the man my aunt had loved and I felt a certain loyalty to Aunt Cordelia. I loved Mrs. Eltwing, however, in spite of myself, mostly I think, because she was so tiny and delicate, so tragic. I believe that Dr. Eltwing saw the feeling in my eyes for he suddenly smiled at me, told me how fond he had been of my mother, hoped that I would visit him and his wife when they were settled in their new home. I was greatly flattered and pleased; it seemed to me something very special that I was a friend of Jonathan Eltwing.

But I spoiled it all as they were leaving. I smashed my hopes of a fine friendship as suddenly as I had smashed many a cup and plate in Aunt Cordelia's kitchen.

It happened as we stood on the wide porch saying good-bye. Dr. Eltwing held out his hand to me after he had shaken hands with Aunt Cordelia, and he said, "Good-bye, Julie, dear child. You know it's amazing how much you look like your Aunt Cordelia."

His words roused a quick fury inside me. I would have agreed with him that Aunt Cordelia looked rather nice that afternoon in her new golden colored wool with the brown velvet bow at her throat. But she looked only nice for Aunt Cordelia, and I was not flattered that I was compared to her, even when she looked her best.

83

I hadn't Laura's beauty, of course, and that was a sore spot which had always rankled, but I knew that I was prettier than Aunt Cordelia. My cheeks were *not* thin and flat, my mouth was *not* a thin, straight line, and my neck did *not* have a strange, flabby fold running down the center. I hated Dr. Eltwing at that minute. To humiliate me — me, Julie Trelling in my new scarlet wool with a scarlet velvet ribbon holding back my hair!

They were all looking at me, they were all seeing the furious anger in my face. Father's face was red, and his mouth looked hard; Aunt Cordelia was calm with just the shadow of a smile on her lips; Mrs. Eltwing looked wistful, wondering. It was Jonathan Eltwing's face that hurt me most. It had suddenly become cold, severe. He dropped my hand and nodded briefly. Then he turned to Aunt Cordelia and did not look at me again.

I was completely miserable when Aunt Cordelia and I came back into the living room. The cups with small quantities of cold coffee in some of them did not look so sparkling as they had that morning; the whole room seemed cluttered; even the flowers I had arranged so proudly looked a little weary.

If Aunt Cordelia had given me the scolding of my life I wouldn't have been either surprised or resentful. I knew that I deserved one; I felt as if a few good lashes would help me to live with myself. But she didn't scold; she just sighed and shook her head as she looked at the cups and plates.

"Somehow I don't quite feel up to washing them right now." She smiled apologetically. Aunt Cordelia did not hold with people getting too tired to put a room to rights.

"I'll do them for you if you'll trust me," I said in a small voice. "I'll be terribly careful."

She looked at me absently for a moment and then nodded. "Yes, I know that you'll be careful. And if you *should* have an accident — maybe I have put too much value on a piece of china. Your wish to help me has value too." She went to the closet and took out an old sweater. "I think that I'll rake leaves for a while, Julia; the air smells so fresh. Maybe the exercise will do me good."

I changed my dress quickly and carried the dishes into the kitchen, lifting only one piece at a time into the soapy water, rinsing, wiping and setting it on the cupboard shelf before I picked up another. Then I swept up the crumbs and pushed the chairs back into their places, put more wood on the fire and carried the silver coffee service out to its place in the dining room. All during this time the tears were slipping over my cheeks; every so often I had to stop my work and use a handkerchief.

It was an empty, shamed and remorseful evening, terrible really. I stood at the window for a long time when my work was done and watched Aunt Cordelia as she raked up great piles of leaves and pushed them into a deep ditch that ran on one side of our woodsy lawn. It was so foolish to be raking leaves at that time, a completely futile gesture, for the trees were still full of leaves, and as quickly as Aunt Cordelia raked one section of the lawn, it was again covered with the bright rain from the boughs above. It was a foolish expenditure of energy — that is what Aunt Cordelia would ordinarily have said to me had I been occupied by this pointless task.

Another thing struck me: Aunt Cordelia had not changed her best dress before going out to work among the dusty leaves. It was unprecedented behavior on her part. Not on mine. I often forgot, and I had been reprimanded many a time for my negligence. And now, there was Aunt Cordelia hard at work in her best dress, her fragile stockings and high heels. I wouldn't have believed it possible.

Darkness came to our house sooner than it did elsewhere because of the many trees surrounding us. I watched the sunset, hardly brighter than the leaves had been that afternoon, and I thought that surely Aunt Cordelia would soon come inside. I started a kettle of water heating slowly for tea and I planned to make hot buttered toast and scrambled eggs when I saw her putting her rake in the tool shed. But I waited and waited, and when she set fire to the great piles of leaves she had raked together and the blue-gray coils of smoke started rolling, I knew that she would stay outside until every leaf in the ditch was burned and every ember carefully extinguished.

It was quite dark when Aunt Cordelia came inside, her hair disarranged and her face and dress grimed lightly with the smoke. If I had been in a different mood, I might have gloated over the fact that it was her carelessness, not mine, that was going to cost us a cleaning bill the next week. But I was not in a mood for gloating; my spirit was too much abased.

"You have made tea, Julia? Good. I'll be down as

soon as I've changed and freshened up a little." She glanced at her smudged skirt and then looked at me with a wry little smile. "I've been very foolish, Julia. Somehow I forgot to change. I must remember this before I scold you when you forget."

I wanted to say, "Don't be kind to me. Hit me; scream at me. It will make me feel better." But, of course, she did no such thing. She went upstairs, quick and light of step, and I prepared our little snack which I carried into the living room and set in front of the fire. I then turned on two shaded lamps and sat down to wait for her.

She came down soon, wearing the long rose-colored robe that was her favorite, and carrying a large manila envelope which meant, I supposed, that she was going to spend the evening working on her household bills. When she had seated herself in an armchair before the fire, she drew a long breath and reached for a piece of toast.

"This is very nice," she said quietly, "I didn't realize that I was hungry, but I am."

I tried to begin the little apology I had been working on all evening. I cleared my throat and began shakily, "Aunt Cordelia, I want to say —"

Then she did an amazing thing: she interrupted me. Interrupting another's speech was almost as horrendous an act in Aunt Cordelia's code as neglecting one's homework or calling Jane Austen a bore.

"Mrs. Eltwing is a pathetic little woman, isn't she, Julia? So lovely, so gifted — and so lost. Did you notice how exceptionally kind and understanding Jonathan is?

But he was always like that — the gentlest and best person I have ever known."

I felt that for some reason she did not want me to voice an apology, and so I sat beside her, feeling very wretched and awkward, trying to eat a little of the food for which I had no appetite.

Aunt Cordelia took her time over the meal, sipping her tea slowly and helping herself to a second piece of toast. When she had finally finished she wiped her fingers carefully on her napkin, and then getting up, she reached for the envelope on the mantel.

"I've had this in my bureau drawer, Julia. I should have shown it to you before. It would have helped you to understand this afternoon."

She drew out a sepia colored photograph, rather faded but still clear, of a young man and woman and a younger child. I knew in a flash who it was. The blond, graceful young man standing in the rear with his face turned carefully, no doubt in order to give posterity the full benefit of his beautiful profile, could be no one other than Uncle Haskell. And the child, leaning against the young woman's knee and smiling directly into the camera looked like a miniature Laura, but was, of course, my mother.

However, it was the young woman seated on the photographer's velvet-covered bench that held my attention. The other two I would have recognized, but not the lovely girl in the center. Her head was thrown back a little as if some word that had brought the smile to her pretty lips had also brought the small oval chin up in a mood of gayety. Her cheeks were full and rounded, her dark hair was brushed back but little curls had sneaked out at her temples. And the neck — that girlish neck was smooth and firm; there was a thin black ribbon tied around it and a small heart rested in the hollow of her throat.

"This was taken the first year I taught," Aunt Cordelia said in a matter-of-fact voice. "That was the year that Jonathan and I worked together to prepare him for his entrance examinations."

Of course. That was the year. And no doubt the photographer had said coyly, "Now think of someone you love, and let's have a big smile." And she had thought of Jonathan Eltwing; you could almost see his image in her large, dark eyes.

I put the photograph on the arm of my chair and then I knelt and buried my head in her lap. I seldom touched Aunt Cordelia; she never invited demonstrative behavior, but that night as I shook with sobs, she patted my shoulder and smoothed my hair back from my forehead.

"I'm a beast, Aunt Cordelia, an ungrateful, bad-mannered beast. I'm cruel and hateful —"

She gave my shoulder a little shake. "Now, now, that's enough. Let's have no more of this." She lifted my face with her hand under my chin and looked at me with a little smile. "You're neither cruel nor mean; basically, you are a very good child. You're just young," she added, and it was as if she said the last words to herself.

6

My last year in elementary school was Aunt Cordelia's last year of teaching. The decision to leave her position was not her own; rural schools were being consolidated that year, and children who would have learned under Aunt Cordelia were taken by bus into the town schools. The white schoolhouse where she had taught for forty years was sold at auction and used for the storage of grain.

Aunt Cordelia was very quiet as talk of these changes went through the community. She didn't approve of many things she heard of the teachers in the town schools. They were a permissive lot, and Aunt Cordelia believed that children were happier if the boundaries of their behavior

90

were established early and they knew exactly where they stood with reference to authority; neither did she approve of something called "social studies," which she felt was a hodgepodge of watered down ideas being substituted for honest and scholarly courses in history and geography.

When she was invited to take a class in town, she refused promptly. "I have taught in my own way, following the dictates of my own judgment for too many years," she said. "The philosophy and the restrictions of city schools would be too much for me." So saying she gave up her profession, and no one was ever quite sure just how she felt about it.

She brought home the brass handbell from her desk, the framed pictures of many groups of children with which she had decorated the drab walls of the classroom, and a great stack of old class rosters dating back to the year when Eltwing, Jonathan, was one of the names inscribed. I spent hours going through those lists of names with her.

"Trevort, Charles," I read. Danny's father. A fine boy, Aunt Cordelia said. One of the younger ones. It had only been a very few years in her reckoning since Trevort, Charles, had helped her with the heavy coal buckets and the Monday morning fires as Danny had done in my time.

Aunt Cordelia read the names with me and commented upon the personalities. "That girl had a way with words when she was no more than six; she's published three volumes of poetry so far. I'm not surprised; I recognized her gift." Or, "Now that one was bound for trouble from the first. She was boy crazy before she was quite aware that there *were* two sexes."

She remembered them all; she had indicated the universities to which some of them had gone, the careers many of them had followed, the persons they had married. The word "deceased" was written after many names. "Kilpin, Agnes — deceased," I read on a late roster.

As autumn approached that year everyone supposed that Aunt Cordelia would be very sad. It was the first September since she was six years old that she had not entered a classroom either as a student or a teacher. "She will be lost," the family feared. "She will be heartsick and lonely."

But Aunt Cordelia didn't seem heartsick. "When the first day of school comes this September," she told me, "I intend to stand quietly in the sunlight and lay my hands on the bark of one of the tallest trees. I'll say to myself, 'Well, good! Now *that* part of my life is finished.' And after that I may gather an armful of autumn flowers, and I'll move slowly while I do it and breathe deeply of good, clean air that is free of chalk dust. Maybe I'll make peach preserves in the afternoon or reread a few chapters of *Pride and Prejudice;* I may take a long walk in the woods or call on Helen Trevort or Cora Peters. I may fix a nice dinner for Jonathan and Katy Eltwing. Whatever I do, it will be as I please, and I intend to savor every minute of it."

Aunt Cordelia didn't talk like that ordinarily. She seemed to be anticipating her freedom in September, and yet I couldn't quite believe it. It struck me uncomfortably that if it *were* true, she might be also anticipating the fact that she was getting rid of me as well as the labor and problems and smells of a country classroom. She hadn't once mentioned my leaving her — no little moan for Julie.

I had overheard remarks that summer. "Being responsible for an adolescent is too much; Cordelia has done her share." And again, "Julie is a dear child, but — well, you know — temperamental, a bit headstrong, impetuous. And there will be the boy-problem before long and all the turmoil of growing up. It's too much to ask of Cordelia now that she is getting old."

And so, in spite of all the plans I had for the years in high school, I felt a wave of wistfulness. Aunt Cordelia was waiting to be free of me, perhaps was good and tired of me. It hurt. I couldn't help it; it bothered me.

Of course I was eager to go home. In my desk drawers were little calendars that I had made from time to time, with notations of the number of years, months and days until I would be old enough to be free of Aunt Cordelia's lectures, her stern routine of duties, her authoritarian attitude. I had long looked forward to the day when I would no longer be a "country girl," when I would be living with a parent rather than an elderly aunt not too much admired by many of my peers, when I would have Laura's old room at home where I could look out over the flower garden that seemed to evoke Mother's presence.

I had visited Father frequently during my years with Aunt Cordelia, and the visits were nearly always a delight, a foretaste of the life we'd lead when I was in high school and also Father's "hostess" as Laura had been. We often went out to eat, because Father liked to take advantage of any excuse to get away from the food served by his housekeeper, Mrs. Coffers, who was certainly a wretched cook, but so old, and so unskilled that she couldn't find another job. She thus escaped being dismissed, because Father was unable to hurt anyone unfortunate and helpless.

"I really must take my little girl out for a celebration, Mrs. Coffers," he would say, and the old woman would give us a gimlet-eyed look that made me suspect she knew the real reason behind our visit to an expensive restaurant. She didn't believe in squandering money on "high living," she grunted, and wondered since when professors in small state colleges earned salaries that allowed them to go out and buy lobster when fried steak and canned peas in white sauce made a meal good enough for anyone.

But Father and I dined out often all the same, and I felt very proud to follow the head waiter along a thickly carpeted dining room with my well-dressed and distinguished-looking father close behind me. When we were seated, I studied the menu with what I hoped was a slightly bored air, although I nearly always grew excited over the strange, delicious dishes and it was difficult to hide my enthusiasm. Then as Father gave our orders, I daintily drew off my gloves, one finger at a time and wondered if people around us thought that I was sixteen — possibly older — and was dining with some elderly admirer. Father was always amused, and I greatly enjoyed my acting until one night a sudden realization of what I was doing struck me.

"Father, am I like Uncle Haskell?" I asked him in consternation.

He patted my hand reassuringly. "Acting is rather good fun, Julie, if it isn't carried too far; Uncle Haskell went overboard with his acting a very long time ago, but I don't think you need to worry. Your reasons for it are quite different from his." Then he frowned at me slightly. "Still, I'm glad that you've recognized a pattern; think about it if you ever feel yourself getting carried away."

Often he read to me when we sat before the fire in his study, and we discussed the books that I had read, and I tingled with delight at his pleasure in my understanding. Once he took me to a faculty reception where he danced with me and some of his male graduate students made quite a fuss over me. Aunt Cordelia had a bit of a time getting my head out of the clouds after that experience.

I always slept in Laura's old room. It was the prettiest room upstairs, where I had often gone late at night when I was little, pretending that I'd had a bad dream so that Laura would take me into her bed and kiss me and comfort me. Now, when I visited Father I would sleep in Laura's room and I would pretend that my hair, scattered across the pillow, was thick, rippling gold like my sister's. I'd pretend that Mother was still alive and that I, being much the oldest daughter, was Mother's confidante; that I had a younger brother and sister, whom I loved very much.

Quite often on these visits Alicia Allison was invited to be with us. She was as pretty as when I first knew her, and always beautifully dressed; there was a gayety about Alicia that made her seem almost as young as Laura. It was obvious that Father liked her, and I noticed that she now called him "Adam"; when she had talked to him at Laura's wedding, she had called him "Dr. Trelling."

I was long past the pettishness I had shown when Laura suggested that it was about time Father married Alicia and got me away from Uncle Haskell's influence. I liked her; furthermore, I thought that it might be advantageous for me to claim the highly popular Miss Allison for my stepmother when I entered high school. I certainly was not jealous of her; actually I rather looked forward to the day when the three of us would live together.

We went ice-skating during the winter, Alicia, Father and I, or we took long tramps through the snowy woods and then came back to her small cottage where we drank spiced cider and munched the pleasant little pastries she had prepared for us. On a few occasions I spent the night with her, and we talked of frivolous things like face creams and the weight one should be for her height, and once she let me do her hair a new way and seemed really pleased with the effect. They were the kind of evenings one would never spend with Aunt Cordelia.

Then, finally, the spring before I was to enter high school, Alicia and Father were married. It was a quiet wedding, but a very lovely one. Laura and Bill were there with little Julie; Danny escorted Aunt Cordelia, and besides these, Dr. and Mrs. Eltwing, Mr. and Mrs. Trevort and a few faculty couples made up the guest list. Chris was Father's best man, and I was Alicia's one attendant. It was very nice of Alicia to ask me; the honor might well have gone to Laura, because Alicia and my sister had been close friends since Laura's high school days. But she chose me, and Laura seemed pleased; I had the feeling that the two of them had talked it over. Anyway I was happy in my important role, and much impressed with the ankle-length dress which Alicia had bought for me.

We had fun that summer. I was to move in with them at the beginning of school when the redecorating of our old house was completed; until then I often visited them for the weekend, and it was a delight. Mostly. It wasn't quite as much fun to go to a restaurant with Alicia and Father as it had been to go with him alone. There was no longer any doubt but that I was just some outsized kid tagging along and that she was Father's dinner companion. She and Father could have wine together and touch their glasses over some private little toast; they offered to buy me a carbonated drink so that I could join them, but I refused. It seemed rather artificial; too much like Uncle Haskell's *Le Vieux Corbeau*.

Most of the time, however, everything was perfect. Like one night when we had come home late from a movie, and Father had declared that he was starved and Alicia and I were suddenly ravenous too. We had cooked hamburgers and coffee, and Alicia had whirled up a milkshake for me. Then we had talked until we were half dead with sleepiness and Alicia had said, "Oh, bother with the dishes," and we had put them in the sink to wait until morning. That might not have been a thing of any importance to many girls, but it impressed me, because never, in all the years that I had been with Aunt Cordelia, had we fixed a snack late at night; most certainly, we had never left a dish unwashed in the sink. "What if illness should strike in the night?" Aunt Cordelia had said to me once when I wanted to leave the very few dishes we had used at supper until the next morning. "What if strangers came into our home and saw evidences of such slothful habits?"

I told Aunt Cordelia of the fun we had had with our midnight meal and our unconcern with evidence of slothful habits.

"You mean, Julia, that you enjoy coming down to a disheveled kitchen when you get up of a morning?" she asked.

"It isn't *that*, Aunt Cordelia, it isn't the cooking at midnight or leaving the dishes. "It's just —" I tried to find the right words. "It's just the flexibility of a way of living."

Aunt Cordelia raised her brows. I had used the words "inflexible" a time or two when we had had an altercation. She understood me perfectly — but we still washed the dishes every night!

But little things happened at the house in town that summer, things of no special importance, but the sum of them began to bother me. One thing was the mirror. It really was of little moment, but it made me realize that there were adjustments which I would have to make now that there was a new mistress in our home.

The mirror had hung in the living room for as long as I could remember, a beautifully cut glass just above the back of the davenport; Chris and I used to stand there when we were little and play with our reflections in the faintly blue depths that made us look a little strange, a little like children in some softly illustrated fairy tale. Alicia decided to move the mirror; she thought it would look better over the buffet in the dining room.

"But Mother always —" I began in a rather severe tone, and then stopped myself.

Alicia smiled at me. "I know, Julie, I know very well how you feel. But your mother and I were very good friends. She would want me to arrange the house to my taste, I feel quite sure."

Well, I wondered! But it was a little thing. Later I told Alicia that the mirror did, indeed, look nice in the dining room and she seemed pleased.

After we had removed the mirror, it was plain that the walls needed redecorating, and when they were done in a beautiful French gray, Alicia confided in me that she was going to be profligate and buy the outrageously expensive draperies that she had long wanted. We had a wonderful time selecting them together, and it was pleasant to find that our tastes were quite similar. We bought a heavy tapestry the color of the walls but brightened by great irregular splashes of cerise, a bold color that delighted both of us.

We were all quite pleased with the effect in the living room, but when the kitchen was done over, and the old dining table under which Chris and I used to hide and pinch Father's ankles while he dined, was discarded in favor of one very smart and modern, I felt as if this were no longer my home. I got a lonely feeling in it, although I had to admit that it was beautiful.

But it was Laura's room that mattered most. Somehow, it had never entered my mind that this room would

99

be other than mine. It had belonged to me in every dream that I'd had of coming home; later I thought how strange it is that your dreams can be so real as to make you sure that other people are aware of them too.

I seemed to feel faint warnings of a deeper shock to come when, on one weekend visit, I found that Alicia had had Mother's old flower garden put to sod so that it stretched out as a continuation of the green lawn.

"Don't you think it makes the lawn lovelier, Julie?" Alicia asked, apparently certain that I would agree with her. "The garden hasn't really been carefully tended for so long and was actually getting very shabby. If either your father or I had green thumbs — but we don't. Neither green thumbs, nor time for gardening, if we're to get term papers and final examinations graded."

"Yes, I think it's an improvement — I do, really, Alicia." I tried to make my voice enthusiastic, but my dream was beginning to be upset. The view of the flower garden from Laura's window was part of the memory I wanted back.

Later, Alicia wanted to show me what she had been doing to the rooms upstairs. That's when I saw Laura's room.

The white curtains were gone, and draperies of coarsely woven cloth in blue and copper were at the windows. The shell-pink walls had become beige and gold, and a thick beige carpet covered the floor which Laura had always left bare with fluffy white throw-rugs here and there. The pink and white bed was gone too, and the only furnishings in the room were a massive walnut desk with a special niche for a typewriter, a few straight chairs and several bookshelves against the walls.

"My home office," Alicia said with a pleased sigh. "Your father has the library — I insisted that he keep it to himself; up here I'll wield my red pencil over high-school themes and when I finally explode, at least I'll do it in privacy. I'd hate for you or your father to see me when I begin pulling my hair —"

I couldn't keep from wailing, "Oh, Alicia, *what* have you done?"

She was amazed. "But Julie, your father told me that this was Laura's room — not yours. I'm having your own little room all done over with a matching desk and bookcase and draperies that I think are the loveliest. I thought I'd be making you so happy — I didn't dream —"

Well, there were reassurances and apologies and more reassurances until finally I convinced Alicia that I was, of course, delighted with my old room and that she should never think of my outburst again. Everything was settled, but that night we were a little quieter than usual at our meal, and Alicia and Father glanced at one another as if they were thinking that it certainly was too much of a chore for Aunt Cordelia to look after a girl of my age; that they saw it as being something of a problem even for themselves.

During the next few weeks everything went smoothly; then one morning I came downstairs in my house slippers and walked into the breakfast nook without their hearing me. It really wasn't anything — just a recently married husband and wife giving one another an exceptionally warm embrace and good-morning kiss. Nothing wrong with that, but it was their surprise, their sudden

101

standing apart with a half-embarrassed, half-irritated look that struck me full force. I said, "Oh, excuse me," and they said, "Not at all, dear," and we all laughed a little, and they poked a bit of fun at themselves for romancing before breakfast.

But the experience left a strange feeling inside me; it wasn't the jealousy I had felt at Laura's, for I certainly wasn't trying to stand in the Number One place with either Alicia or Father. It was, rather, the feeling that I didn't belong anywhere — not in a house that was no longer my old home but a beautiful, strange place where I might at any moment invade the privacy of two people very much in love; not at Aunt Cordelia's if it was true that I had become a burden to her.

I went out from town on the rickety old bus that passed within a mile of home that afternoon. It seemed strange that I should think of Aunt Cordelia's place as "home"; always before it was the house in town that had been closest in my affection. But as I walked the dusty mile from bus-stop to the old house in the woods I thought about my room at Aunt Cordelia's with more warmth than I ever had before. It was twice as large as my old one in town, and while the furnishings were old, they were mellow and held more significance for me than did the desk and bookcase that Alicia had selected for me. Aunt Cordelia and I had worked together refinishing my bureau, a walnut one that had been old even when she was a child; I knew how much sanding and rubbing and polishing had been necessary to bring out the beauty of the fine wood. It suddenly seemed to me that I couldn't bear to give up my beautiful old furniture

102

for the glossy new things that should have been giving me so much happiness.

I wondered, too, how it would seem waking up of a morning and being unable to look out at the woods, my beloved woods that were hardly the same two days in succession. There would be a veil of fog one morning, and bright sunlight or gray rain the next; there would be snowy branches, or little, tender, new leaves, or colorful autumn ones — always a new picture to put away in my memory. I wanted my woods as I wanted my big room and my old bureau. I wanted, too, the freedom of the old house where I could run through the many rambling, high-ceilinged rooms singing if I cared to sing, exploring some ancient trunk or nook or closet that I had missed, never wondering if I were going to startle two persons burdened with someone like me in too small a house. For the first time, I was conscious of Aunt Cordelia's home as a haven, and I wanted desperately to know that I was welcome there.

Uncle Haskell called to me as I walked up the long driveway. "Well, Julie, my sweet, are you happy at the prospect of shaking the dust of this estate from your little feet?"

I linked my arm in his, and we walked on up the path without my answering. Uncle Haskell seldom noticed whether one replied to his remarks or not; he was interested only in his own voice.

"And how are the impeccable Adam and his beautiful bride?" he asked maliciously.

"Quite well. Not wholly impeccable, but they're both very nice people," I answered.

He bent down suddenly and looked into my face. "Come to think of it, you look a bit drawn, my pet. What is it? Were you pushed a little backstage away from the footlights?"

I thought, "That is *your* idea of pain, isn't it, dear Uncle?" But I said, "There's not a thing wrong except for that old bus and the ghastly heat." And then I changed the subject. "How is the magnum opus coming along?"

"Beautifully," he answered, smiling blandly and without the slightest embarrassment or anger. "Magnificently, really. I'm very pleased — so much so that I think I'll go out for a spot of twilight golf this evening. One must relax a bit, you know."

"Of course," I agreed, going along with the time-honored hokum. "Have a good game." We smiled at one another and parted at the end of the lane. Uncle Haskell and I had a tepid sort of liking for one another.

The drawn look that he had noticed in my face must very well have been evident, for as Aunt Cordelia and I sat in the living room that evening, she looked at me in her direct way and plunged into my anxiety bluntly.

"Tell me all about it, Julia," she said without prelude.

I had not told her about the little things that had bothered me, the mirror and especially Laura's room. They seemed to show up a childishness in me that I didn't like. But the breakfast-nook incident was different; it pointed up their discomfiture as well as mine. I tried to show in my telling of it that I held no rancor, only a sense of insecurity, of loneliness.

Aunt Cordelia nodded when I was through. "I think I understand how you feel, though I believe that you have misinterpreted Adam and Alicia. It's unfortunate that in our culture, where the accent is so much upon youth, that people of middle age feel awkward and absurd if they demonstrate their love. They feel that they're playing a role that belongs to nobody over thirty. I'd guess that is how your parents felt this morning — a kind of embarrassment rather than annoyance."

I thought for a while. "I'm egotistical, isn't that it, Aunt Cordelia? And egotistical people are supersensitive, aren't they?"

Aunt Cordelia smiled. "In a few years you'll love someone, Julia, and it will make a great difference in you. You'll see. A woman is never completely developed until she has loved a man; when that happens in the right way she is happy in other people's love as well as her own; she is more generous and understanding about the feelings of others. You might say that she knows completeness."

Then I asked a question that I shouldn't have, one that might well have brought me a rebuff, although it didn't.

"Did you feel that completeness the year — the first year you taught, Aunt Cordelia?"

I was immediately full of consternation at having asked the question, but to my surprise, she answered me readily.

"Yes," she said, "I did."

We were silent for a while, during which time my worry over a home came uppermost in my thoughts.

"Am I a pain in the neck, Aunt Cordelia?" I asked finally.

She came quickly from the "woman who had known

completeness" to the spinsterish schoolteacher.

"I dislike that expression very much, Julia; it is flippant and in poor taste. However, I fully understand your meaning, of course. No, you are neither troublesome nor an annoyance to me."

"I thought that maybe I was getting to an age where I am too great a responsibility," I quoted.

"I never said that. Laura and Adam and Alicia decided that."

"You wouldn't mind if I stayed here then — if I lived with you while I'm in high school. I'll try to be mature, Aunt Cordelia, honestly I'll try. I don't want to be a burden, but when you get down to brass tacks, this is *home* so far as I'm concerned."

Aunt Cordelia closed her eyes for a second and shook her head ever so slightly. But she was smiling as she made the gesture; I had never seen her look like that before.

"If you choose to stay with me, Julia, I shall be much, much happier this fall than I had expected to be. You have come to seem like my own child, and I haven't wanted to think of what it would be like this winter with no girl coming in from school, no young mind to guide —" She stopped then, apparently troubled. "How are Adam and Alicia going to feel about this, Julia? They've been expecting you, getting things ready for you. Are they going to feel hurt?"

My spirit was soaring. I would be a part of the old, the familiar. The roots that I had put down during the past six years need not be disturbed. I could be realistic about Father and Alicia without pain: they would welcome me, of course, if I moved into town, but they wouldn't suffer any sharp agony if I only came in for an occasional weekend. And that was all right. Don't try to get into the Number One place, my girl. Father and Alicia had as much right to their privacy as had Laura and Bill. Anyway, I had Aunt Cordelia.

"I'll make them understand." I tried to put into words the feeling I had for Father and Alicia: "I like them very much, Aunt Cordelia; I admire them too, but it's as if they are sort of holiday parents. Everything is just fine and new and beautiful; we're all polite and careful of one another's feelings. But they'll just have to understand: you and I are closer."

Aunt Cordelia sat very straight in her chair for a long time without speaking. Then she said quite casually, "Well, I suppose we'd better get to our beds. Be sure to hang your dress up properly, Julia; you left some of your things lying about the room when you left for the weekend."

It was cool and quiet and wonderful in my room. I lay in the wide old bed between my two windows, and looked up at the stars which were thick above the trees that night. This was home, this was contentment, a warm and good contentment in spite of the fact that I knew in winter the room would be icy and I'd have to leap downstairs to dress beside one of the big stoves, in spite of the fact that I would not be one of the town-clique and so would probably have fewer beaux, in spite of the fact that I knew there would be altercation between Aunt Cordelia and me. It didn't matter. Here on the wall were the bookshelves that my grandfather had made for Aunt Cordelia when she was young; out in the stable there was Peter the Great, getting old, but still showing his blood; there were the country roads and the woods; there was good old Danny down the road, and silly little Carlotta.

I thought about things Aunt Cordelia and I had talked about that evening. Especially love. I wondered if I would ever love anyone; if any boy would ever love me. I wondered what it would be like to have a boy's kiss — oh, not that silly kid-play of Danny's when Chris and Jimmy held my arms. What interested me were the kisses I read about or the ones I had watched with a kind of a hypnotized distaste when I had seen them in the movies. I wondered what it was like to be married, and then I wondered about babies and the bits I'd heard here and there. Once I had asked Laura shortly after little Julie was born, "Was it very dreadful, Laura?" And she had answered, just as bright and sparkling as she usually was those days, "Not really, darling. A bit rough for a few hours and after that, pure joy." I wanted a baby very much, one that was all mine, beautiful and soft. I wanted to be grown up and to know all about the things I wondered about. I sighed and turned in my bed luxuriously. "I do so want to be complete," I thought.

7

Dr. Jonathan Eltwing did not forgive easily. I soon learned that he would not be quick in forgetting my behavior on that day when he and his wife first called on us, and I knew that I couldn't blame him. I admired and respected the huge, sad-eyed scholar who was equally kind to Aunt Cordelia and to his sad little wife, but it was a long time before he was anything but cool and distant toward me.

The Eltwings had established themselves in a pleasant old house about three miles from Aunt Cordelia's, shortly after their initial visit to us. It was as lonely and isolated as ours, but much smaller and out of keeping with the handsome furnishings they had sent out from the East. People wondered what had brought Jonathan Eltwing back to our part of the country after so many years in which he had apparently forgotten his birthplace. No one was ever quite sure although it was generally believed that he had sought out a place where he could shield his wife from curious eyes and tongues. Mrs. Peters had her own idea which she confided to me. "Sometimes old memories have a strong pull, Julie. I can't say this to many people, but it's my own conviction that Jonathan Eltwing has never been able to forget the winter he and Cordelia were eighteen."

Whatever the reason for their return, they were a sad and tragic couple. Within a few months after their arrival, it was obvious that the state of Katy Eltwing's mind was worsening. She was fearful when neighbors called in the casual, friendly way of country people; sometimes she strayed from home and had been found, frightened and bewildered, in the adjacent fields and woods. The housekeeper from town gossiped of days when Mrs. Eltwing sat at the piano and wept because her hands had lost their skill; she told how Jonathan Eltwing would leave his work to hold the distraught woman in his arms, soothing and comforting her until she forgot her sorrow.

Often when his wife was safely under the care of others, Jonathan would come down to Aunt Cordelia's and sit before the fire, talking quietly with her, sometimes leaning his head against the back of the chair as if he savored a tranquil moment removed from care. He spoke politely to me on these occasions, but that was all; he never saw Uncle Haskell nor did he ever ask of him.

110

My uncle and I did not share Aunt Cordelia's place in the affection of our new neighbor.

There came an autumn night of fog and mist just a year after the Eltwings' arrival, however, when it was necessary for Jonathan Eltwing to talk to Uncle Haskell and to me.

It was on one of those rare occasions when Aunt Cordelia had gone into town to attend a lecture with Father and Alicia. I was up in my room polishing off the last of my homework when I heard Uncle Haskell's voice, its habitual jauntiness submerged in anxiety.

"Julie, come down quickly," he called, and I ran downstairs wondering at the note of alarm in his tone. Once outside in the dooryard I understood his concern, for there, holding his hand as if she were a child clinging to a parent, was Mrs. Eltwing. Her grayish blonde hair, dampened by the mist, had come unpinned and fell in a tangle about her face and shoulders. Those shoulders were bare, still beautiful in spite of mud and scratches, and they rose from what had once been a lovely dress of blue velvet, now torn in a dozen places by brambles or underbrush that she had encountered, the long full skirt splashed halfway to her waist by mud and water.

"She was in the middle of the old creek bridge," Uncle Haskell told me in a low voice. "She was crying — afraid to come on across or to turn back. See if you can take care of her, Julie." He was as agitated as if someone had placed a day-old infant in his arms.

I knew the creek bridge. It was narrow and without railings. When the creek was high, as it was that night, the dilapidated old crossing seemed a little hazardous

111

even to sure-footed kids such as Danny and I were. I felt a rush of sympathy for the lost woman who had attempted to make that crossing alone and in the night, but when I tried to take her hand in order to lead her inside, she cried out shrilly, refusing to allow me to touch her, and turning to Uncle Haskell as if for protection.

He led her inside while I ran to the telephone and called her husband. "I'll be there," Jonathan Eltwing said as soon as I spoke his wife's name; I heard him drop the receiver without bothering to put it back on its hook.

In the living room I turned on the lights and Uncle Haskell helped the disheveled woman into an armchair where he stood looking down at her, apparently perplexed and uncertain as to what he should do next. Mrs. Eltwing looked up at him, and the fright seemed to leave her eyes as if she suddenly recognized a friend. The light shone on tiny beads of mist that covered Uncle Haskell's blond hair; she seemed to be fascinated by them.

"Beautiful — beautiful," she whispered after a while. "You are a kind and beautiful man. I am not afraid now." She took his hand and pressed it against her cheek.

Uncle Haskell glanced at me in consternation. "Dear Mrs. Eltwing," he stammered, "dear little lady —"

She apparently did not notice his discomfiture, but continued to look at him as if just seeing him gave her complete happiness. If it had not been for the sadness of her condition, I could have laughed at his incredulous and frantic expression.

I noticed that her slippers were gone, that her feet in the torn stockings she wore were cut and bleeding. I brought a basin of warm water and a soft towel, but when I prepared to bathe her feet she again resisted me and turned imploringly to Uncle Haskell.

He hesitated when I extended the basin toward him; I doubt if Grandmother Bishop's darling had ever performed a personal service for anyone, but after a few seconds, he knelt before Katy Eltwing and bathed and dried her little feet as tenderly as Father would have done for me under like circumstances.

He was still kneeling on the floor, touching the cuts on her feet with iodine which I had brought from the medicine chest when Jonathan Eltwing ran up the porch steps and into the living room. His face looked haggard as he bent over his wife and lifted her in his arms.

"Katy — Katy, I thought you were sleeping," he said brokenly. "Poor little girl, I never dreamed —"

"The golden haired man found me, Jonathan — I wasn't afraid after he found me. But I'm so tired — so tired. I think you'd better take me home, darling."

He laid her on a couch in the library and sat beside her, soothing and reassuring her for a long time. Finally he came back into the living room, closing the door softly behind him.

"She is asleep," he said with a heavy sigh. He slumped down in an armchair without looking at either Uncle Haskell or me. "Where is Cordelia?" he asked abruptly.

"She's in town with Father and Alicia," I answered. "They'll probably be bringing her home in a little while."

He nodded. "Now tell me, Haskell, where did you find Katy? What happened?"

His voice was harsh with dislike. I glanced at Uncle

113

Haskell quickly, half expecting a stinging reply, but he answered Dr. Eltwing civilly although with an unmistakable coldness.

"I had gone for a walk down toward the creek. I heard crying from the bridge. I went to her, brought her here as you can see."

"Did she recognize you?"

"No, it was quite dark in the woods. We have only met the one time; she could have had no idea who I was. I'm sure of that."

"But she allowed you to take her hand — to lead her?"

"Yes. She was like a lost child, happy to be rescued."

Dr. Eltwing ran his hand across his forehead. "I can't understand. For months she has allowed no one to touch her except me, even when she has been lost and frightened. And yet, she allowed you to lead her — to wash the cuts on her feet."

I felt a little sick. I thought that if this sorry business fed Uncle Haskell's ego, that if he boasted of the special place he held in this deranged woman's feelings, I would die of shame for him. I watched his face to see if I could read his reactions.

But there was nothing in his face that night to substantiate my fears. He stood there, silent and perplexed, as he looked down at Jonathan Eltwing's bent head. For the first time, I thought that he looked old.

Finally he said, "If it will help her — if my listening to her music will make her happy —" he broke off and started for the door. "Feel free to call on me if I can help her, Jonathan," he called back, and was gone.

114

Dr. Eltwing did not talk to me after Uncle Haskell left. He went into the library and, lifting his wife in his arms, carried her as if she were a sleeping child, down the long lane to his car. I followed with a soft pillow from the couch, and when he had placed his wife in a half-reclining position on the seat, I adjusted the pillow beneath her head and shoulders. Then I looked up at his sad face as he stood watching me, and for a second I forgot that he was "Dr." Eltwing and that, in any case, I was too young to address him by his given name. But before I realized it, the name had slipped out.

"She will be all right now, Jonathan," I said.

Dr. Eltwing apparently forgot something too. He said, "Thank you, little Cordelia." Then he patted my shoulder and drove away.

In the months that followed, Uncle Haskell became a lay physician to Mrs. Eltwing. It happened shortly after the night when she had been lost in our woods that Uncle Haskell and I were riding past the Eltwings' place one evening and found her standing at the gate, her face swollen with crying, her eyes wild, her hair and clothing disarrayed. The housekeeper was trying to coax her to come inside, but whenever the woman tried to touch her, Katy Eltwing screamed and clung to the wooden pickets of the fence. I noticed that Uncle Haskell's face looked pale as we reined our horses and sat for a moment in our saddles watching a scene that was both sorrowful and revolting.

Then Uncle Haskell dismounted and walked over toward the fence where Katy Eltwing stood.

"Mrs. Eltwing," he said pleasantly, "do you remember me? May I come in and talk with you for a few minutes?"

She stared at him for a brief time and then ran to him, her face like that of a child restored to sweetness after a tantrum. He took her hand and the two of them walked slowly into the house, Uncle Haskell talking to her softly, the housekeeper and I following in silent wonder.

When Jonathan Eltwing came home at twilight he found Uncle Haskell at the piano playing a few simple melodies which he remembered from his youth, and Mrs. Eltwing sitting beside him, subdued and apparently content. She held out a hand to her husband when he came toward her.

"The golden haired man came to me when I was frightened, Jonathan. Please don't let him go away again."

Jonathan Eltwing may not have liked to do it, but there were many days when he was forced to call upon Uncle Haskell for help. And Uncle Haskell, on his part, may not have liked to have his self-centered way of life upset. He never, however, refused to go to Katy Eltwing when she needed him although he always insisted that either Aunt Cordelia or I go with him; sometimes it seemed to me that my poised and self-confident uncle showed signs of being a timorous boy when he was summoned to the Eltwing home. He was always tired and silent when his hours of providing therapy for Katy Eltwing were over.

She wanted him to play for her when her hands, which had so recently held the high skill of the artist, now stumbled and faltered over the keys. Uncle Haskell was not an accomplished musician, but he was able to play excerpts from the musical plays that were popular when he and Mrs. Eltwing were young, as well as the familiar aria from some opera. He had a pleasant baritone voice, and this compensated in some measure for the occasional false note he struck on the keyboard.

She loved to hear him sing *My heart at thy sweet voice* from *Samson and Delilah;* sometimes she wanted him to sing it over and over again as a child wants to hear a story retold time after time. I used to wonder what Jonathan Eltwing thought about in his study as he listened to that tender love song sung a dozen times over while he tried to concentrate upon the ordeal of Dostoievsky.

The pattern of a lifetime did not change for Uncle Haskell except for these sessions with Katy Eltwing. He still had occasion to fill his old golf bag with empty bottles every so often; he continued to perpetuate his myth of being a busy writer; he still clung to his role of a gentleman born to a gracious way of life. He still was completely ridiculous (that's if you loved him at all) and completely disgusting (that's if you were a stranger to that side of him which was seldom seen).

But as far as his attitude toward Mrs. Eltwing was concerned, Uncle Haskell was truly the gentleman he would have liked to be. He was gentle and patient with her, and he was unfailingly silent about her. He never discussed her condition even with Aunt Cordelia or me.

There was very little that either Aunt Cordelia or I could do for the Eltwings; sometimes my aunt prepared

117

little Sunday night suppers for them — strange supper
parties in which Aunt Cordelia did not dare approach
Katy Eltwing, but would sit talking to Jonathan when
the meal was finished while Uncle Haskell took Mrs.
Eltwing for a walk, or sat at the piano playing for her
and singing the songs she loved. Often she would fall
asleep against his shoulder and he would lift her in his
arms, carrying her to the couch in the library, where her
husband would cover her carefully and sit close beside
her. It was like a strange, unreal play. Sometimes I was
happy to escape to the Trevorts and taste the air of
reality again with Danny and his kindly, very normal
parents.

As the months passed, we watched Katy Eltwing become feebler, farther and farther removed from everything about her. It was very hard to persuade her to eat
enough for the maintenance of her strength. Aunt Cordelia used to cook every nourishing delicacy she could
remember, and send me over with covered bowls of
food that might tempt Mrs. Eltwing's appetite. Jonathan
used to coax his wife to eat whatever I brought over,
but after a few spoonfuls, she would turn wearily away,
shaking her head.

"She used to enjoy food so much," Jonathan Eltwing
told me on one such occasion when we had tried to
tempt her into eating. "She enjoyed all good things —
good food, beautiful objects, beautiful people. She had
a great fondness for gold; every piece of jewelry she
selected was of gold. I used to think that the metal pins
and necklaces she bought were too heavy for her, but
they were what she wanted. And velvet for her dresses

118

— soft velvets and gold. How she loved that combination."

I thought of Uncle Haskell's bright hair and the dark velvet of his smoking jacket on that autumn afternoon when she first saw him. Soft velvet and gold; that combination and with it high praise for the turbulent music that obviously had shaken her as she played it.

As she became weaker, she no longer cared for the songs that previously had given her pleasure. For weeks she lay in her bed, silent and uncomprehending. Uncle Haskell and I went to see her almost daily; then one evening he turned to Jonathan Eltwing as if he had come to a sudden decision. "I can do nothing for her, Jonathan; I will not come here again."

"It is possible that she recognizes you, Haskell," Jonathan began.

Uncle Haskell almost plunged from the room. "No, she doesn't, I'm sure of that. If I could help her, I would, but it's no use. Surely you understand, Jonathan. I have my work — there are many pressures upon me . . ."

It was the first time he had resorted to his lies in connection with anything that had to do with Katy Eltwing.

She died one bright summer morning. When I told Uncle Haskell about it, he turned his head and had nothing to say. He did not go to her funeral.

According to Mrs. Peters there was an old cliché among the men of the neighborhood, the gist of which was the fact that they had never known Haskell Bishop when he wasn't drinking, but neither had they ever known him when he was drunk. He was drunk, however, the day Katy Eltwing was buried, sadly and pathetically drunk. He never spoke of that day afterward, nor did he ever again mention the little woman who had loved him — or who had loved something he represented.

8

Carlotta thought that I was completely bereft of my senses when I chose to live with Aunt Cordelia during my high school years.

"You won't have any dates, Julie; you simply won't. How many high school boys will have a car to drive out into the country, or how many of them — unless you date upperclassmen — are going to be old enough to drive? And anyway, Julie, how many boys are going to want to face Miss Cordelia if they should bring you home five minutes late some night?"

Carlotta was taking a room in town; when she heard that I was staying with Aunt Cordelia, she tried to rent my old room at home, but Father and Alicia would have none of it. "That room is Julie's whenever she wishes to stay in town," they said, and so Carlotta found an even more desirable place with a young couple, neither of whom paid the slightest attention to the whereabouts of their pretty tenant.

For two years while Carlotta sailed from one boy to another, attended every dance and football game, and shook her head pityingly at me as she realized the fulfillment of her prophesies, I might still have been twelve years old and a student in the old one-room rural school, for all the social life I had. Occasionally Father invited me to a college affair and introduced me to some of the young men in his classes; but young college men were interested in young college women for the most part, and their attentions to me were more or less in the line of duty. And Carlotta had been right about the high school boys: they dated the girls who lived in town. The girls who lived in town constituted an "in-group"; if you lived five miles out in the country and were looked after by an austere aunt — well, you simply were not considered eligible for the "in-group."

I was not too unhappy during those first two years. Danny or Jim Ferris saw to it that I got into town for the football games; Alicia insisted that I try out for dramatics and I had parts in a couple of school plays; there were occasional weekends with Father and Alicia during which I had sophisticated experiences that many of the "in-group" girls might have envied. My existence was hardly that of a recluse.

There were, however, many times when I felt lonely,

when I had the aching feeling that life was passing by me and that I was missing something very desirable. Sometimes I leaned on the sill of my window and looked out at the night with a longing that I was not able to define, but one which was responsible for many a sigh and even a few tears.

And then suddenly, there was Brett Kingsman. Suddenly there was a new chapter of my life opening before me. It seemed very beautiful and marvelous, but there were tensions and anxieties arising as suddenly as love had arisen, and I felt bewildered as I tried to face them.

It was Alicia who sharpened those tensions and anxieties for me. She did it indirectly, of course, and without malice. Actually, she set things in motion through an assignment given to her third hour English class where I sat beside the handsome transfer student who had created a sizable furor among the girls, "in-group" as well as outsiders.

My stepmother came to her classes each day beautifully groomed, poised, alert, and with a sweet-sour quality to her comments that made them palatable in spite of an occasional sting. I was quite proud of her, really, although for a long time the memory of Laura's room and of my lonely, bewildered feeling that morning in the breakfast nook tinged my feeling for her ever so slightly. But I couldn't deny the fact that she was a charming person and an exceptionally fine teacher. There was no loafing in Mrs. Trelling's classes; we had to dig ideas out of our own minds instead of reference books; we were treated to no pablum feedings of "true-false" or "fill-in-the-blank" tests. And our themes were not devoted to accounts of a vacation trip or a résumé of *Silas Marner*. Alicia liked originality and independence of thinking; sometimes, however, she had considerable difficulty in discovering either among the adolescents who sat before her.

I remember how fresh and radiant she looked that morning, her blue eyes cool and smiling under her smooth black brows. It occurred to me that my father's wife was still very happy after almost three years, and I envied her a little. I kept telling myself that I was happy, but I wasn't. There was too much anxiety, too many half-hidden uncertainties in my feeling for Brett Kingsman. I had no wish to be as old as Alicia — her forty-odd years seemed quite appalling to me — but I wished for her confidence, her air of what I had recently learned to call *savoir faire*. Uncle Haskell had this quality too, but there was a difference; with Alicia, it was genuine.

I was thinking of these things when I suddenly became aware of her assignment.

"I assume that each of you has read Thoreau's *Civil Disobedience* since it is on the list of required readings — if not, perhaps this assignment will provide motivation for doing so over the weekend." Alicia leaned her elbows on the desk, lacing her slender fingers together and smiling in a way that took the edge off her words. "For next week's assignment I'd like you to write a paper on *Civil Disobedience,* explaining Thoreau's justification for his position and your own reactions to that position." Alicia paid no attention to a slight moan that swept heavenward from the class, and continued serenely. "I will throw out a few points that you might think about in organizing your paper: for example, remembering that *Civil Disobedience* was written in angry protest against the Fugitive Slave Law and the prospect of war with Mexico, what do you think Thoreau's reaction would have been to the secession of the southern states a few years later? And in our own century, how would he have stood with those who violated the 18th amendment? Incidentally, how do you think he would have felt about Federal Aid to Education?"

It was plain that Alicia was enjoying herself. "You may wish to explore the growth of Gandhi's passive resistance struggle in India and its relation to Thoreau's theory. Or again, you might like to discuss in terms of Thoreau's convictions, such a statement as I have placed on the board." She pointed to a sentence which most of us had read idly when we entered the room: "The goal of counseling is to help the individual adjust to his environment."

I commenced jotting down a few notes hurriedly; it was not going to be an easy paper, but I felt a bit of excitement growing in me as I thought of some possibilities for discussion. It was while I was writing that Brett slammed a book down on the arm of his chair, sent a couple pencils rattling to the floor and then leaned back, glaring at Alicia.

She was as smooth as ice cream. "You will have a week to complete your paper. I'd like it typed, please, double-spaced. If any one of you wishes to talk with me about the assignment, you may make an appointment with me during one of my office hours." She flipped a few cards through her fingers as the bell rang, studied

125

the notations briefly and then added, "I should like to see Jim Ferris for a short time at eleven; Norma Grayson at four this afternoon; Julie Trelling at four-fifteen. That is all. You are dismissed."

Out in the corridor Brett got rid of his rage, employing me as a sounding-board. "Lord, how I hate schoolteachers," he railed, "how I hate 'em in general and your highbrow stepmama in particular. What did your old man mean, I wonder, getting himself tied up to that she-encyclopaedia." He turned toward me savagely. "She's out to get me, Julie; she's going to see to it that I flunk English again."

And I, who in former years would have had a biting answer for this sort of attitude, was soft as a mound of mashed potatoes. "I'll help you, Brett; I'm not going to see you flunk, darling."

He pressed my arm a little at that. "I wonder what the old girl wants to see you about, honey?"

I had been wondering about the same thing. "I don't know, Brett; maybe something about my schedule for next year." I could hardly tear myself away at the door of my next class. "Will you meet me outside her office about four-thirty?" I asked.

"I don't know, Julie, baby; I will if I can. Anyway, I'll give you a ring sometime this evening." He slipped his arm around me for a second, and Danny Trevort, who was coming down the hall toward us, gave me a disgusted look. "How are you, Julie, *baby?*" he hissed, as we walked into class together.

How Danny knew it, I don't know for I had never discussed it with him, but it was true that Brett's pet

126

names for me sometimes sent a shiver of distaste down my spine. I had lived with Aunt Cordelia too long to enjoy being called "Julie, baby" or "Honeybun" or "Sugar." They were foolish in the first place and rather revoltingly sticky for someone who was strictly a high protein girl. Still, it was Brett who gave me those names and Brett was the boy whom I called "my beloved" in the secrecy of my own dreams. When one loves, one must learn to adjust, to be understanding, I thought.

There had been moments when I very nearly forgot that bit of wisdom; moments like the ones when we sat together in the darkened theater over at the college and watched a famous pair of actors in *Macbeth*. I remember sitting tense as the door to King Duncan's bedroom opened and Lady Macbeth came out, leaning against the wall for support, looking in horror at her blood-drenched hands. I pressed Brett's arm in my excitement, but he did not share my mood. He yawned overtly and leaned his cheek down to mine. "Are you bored too, honey?" he asked hopefully.

I felt strongly out of tune with Brett that night after the play, and he noticed it.

"The whole thing was a lot of hogwash as far as I'm concerned," he said belligerently as we left the theater.

"It has done pretty well for the past three centuries in spite of your opinion," I said sharply, the Aunt Cordelia-influence getting the upper hand of me.

Brett dropped my hand abruptly. "Well, you can have it, schoolmarm," he said, and the contempt in his voice was unmistakable.

Our romance trembled in the air for a while that evening, but it soon became steady again, for I was not long in feeling contritely apologetic for my sharpness, and Brett, who was in immediate need of help with an English assignment, was sweetly forgiving. We reassured one another of our love, and I told myself that I must expect to make adjustments to Brett's tastes. Wasn't that what love was all about — a mutual understanding, a give-and-take relationship? I didn't like it when a small thought intruded itself, suggesting that so far, our understanding was hardly mutual, and that up to the present, I was doing all the giving and Brett was doing the taking.

At any rate, I was not going to risk losing Brett because I had learned to enjoy Shakespeare and he hadn't. Never, I thought, for Brett was a shining wonder to which I could never quite grow accustomed. He was tall, wide of shoulder and narrow of hip, beautifully bronzed. His eyes were blue and heavily lashed, his black hair slightly wavy, his square chin cleft. There was just one feature of Brett's handsome face that I found to be not quite perfect: his mouth was too soft looking, too loose. That was all, and I felt that I was being far too critical in noticing that one defect at all. Almost all the girls in school had been dazzled by him when he entered as a transfer student early in the year, and wonder of wonders, of all the girls he had chosen Julie Trelling. Carlotta was deeply impressed; she remembered after a long lapse that she and I had been close friends since we were little seven-year-olds.

Aunt Cordelia had no comment to make upon my Brett other than the fact that he was, indeed, handsome. She asked me a few questions about him — he had trouble

128

with English, she knew, but that was not uncommon; some of her most intelligent boys had faltered before noun clauses and Shakespearean sonnets. Brett was, no doubt, more inclined toward mathematics or science? No? Music or art, perhaps? Athletics? When I had to admit that Brett had no talent or inclination in any of these areas, Aunt Cordelia only raised her brows expressively.

I wanted to say, "What about your own brother?" but with the thought I realized that I was admitting a likeness between Brett and Uncle Haskell. It was not an admission that pleased me; neither was the fact that Uncle Haskell was the one older person in my family for whom Brett had expressed an interest.

"Fine old boy — I really like him," Brett told me with some admiration after listening for an hour to Uncle Haskell's empty boasting.

Being in love with Brett was not pure joy. I thought about it that afternoon on the Thoreau assignment day as I walked down the corridor in the Administration Building and seated myself outside Alicia's office. The nameplate on her door said simply "Mrs. A. Trelling"; it seemed rather nice, I thought, that Alicia and I had the same name. I never could quite get used to it. In my early months of high school I used to go inside her office and say, "Good morning, Mrs. Trelling," and she would grin at me and say, "Try 'Alicia' when we're in here alone, Julie; it's much friendlier."

I smiled to myself as I thought of the relatives who had been my teachers; I supposed there would be Father in the future, possibly Bill.

We were a schoolteacherish family, there was no doubt of that. But we were a nice family; I liked us. Father and Alicia had been very fine about my deciding to live with Aunt Cordelia; they had looked at me a bit thoughtfully when I told them as gracefully as I could that somehow the big house among the trees had come to seem like home to me, and they nodded although they may have felt some doubt when I added a bit of embroidery to my decision by implying that Aunt Cordelia was hardly able to face my leaving her. But they had neither remonstrated nor pled; they told me that their home was mine, come homesickness, a bad storm, a hankering for a holiday or a complete change of mind. And thus we had left it. We three had been very good friends; in some ways having Alicia was a little like having Laura again. She used to call and ask me if I'd do her hair for a special occasion, and we would chat by the hour as I tried to achieve the effect she particularly liked. Sometimes I would see Father smiling above the book he was reading, and I knew that he was pleased at the friendship between Alicia and me.

They were younger and gayer than Aunt Cordelia, of course, and could offer me many advantages that she could not. If there was a special concert or play to be given over at the college, there was always an invitation for me to stay in town and accompany them. Sometimes they invited Danny Trevort too, not that Danny was anything more to me than the kid I'd grown up with, but they liked him and the four of us had had great fun together. They even took Danny and me to New York once, picking Chris up on the way, and we had gone on a

130

dozen or more interesting forays into the big city, having the gay and carefree kind of vacation that none of us would ever forget.

All that had been before Brett. They didn't invite Danny with me any longer, because he and I had become virtually enemies, but they didn't invite Brett either. And the more coolness they showed toward Brett, the more I saw him as being wronged and misunderstood; therefore the more I was determined to stand by him.

Norma Grayson emerged from Alicia's office at last, looking weary but triumphant. "You're to go in now," she said, nodding toward the door. Then she laid her hand on my arm. "She was real nice, Julie; she went through that *Civil Disobedience* thing for me, and I think that I halfway understand what the guy was talking about. It's pretty ghastly, though, isn't it?"

The whole world seemed a little ghastly to me that afternoon. I said, "It certainly is," to Norma, and then went into the office and took a chair beside Alicia's desk. She looked a little worn, too, I thought.

"How are you, Miss Julie Trelling?" she asked, smiling at me. "You haven't quite seemed yourself lately; I've been concerned about you."

"I'm perfectly well, Alicia, really," I said and settled myself to hear whatever she had to say.

"Good. I suppose it's the end-of-the-year pressure that's moving in on all of us, isn't it? Well, first of all, there's the concert at Collins Hall next week. Your father and I wondered if you would stay in and go with us Saturday evening. You know Ted Bolling, the young assistant in your father's office? He's going as our guest, and he very

131

definitely brightened up when I suggested that you might be able to come along."

I stiffened. Saturday night. They knew I'd have a date with Brett on Saturday night, and they were deliberately trying to hurt him by getting me out with someone else. I wanted to hear that concert; I'd wanted to hear it for weeks, and there was nothing particularly wrong with Ted Bolling, except that he wasn't Brett Kingsman. But I was not going to be sucked in by intrigue.

"I'm sorry, Alicia, but I can't possibly. I always have a date with Brett on Saturday night. I thought that you and Father knew that."

Alicia's brows moved ever so slightly. "Oh, yes, of course. Well, your father will be sorry; he has been looking forward to seeing you. You haven't been over to talk with him lately."

I didn't say anything, and for just a few seconds there was silence between us. Then Alicia opened a drawer, took out a sheaf of papers and said briskly — artificially, I thought — "Apropos of Brett, I have a number of his papers here, Julie. The later ones have shown quite a lot of improvement over his earlier work; however, it's rather an erratic improvement. What I mean is that there will be an intelligently stated idea in one paragraph followed by a meaningless string of words that Brett seems to feel I'll recognize as a sentence. Would you have a theory concerning this discrepancy in quality?"

I knew what was coming. I hadn't meant to do another person's work for him at first, but Brett had a way with him, and week after week his papers had become more and more nearly complete copies of my dictation. I had never cheated before, and I was hard put to rationalize the whole sorry business. It helped to remember that Laura had once said that it was a privilege for her to be able to help Bill with his thesis; now, I tried to tell myself, I could understand exactly how she felt. But my message didn't quite ring true; in my heart I knew there was a difference between Laura's situation and mine. After all, she had only *helped* Bill.

It had all commenced quite early in the year. The first time Brett ever noticed me had been one day in class when papers were being returned to us. He had smiled at me rather sourly and asked, "Are you really that good or do you get this kind of grade because her highness is your stepmother?"

I hadn't liked that much, but I just said, "I think it's because I happen to like English. I don't always make such grades in math."

He looked friendlier. "Well, congratulations, sugar. You're pretty smooth, no matter what kind of grades you make."

When we were dismissed that day, Brett walked close behind me. Out in the hall he said, "Look, baby, how about giving me a hand with this paper? The old girl says I have to correct and return it by tomorrow —" He unfolded a paper that was plastered with red code signs made by Alicia's pencil.

I said, "Of course, Brett; I'll be glad to help you." And that is the way the relationship which I thought of as a romance had started. A lot of very popular girls in high school thought of it as a romance too, and I was suddenly the object of their envy. I hadn't been particularly envied before; I had been simply a little grind who lived out in the country and who made good grades because a grim old aunt saw to it that every scrap of homework was completed and turned in. Brett Kingsman's attentions had changed that picture in their minds.

But I had become worried about the help I was giving him. "This is the idea, Brett; now put it into your own words, just as simply and clearly as you can," I'd tell him. And then I'd get a kiss, a compliment or two, and finally a plea that was almost a command: "Now, what was that again, sugar? How did you say it just now?"

Alicia was speaking again. "I have read your papers for quite a long time, Julie, and I recognize your style of writing, your approach to ideas. What I find here are papers done by you with a few semiliterate lines contributed by Brett. It's a bit on the shabby side, isn't it?"

I was close to tears, but I forced them back and tried to summon strength for a counterattack. "I've only been trying to give him a lift, Alicia. Your course *is* difficult, and Brett has lost so much schooling because of his family moving around from place to place. Anyway, everybody is against him. You know that neither you nor Father can stand the sight of him."

Alicia squared her shoulders, and there was really an air of Aunt Cordelia about her. "Julie, any person in my classes is welcome to come into this office to discuss his difficulties. Any person who takes the trouble to read assigned material, who makes any effort on his own to discover a few ideas and arrange them — that student can depend upon my help whether I like him or not.

134

Kingsman hasn't made the slightest effort. He is sullen, lazy, smart-alecky and dishonest." She paused a minute and looked at me steadily. "What in Heaven's name do you mean by getting involved with this boy, Julie?"

All the fire that I withheld from Brett was ready for Alicia. "You wouldn't know, would you, Alicia? You have Father just as Laura has Bill. You have someone to love you and a home where you feel secure, and you don't have to be lonely and not sure where you really belong. Well, I'm not so lucky as you. I need love very much, and when I find someone who gives it to me, I'm going to hold on to him — and you can tell Father that — and Laura — and everybody."

I was half-crying, half-shouting at her; even in my overwrought state I noticed that she looked pale. It was a rough session for both of us.

"Julie, believe me, I am not unsympathetic. I know what it means to be lonely, and I know that insecurity is frightening. But you never gain security by selling out for a shoddy something that only resembles love."

"You're saying then, that Brett is shoddy?"

"I think that he is very immature and that he is using you for his own purposes. He is giving you nothing and taking all he can get. He may change some day; I doubt it, but he may. Until he does, yes, he's shoddy."

"Not in the same class with Father or Bill or — or —"

"That's right. Or Dan Trevort or Chris or Ted Bolling. Or a dozen others I could name for you."

I got up with what I felt was considerable dignity. "Well, Alicia, I'll say just this: I don't care whether you or Father or Laura or any of the people you've named like

Brett or not. I love him, and I'm going to stand by him."

Alicia also got up with dignity. "Very well, Julie. That is your right. But understand this: if any more papers done by Julie Trelling are handed in by Brett Kingsman, you are both going to the Dean's office. Brett will flunk the course, and you will be disciplined as the Dean sees fit. You had just as well begin learning what Brett is going to mean for you."

I walked out of the office without looking at her. It didn't seem possible that we had ever been friends.

Brett wasn't there to drive me home; neither was Danny, who probably had thought that I was staying in town when I hadn't shown up at our usual meeting place for the drive home. I could have asked Father to take me home or I could have called Aunt Cordelia, or have waited an hour for the next bus, but the spirit of martyrdom was strong upon me and I decided to walk the five miles home. I rather hoped that they'd find me along the wayside sometime before dawn, perhaps, in a state of complete exhaustion.

I'd only walked a little over a mile, however, when a car came tearing down the dusty road toward me. It made a U turn a few yards in front of me and then stopped at the side of the road. A very grim-looking Danny sat behind the wheel and watched me approach.

"You could have told me your plans, Julie," he said angrily. "How was I to know that you didn't have a way to get home? Couldn't gorgeous Kingsman afford the gas to drive you out or is he having his beauty-nap?"

"I wasn't with Brett in the first place, and I'm under no compulsion to tell you my plans in the second place. I

136

don't know why you've come out here to meet me; I'm nothing to you."

Danny was pretty furious. He said, "You've just made the most doggoned accurate statement that I've heard in days. You are absolutely nothing to me. Absolutely. But you're wrong about my coming out to meet you. It's just a coincidence — even now I have half a mind to make you walk the rest of the way —" He jerked the car door open. "Get in," he barked at me and I did, ungraciously accepting his favor while I remembered with satisfaction that I had once blacked his eye.

The world was against me that evening. Alicia was mad. Danny was mad. Aunt Cordelia was irked because I hadn't told Danny that I was staying after school, thus causing him to make another trip. I told her that he had not come back to meet me, that he was going into town for some other reason — he hadn't told me what — but she said, nonsense, that he'd called to find out if I was home and a few minutes later had started down the road.

I went up to my room and tried to think of what it would be like when Brett and I were married; I thought about how I would inform my entire family that be it Thanksgiving or Christmas or any other holiday, if Brett were not welcome, then they could count upon it, Julie would not be on hand either. I thought of how I'd stand by him and comfort him with my love and loyalty. But try as I would, I couldn't get Brett to emerge in my daydream as a wronged but valiant and heroic figure; I kept seeing him behave like a sullen child in spite of all my efforts.

It was getting late when Brett finally called to ask if he could come out for a while and talk over our English assignment. He sounded sleepy and morose; I thought of what Danny had said about his having a beauty-nap, but I pushed the thought aside and told him joyfully that yes, he might come out. Aunt Cordelia, who sat beside the table reading, said, "Until ten, Julia; no later." She didn't lift her eyes from her book.

Brett and I sat in the living room and talked; Aunt Cordelia did not come in to meet him. If it had been Danny who was calling on me, there would have been a pleasant welcome for him and some sort of refreshment. Not for Brett. She remained seated with her book at hand, her knees crossed, and her foot swinging back and forth with what appeared to be mild agitation after some of Brett's remarks.

He wanted help, of course, with the paper on *Civil Disobedience*. He had a notebook ready and his pen poised above it. "Tell me how to begin it, sugar," he said wearily, knowing, I suspect, that it was going to be tiresome business in getting a clear dictation from me and then expending precious energy in putting my words down on paper.

"I can't tell you what to say, Brett; I just can't do that. Why don't you write in your own words just why you think Thoreau felt that a man is justified at times in not paying his taxes, in not fighting for a cause in which he —"

Brett slammed his notebook shut. "How am I going to say it in my own words? I haven't read the stupid thing, and I have no intention of reading it. If you don't

138

want to help me, just say so."

I thought that foot beside the dining room table was going to fly through the door. Even my love cracked a little.

"Well, I can't do your paper for you, Brett, if that's what you mean. I've been doing too much as it is. We're going to get in trouble, both of us; Alicia told me so this afternoon." Let Aunt Cordelia hear it, I thought; I supposed that it was just as well.

There wasn't any love in Brett's eyes as he sat staring at me. Finally he said, "So that's it, is it? You're afraid of getting your own neck in the noose. It's all right if I flunk English again, but you're not going to get in bad with your precious stepma. Lord, how I hate schoolteachers," he said, for the second time within twelve hours.

We sat for a while in silence, and Aunt Cordelia's foot quieted down as if it were waiting. I was so mad at that point that I was ready to tell Brett that our romance was over. But Brett changed his tactics suddenly and swept down my defenses.

He said, "I'm sorry, honey. Forget the whole lousy business. I might just as well flunk English again, because it's a sure thing that math is down the drain." He shrugged, and taking both my hands, drew me to my feet. "Don't be mad, little sugar; come out to the car and say good night," he whispered.

He was so handsome, so masterful looking with his height and his beautifully wide shoulders. I commenced to melt in the warmth of his sudden tenderness. We went down the long path toward his car, Brett's arm around my waist, his cheek resting against my hair. When we reached the end of the path, he said, "Let's go for just a little walk, honey; just a few minutes together."

"I can't, Brett — it's getting late. I simply can't. Aunt Cordelia will —"

There was another flash of anger. "Look, Julie, are you letting that old woman run your life? If you are, you can count me out. I'm not coming out here to be told that you can't help me out of a tight spot, you can't take a little walk in the woods, you can't do anything. I thought you loved me, but if you don't, all right, say so. I'll begin looking around somewhere else."

The next minute we were walking back into the woods — just a short, little walk to show that I loved him.

It was a wonderful night; the world looked as if it had been dipped in some liquid silver poured out of the moon. The woods were so still and radiant that it brought a catch of wistfulness to my throat. Such beauty ought not to be wasted in small talk. I thought of Jessica and young Lorenzo watching that moon together, matching their flashes of imagery, fitting them together into a perfect mosaic of poetry:

> "The moon shines bright: in such a night as this
> When the sweet wind did gently kiss the trees
> And they did make no noise; in such a night
> Troilus methinks mounted the Trojan walls
> And sighed his soul toward the Grecian tents,
> Where Cressid lay that night."

I wished that Brett would say those lines to me as

we walked in the moonlight, and that I could then say:

"In such a night
Did Thisbe fearfully o'ertrip the dew,
And saw the lion's shadow ere himself
And ran dismay'd away."

I felt a longing for Brett to understanding my feelings, for an affinity between us such as must have existed between Jessica and young Lorenzo that radiant night.

But Brett had not read much of Shakespeare, and even if he had known every play and every sonnet by rote, he would not have been at that moment in a mood to quote any of the immortal lines. His arms were suddenly holding me very tightly. "I love you so much, little honey-bun, little sugar —" I didn't much care for the pet names, but that night he could have run down the entire dessert menu of a well-stocked restaurant and I wouldn't have objected.

We stood close in one another's arms and Brett was whispering, "You understand, don't you, sugar, don't you, Julie, baby —?"

Julie, baby, was indeed beginning to understand. The word was beginning to come through clearly to her, and Shakespeare was fading away into the background like muted music contrasting with the tumult of a mighty drama.

Then, as if on cue, there emerged from left wing a dapper, slender figure which advanced airily to center stage, laid aside an ancient golf bag, and extended a cordial hand toward the leading man.

141

"Kingsman, dear boy, what luck to have run across you," Uncle Haskell exclaimed gaily. He immediately pretended to be chagrined at having burst in upon us, but I knew Uncle Haskell; he did not know the meaning of chagrin.

"So awfully sorry to have intruded upon a tender moment, children," he said playfully. "Still, it's my good fortune to have found you, Brett. Do you know that you were the subject of a telephone conversation between me and one of the best known producers in New York not more than two hours ago?"

Brett was staring at Uncle Haskell a little stupidly, but I could see that his interest was beginning to come through the fog. He liked Uncle Haskell; he wouldn't for very long, but that night my uncle seemed to be opening up new vistas for Brett.

Uncle Haskell disposed of me in a hurry. "Julie, my pet, I think you'd better run along now. Brett can tell you his good news tomorrow. I have an idea that Aunt Cordelia would like you safe inside. Ten o'clock comes on apace, you know."

I felt weak and ill with humiliation, anger, anxiety, and uncertainty. I lingered a few yards away and listened for a minute or two while Uncle Haskell unfolded his story. He would never have considered merely sending an amorous young man on his way and giving an amorous young niece a brief bedtime lecture. Uncle Haskell's soul would have revolted at the image of himself as an upholder of morals; he preferred to achieve the same result by means less hackneyed. Thus, his story that a producer in New York, beside himself with

142

joy in producing Uncle Haskell's play, had telephoned to ask about a prospect for a part — "a minor part, mind you, but not an unimportant one —" My uncle was pouring the soothing unguent on Brett's bruised feelings. Brett, of course, was young and inexperienced; still, Uncle Haskell had told E.J. that this young fellow was extraordinarily handsome, had a natural grace and flair for the dramatic —

I had heard enough. That Brett was weak, I had to admit, but he didn't deserve cruelty like this. I ran through the woods and up the steps to the old porch swing where Aunt Cordelia was waiting for me.

I expected a lecture, but she was strangely quiet. Let me forget to dust the living room or mend a torn blouse, and she would hold forth at length; let me run off into the woods with Brett Kingsman, and she had nothing to say. Finally, when she didn't speak, I said, "I'm sorry, Aunt Cordelia; I shouldn't have gone out there tonight."

She put her hand on mine for a second; that was all, just the faintest pressure on my hand. After that we sat in silence.

We heard Brett's car roar down the road after a while; then later, a long time later, we heard Uncle Haskell emerging from the woods, his pleasant voice humming, *My heart at thy sweet voice,* and I wondered if he were deliberately hurting himself by remembering that aria which Katy Eltwing had loved to hear him sing. He seemed cheerful enough, however, when he glimpsed us among the shadows and waved to us.

"Good night, my girls," he called, and strode away

143

toward his carriage-house apartment.

"You sent him out there for me, didn't you, Aunt Cordelia?" I asked after a while.

"He went of his own accord," she said quietly. "I was frightened tonight, Julia. For the first time that I can remember, I gave way to panic. Then I called Haskell. I guess you realize that he has never in his life lifted a burden from me; that is why your father and Jonathan have disliked him so much. But tonight, he did. He treated me the way a strong brother treats a sister when she is weak."

Upstairs in my room I stood at the window and looked out at the silver world.

"On such a night," I thought, "were ill and good,
Bright and unlovely; precious, tawdry,
All mingled into one
And pressed against my heart."

It was a long way from Shakespeare, but it gave me a bit of comfort to think in blank verse at the close of a particularly wretched day.

144

9

That spring which marked the end of my junior year in high school was a difficult one for me. When Brett had the hard news straight from Uncle Haskell that E. J. had felt the academic record of Bishop's protegé made an interview unnecessary, Brett was through with me, my family, and any person who had a kind word for any one of us. He immediately began taking Carlotta Berry to all the spring activities at school whereupon Carlotta glowed and began regarding me as if I were a country cousin. Even Danny refused to let bygones be bygones, and he invited Eden Brownlee to go to the prom with him when he knew that I had no choice but to stay at

145

home. Ted Bolling, who, Alicia said, had brightened at the mention of my name, had in the meantime brightened at the presence of a young secretary from the English department. I was a social outcast as suddenly as I had become the envy of half the girls in school when Brett first paid attention to me.

The loneliness and sense of loss left an aching void inside me, and the knowledge that everyone knew I had been jilted was an added stroke of bitterness. I chose not to remember Brett's inadequacies; but to dwell upon his attractiveness, his moments of tenderness; there were many sweet memories, and they made the bitterness of Carlotta's taking over everything that had belonged to me very hard to bear.

I wrote a little poetry as a release, and it helped somewhat, although even in my misery, I knew that it was not very good poetry. I grew apathetic about my schoolwork and did a C paper on *Civil Disobedience* for Alicia, who made no comment, but shook her head ever so slightly when she handed it back to me. It was a pity; I had intended writing a really superior paper for her on that day when she made the assignment.

From my window I watched the full moon — a moon that reminded me of Brett — become shadowed, little by little until there was only a deep blackness in the woods at night. I would sit there wakeful, hour after hour, and wonder if this aching around my heart, this sense of being alone, forlorn and unwanted in a world where there was gayety and love for others of my age, was going to continue for all of my days.

Everyone in my family was kind to me that spring.

Father came out and took me for long drives; Alicia gave me a crisp, white suit with a coral blouse that would have sent me into raptures ordinarily; Laura wrote that she and my small namesake were looking forward to visiting me in August. And Aunt Cordelia was wonderful. There was not one sermon or high and mighty word from her. I think that I began to love Aunt Cordelia that spring.

Day followed day, each heavier than the other, for six weeks or so, and then the miracle happened. I have often thought about that miracle: surely the weight under which I had labored had gradually been lessening and the miracle was not a miracle at all. I think not though; it still seems like a miracle and this is how it was:

I had gone to sleep in sorrow and longing; I awoke the next morning — and something had happened. It was a bright summer morning and every leaf on the trees outside seemed to have been polished, glittering as they were in the sunlight. The white curtains at my window moved just a little at the touch of the breeze that drifted inside, and my room somehow became a vivid picture to me as if I had pulled aside some veil of indifference and was suddenly aware of it. The walls were as pale as they could get and still be called yellow; the surface of the old walnut bureau and bookcase that Aunt Cordelia and I had refinished was deep with lights which were absorbed in its brown depths. There were white throw rugs on the floor — white rugs that Aunt Cordelia had allowed me to have against the judgment of her practical mind — and there was the small rockingchair upholstered in worn velvet which had been hers when she was a girl. On my desk stood a framed photograph which my aunt had allowed me to keep, the photograph of a lovely young girl smiling at the thought of Jonathan Eltwing, and of a blond young man standing in a studied pose, and a little girl who looked like Laura, laughing at the camera that photographed her.

All these things I saw in that moment of awaking; it wasn't until seconds later that I realized how I was lying, cool and relaxed in my bed, with a sense of serenity and quiet happiness enveloping me. I made myself think of Brett as one might touch an old wound to determine whether or not it is healed, and the thought of him miraculously did not hurt. I was neither angry nor contemptuous; I just remembered a beautiful boy I had once loved and it was as if something inside me said, "Well, wasn't that lovely? And now, shall we think of other things?"

For a while I was almost afraid to move, fearful that just starting the ordinary duties of another day would break the spell that had descended upon me. Then I stepped carefully out of bed, and stood in front of the window breathing deeply. All was well. Still only a sense of well-being within me. After a moment I ran into the bathroom, turned on a cold shower and exulted while the cold lines of water pelted my body. As I stood glowing after I had rubbed myself with a big bath towel, I wondered why so much had been written about love's pain and so little about the glorious relief of being delivered from love's pain. I regretted that I did not have more talent for expressing myself in poetry; I did resolve, however, that I'd do another paper on *Civil Dis-*

obedience — it was too late for credit, of course, but it would give me a chance to show Alicia my real ability.

I brushed my hair furiously for a good five minutes and tied it back with a strip of rose velvet. I had a new housecoat, a gift from Laura, too beautiful for ordinary occasions, being all of white eyelet cotton over a lining of petal pink dimity, but I put it on recklessly and stood before my mirror in unabashed self-approval. I had sparkle that morning, sparkle that originated somewhere deep inside me and spread outward to my cheeks and eyes, even it seemed, to the gleam of my hair.

Down in the kitchen Aunt Cordelia was preparing breakfast; the aroma of coffee and Canadian bacon and hot, buttered toast met me as I ran downstairs, and I, who for weeks had been growing thinner as I picked indifferently at my food, was suddenly famished and eager.

We often ate our breakfast in a sunny corner of the kitchen, and Aunt Cordelia had placed two blue bowls on the table, two of Grandmother Bishop's best china bowls, and they were filled with raspberries picked only that morning and still frosted with dew. I was especially perceptive to all things beautiful that morning — raspberries in blue china bowls were enough to make the heart sing.

Aunt Cordelia glanced up from her work as I entered the fragrant kitchen, and I saw a light come into her eyes. She liked seeing me carefully dressed of a morning; she was relieved too, I am sure, to see that I had emerged from the despondency that had weighed upon me for weeks. I smiled at her and hurried to pour the coffee.

"Aunt Cordelia," I said in the tones of a Biblical proc-

149

lamation, "I have been visited by a miracle."

The light in her eyes was clouded instantly, whether in concern over my sanity or recognition of the fact that miracles could sometimes be embarrassing to a family. She let a circle of pink bacon fall back into the frying pan, and stood looking at me. I laughed at her expression and poured the coffee so recklessly that it overflowed one cup and filled the saucer.

"There are miracles and miracles, Aunt Cordelia; this one has just given me a new outlook on life. I went to sleep last night still feeling hurt over Brett; this morning I am completely free of him. He no longer matters. It's all over."

She was relieved, there was no doubt about that, but she took her place at the table as sedately as always. "Love is not love which alters," she quoted as she passed a basket of toast to me, "when it alteration finds."

I knew then that she was happy. Aunt Cordelia was likely to be in one of her better moods when she felt like quoting Shakespeare.

As we sat together at breakfast that morning I thought that food had never before tasted so wonderful.

"You know, Aunt Cordelia, there will come a time when I'll eat berries like these some morning, fresh, dewy berries like these, and I'll think, 'What's the matter? These are not like the ones I ate with so much pleasure long ago.' And then I'll tell myself, 'Of course not, for where is the sunny kitchen overlooking the woods, and where is the beautiful room upstairs where you awakened that morning, where is the aunt who quoted from one of Shakespeare's sonnets and above all, where is the sixteen-year-old girl who had just experienced a miracle?' It will never be the same, Aunt Cordelia; I'll never eat raspberries like these again."

Aunt Cordelia just smiled gently. "Maybe not," she said.

I changed into my blue jeans after breakfast. The first evidence that things were getting back to normal was Aunt Cordelia's sharp, "Not in that beautiful housecoat, Julia," when I commenced to gather up the dishes. All that morning I worked in a near frenzy of housewifely enthusiasm, polishing furniture, dusting rows of books, washing windows, arranging flowers. Everything I did was a delight; it was a beautiful morning, and I was free of Brett Kingsman!

When I had the house shining, I called Alicia, who got a little bit into my mood of euphoria when I told her all about recent developments. Alicia and I hadn't talked for a long time, but that morning we ignored the coldness that had been between us. "Julie, I'm so happy I could shout," she told me, and we laughed and chatted like two girls again. Later I wrote a long letter to Chris and then one to Laura in which I enclosed a little story for young Julie with crazy drawings which I knew she would like. It was as if I had been away from my family for a long time, and communicating with them again was a great satisfaction.

After supper that night I saddled Peter the Great, and rode down through the woods to the road that led south of our place and which, incidentally, went past Danny Trevort's home. I saw Danny out in the yard striding behind a noisy lawn mower as I approached; he had grown

151

very tall, and I smiled to myself because I could remember a good many years in school when I had been as tall as he was although he was almost two years older. Then suddenly, he had shot up, leaving me far below; it had seemed very strange for quite a while. His hair, that used to be so yellow when we were younger, had grown much darker except where it was bleached by the sun and there was a taut, well-knit look about him that suggested strength in spite of his slenderness. I waved casually as I passed and he gave me a nod; I wasn't too much surprised, however, when some minutes later I heard the pound of his horse's hooves as he rode to overtake me.

We had often raced when we were kids and that night I spurred Peter the Great, urging him to forget his years and give Danny's younger mount a run for his money. We pounded down the hard-packed road, and I felt exhilarated and joyful with the strength and the gallant effort of old Peter as he strove to do me proud.

Finally, Danny drew rein and called to me; after a minute or two we were trotting quietly, side by side.

"You ride too hard, Julie. You'll break your neck one of these days," Danny said. His eyes were friendly, and he laughed at the way strands of hair had blown across my face and into my eyes.

"I don't suppose I could have grown up without you and Chris to advise me," I said.

"We did seem to have more sense," he agreed amiably. "You were always one to fly apart in all directions."

"You were both Aunt Cordelia's pets — you know that well enough. Two big, disgusting pets, just because you were male."

"Not at all. She just recognized a certain quality of integrity and maturity of judgment in old Chris and me. You could hardly blame her for that."

"Oh, slurp, slurp, Trevort, I can't stand it," I cried, getting Peter the Great into action again, and we were off, laughing and pounding down the road like two kids gone berserk.

It was fun being with Danny again; it had been a long time since we had been friendly, a whole school year, in fact. Ever since I had started going around with Brett. I had never thought of how Danny might fit into the role of sweetheart; he hadn't seemed to care much about girls until very lately. I knew that he had taken Carlotta to a school dance one night; she had giggled and told me that Danny hadn't so much as held her hand on the way home, no good-night kiss, no more romance about him than when we had been grade school kids under Aunt Cordelia's watchful eye. But he had taken very pretty and popular Eden Brownlee to the prom only a few weeks before, and I had heard no criticism of his behavior from her. It stung me just a little to think of Eden. I believe that I had always considered that Danny was my special property if I wanted to claim him. I had a note up in my leather box of secret treasures, a note from Danny which I had received when I was about nine. It read, "I have for many, many years always thought that you was the nicest girl in school. I will always love you till deth us do part. Yours truly, Danny Trevort." With a document like that in my possession I couldn't help but feel that I had certain rights, and I had rather wanted to claim them that lonely night of the junior prom.

"How are you and Kingsman doing these days?" he asked, when we had quieted down a bit. There was no apparent reason for his asking the question; everybody in school knew how Kingsman and I were doing. However, I was somehow glad to tell him.

"A broken melody," I said, "a shattered remnant of the past."

"Your guardian angel must have been on duty," Danny commented.

I didn't answer. I thought to myself, "No, but there *was* Uncle Haskell."

"How about you and Eden Brownlee?" I asked. I was conscious of what I rather hoped he would say.

But he didn't say it. He looked thoughtful for a minute, and then he said, "She's a right sort of girl. I like her; I guess I like her very much."

So that was that. "Deth" hadn't parted us, but Brett Kingsman had driven quite a wedge between us, and now it looked as if Eden Brownlee were going to finish the job. Danny and I were going to enjoy one of those beautiful brother-sister relationships that summer. Maybe not even that. Not if the Eden Brownlee influence became too potent.

Chris came home for a visit that summer; he, like Danny, was ready for college and a bit patronizing toward me who still had another year in high school. But it was wonderful having him home. We rode and swam, played tennis and went dancing with Danny and Eden. I had never felt so happy and relaxed; I even came to like Eden after a while. After all, it was not her fault that I had lost Danny.

Later in the summer there came Laura and Bill and little Julie; then Father and Alicia joined us and for two joyful weeks Aunt Cordelia and I had our family around us. Jonathan Eltwing often came over for the evening, and occasionally Uncle Haskell risked the failure in meeting a deadline in order to be with us. All the rooms upstairs, so long empty, were filled with people very dear to me. Sometimes I would stand in my own room listening to the buzz of talking and laughter, and I would think of how much life had changed since the October day when I had been brought out to Aunt Cordelia's place under the influence of the doctor's sedative.

Young Julie was my roommate during those two weeks, little Julie, all dimples and rosy curves, but with what seemed to me a reflective wisdom in her large eyes. She followed me around with a devotion I had never known before, and at night she lay beside me, begging for more stories until she grew sleepy.

"It's a Laura and Julie relationship all over again," I heard Father tell Aunt Cordelia. I recognized it too, never so poignantly as on the night when she breathed a long sigh of delight over the end of a story.

"We're always going to be like this, aren't we, Julie? We're always going to be two Julies together in your room when I come here, aren't we?"

My heart got out of rhythm for a second as I remembered things long past. "For quite a while, Julie; perhaps not always, but for a long time," I whispered.

"Till you marry a big boy and go away?" she asked.

"I'm not going to marry anyone for a long time, Julie."

155

"Grandpa and Alicia wish that Danny was your boy friend," the small gossip continued.

I laughed. "I don't think there's any chance of that, sweetheart; Danny has another girl."

"Well, I don't want you to have a boy friend and get married. I want you to stay right here so we can always be two Julies together in this room when I come to see you."

Then the summer was over, and the sweet, sad days of autumn moved in once again. Fun was over, and another year of work had commenced. I didn't see Danny and Eden so often after Chris went back to school; Danny still came over to do any heavy work for Aunt Cordelia, putting up storm windows one week, cutting down a tree that leaned too near the electric power line another time. I felt that since he and Eden entered college he treated me as if I were a somewhat dull younger sister. I often sat at my window during the nights of early fall that year, and it seemed to me quite likely that I would, indeed, stay right on being another Julie in the same old room when my little niece came to visit me.

There was another matter that made the autumn days sadder than usual that fall. It was the talk about Carlotta and Brett Kingsman, gossip that everybody seemed to know about before I did. Danny was the one who told me.

He still drove from his home into town where he attended college, and as in other years, I rode with him, sitting in the front seat at his side while the younger freshmen and sophomores were packed in the back. One evening when he had delivered the others at their homes

156

he turned to me suddenly.

"Do you ever see Kingsman these days, Julie?"

"Not if either of us can avoid it," I answered.

"Well, don't. He's no good. There's talk all over town about him and little Lottie. She may be a dumb kid — all right, so she is — but she's far too good for him. And if I ever hear of your being with him, I'll tell Miss Cordelia things that will make her lock you up and —"

"Don't you think, Mr. Trevort, that you're being —"

"Shut up," he said brusquely, and rather to my surprise, I did.

And there was no flippancy about me a few days later either, when I knew that Carlotta had left high school to spend the winter with an aunt in Idaho, an aunt of whom we'd never heard. I met Mrs. Berry one day when I was shopping and hardly recognized the pale, haggard woman as Carlotta's mother who had been so vivaciously excited only a few months before when Brett invited Carlotta to the prom. Mrs. Berry turned away so that she would not have to speak to me; it was a sobering moment.

There was a strange dreariness in the air that fall. At first I thought that I felt that way because of Carlotta, but later I noticed that Danny was dreary too. I didn't know why at first, but little by little, the gossip came through that he and Eden were having trouble.

Eden, it seemed, interpreted the relationship between Danny and me as being more than friendship. She didn't like it that Danny felt he must drive me into town for special events, although she was the one he squired to those events — he only gave me transportation service. She was also annoyed when he mentioned that we had ridden our horses together on some crisp autumn evening — we'd done that for the past ten years — and she didn't like it when Aunt Cordelia invited him to stay for dinner one evening after he had done some work for her.

Then Alicia and I gave a dinner party for a young foreign exchange student to which we invited Eden and Danny as well as two other couples. Eden sent her regrets, but Danny came anyway, and after that they quarreled. Eden was said to have delivered an ultimatum concerning Danny's brotherly concern for me; I could have advised her there if she had only asked me: Danny was a sweet-natured lad, but he didn't hold with ultimatums. Not at all.

And thus things stood. But if Eden (or I either, for that matter) thought that Danny would come running to me with open arms, she (and I) were mistaken. Never had I known him to be as he was that fall — silent, morose, irritable.

After a while as I looked at Danny's somber face, I began to feel sorry for him. If he were suffering as I suffered after Brett, I felt deeply sorry for him although I was angered too, at the way he barked at me sometimes. I offered once to stop riding with him if it would help his standing with Eden, and he nearly snapped my head off. I wondered if Father had ever been sharp like that to Alicia and if she'd stood for it and what she'd done if she hadn't stood for it.

One night in November we drove out toward home in Danny's car after the last class, the last conference, the last lab make-up period any of the five of us had to attend. It was a cold, rainy evening, and the tensions

158

aroused by term papers, love, approaching exams, lack of love, or simply the wretched weather, bore down in varying degrees of intensity upon all of us.

We deposited the three younger ones at their respective dooryards, and then Danny and I drove on through the gathering dusk together, silent, wholly uncommunicative. I remember thinking that even the windshield wipers sounded a little discouraged; their flip across the surface that was cleared one second and splashed with rain the next seemed to suggest futility and despair. "Wherefore?" they clicked wearily in one direction; and "Why?" they wanted to know as they moved in the other.

We passed Carlotta's home after a while; the place was dark except for a lighted kitchen window. I wondered about Lottie, where she was, what she was thinking that November evening. I wished that Mrs. Berry would not turn away from me when we met; I wanted very much to let her know that I would be one to welcome Lottie home when and if she returned. I wished that Mrs. Berry knew how often I said to myself: "Be very kind, Julie Trelling, be very kind in what you think and say about Carlotta."

And then Danny and I saw something at the same moment; something that made our childhood seem very far away. Carlotta's father had just thrown open the doors of his lighted garage as we were opposite it, and there, leaning a bit crazily on one side, we could see a wicker cart looking faded and decrepit even in the rainy twilight.

"The old pony cart, Danny," I whispered. Carlotta

and I had never been very close, even as children, but at that moment I could have wept for her.

Danny looked at me and when he saw the tears in my eyes, he took my hand without speaking and drew my arm through the curve of his own. We sat close together, our arms locked, and the car was warm and dark and peaceful. Outside the rain splashed harder than ever against the windshield, and the wipers seemed to have drawn new energy from some source. They weren't exactly gay, but they were less despairing than they had been moments before.

We rode on like that, still silent, until we came to the long lane that led up to the house. I could see through the trees that there was a fire in the living room fireplace, that Aunt Cordelia was moving about, turning on lights and adjusting shades. The room looked inviting, but I found myself wishing that I could stay with Danny.

"You have a raincoat?" he asked. The first words in over a mile. His voice didn't sound quite natural.

"Here," I said, picking up the folded cape on the seat beside me. "Well," I hesitated. I hated to go in. I wanted to stay out there in the rain with him. But then, I thought he would probably bark at me if I suggested it. "I suppose I must dash. See you in the morning if I don't drown."

And then suddenly Danny's arms were around me, and his lips were on mine, and the crazy windshield wipers commenced singing our names together, much like the taunting of the kids in school a long time ago: Danny loves Julie; Julie loves Danny. I wondered why it had made me so fighting mad in those days.

We sat together for a long time after that, our cheeks

close, our arms around one another.

"It's always been you, Julie. No one ever really except you."

"Not Eden?"

"I said 'no one ever really,' Julie. Eden is a nice girl; I liked her a lot. But she was right; I loved you, and it showed through."

I loved him so much. Without the reservations that I'd had for another boy whom I didn't like to remember. "Danny," I whispered.

"Yes, Julie?"

"I've always wanted to tell you — all these years I've been sorry about that time I hit you."

He chuckled a little. "You were a brat, but even then I thought of you as 'my girl.'"

"Was your mother mad at me?"

"No. She said that Chris and Jim and I had no right to tease you."

"My Grandmother Bishop would have scratched the eyes out of any girl who might have blacked Uncle Haskell's eye like that. He told me so."

"Not my ma."

"I love you, Danny." I felt I had to tell him. And then he kissed me again.

That was the way it was that beautiful evening of cold November rain and muddy country roads and crazy windshield wipers. That was the moment of my greatest security and confidence; it was the time when I realized that love makes one a better person, a kinder and a gentler one. I couldn't believe as I sat there in the car with Danny that I could have been jealous of Laura, that I could have been cruel to Aggie or unkind to Aunt Cordelia. Most of all I couldn't believe that I was the girl who had thought she loved Brett Kingsman.

When I finally entered the living room that evening I noticed that Aunt Cordelia had set a little table in front of the fireplace and was carrying in food from the kitchen to place upon it. This was something new for her; she didn't believe the living room was a place for eating except for coffee and cake when there were guests. Perhaps she was remembering how I had described the little suppers Alicia liked to serve in front of the fire; perhaps she was remembering that a certain pert girl had spoken of "inflexibility" as a highly undesirable trait.

"This is so nice, Aunt Cordelia," I said, taking off my wet raincape. The old room seemed to glow with beauty that night; I wondered that I had ever privately fretted over the fact that we couldn't afford to lower the ceiling or to buy a carpet handsome enough to make a proper setting for Uncle Haskell's piano.

"Well, it's such a bad night — I thought supper in front of the fire might cheer you. There's a good, rich soup tonight, and I have a souffle in the oven. We should have asked Danny to eat with us."

"Some other time," I said, seating myself in a low chair and looking into the fire. I wanted to think quietly, to savor every sensation of peace and happiness inside me.

I noticed that Aunt Cordelia started toward the kitchen to get the souffle and then stopped in the door to look at me. She sensed something. No wonder; the whole universe was singing. But she walked away without saying anything, and returned shortly with the souffle rising high and lightly browned from the platter on which it rested.

"There is dessert in the refrigerator if you want it later, Julia. I am driving into town with Jonathan this evening. Your father and Alicia have asked us to visit them for a few hours."

I had intended telling her about Danny and me, but I suddenly decided against it. We would talk about her; I would tell her that the new crimson wool she was wearing under her big kitchen apron was becoming; I would hope that she and Jonathan Eltwing had a pleasant evening with Father and Alicia. There was no particular reason why the events of my evening should have priority over hers.

"I hope Jonathan is a careful driver," I said after a while. "It's a bad night."

Not really. Not for Danny and me. But a bad night for Father to be driving, or Mr. Peters, or Jonathan Eltwing.

Aunt Cordelia nodded. "Once when we were young, Jonathan and I drove home from town in such a rain as this. I always remembered that night — the rain and wind outside; warmth and security inside —"

It was most unusual for her to confide anything of her early years to me. I felt proud that she chose to give me a brief glimpse of something dear to her.

Then I noticed that she was smiling at me. "Didn't you find that you felt safe and happy with a good driver this evening, Julia?" she asked quietly.

"Yes," I said. "How did you know?"

"You are much like the girl I used to be," she said. "I'm glad it's Danny," she added.

10

Because of Uncle Haskell I had never dared admit to anyone that I had an ambition to write. If I could have suddenly bloomed in print, or if a qualified critic had praised a manuscript of mine, I could have squared my shoulders and looked any doubters in the eye. I might have asked Alicia or Father to read one of my stories; I might have asked Jonathan Eltwing, or even Aunt Cordelia, whose literary background stood up well with any of the other three. There were plenty of people to advise and guide me, but I could not bring myself to admit the fact that I was trying to write. I was sure that any such admission would bring to their minds the

164

picture of Uncle Haskell, allegedly working for forty years on a book that no one had ever seen or was likely to see.

I wouldn't even take the evening course in creative writing which was offered in the college, and for which I, as a high school senior in honors English, was eligible. I was sure that — not my family — but everyone else who knew us, would say, "Well, well, so now it's Julie! If I were poor old Cordelia I'd lock both Julie and Haskell up in a room with two typewriters and feed them on bread and water until they produced a few thousand words between them." Something like that. And, of course, I had no more justification for believing that I could write than had Uncle Haskell. He had done well in rhetoric too, many years before, and it hadn't meant anything in particular. I wondered if I had been around him so long that I might have caught a mild case of delusions of literary grandeur.

I was often troubled by the fear that there was something of Uncle Haskell in my character; if I might possibly have certain weaknesses which had led him to become what he was. I knew that I had a tendency to be overdramatic at times; I wasn't exactly the be-good-sweet-maid-and-let-who-will-be-clever type of girl. And certainly, I had always liked Uncle Haskell, not always warmly, but enough to make me seek out his companionship at times.

Perhaps the loneliness of the old house and the woods helped to foster a habit I had of peopling my mind with characters who loved, hated, despaired, and exulted before my inner eye. Alicia had said once that loneliness

165

could be dangerous in creating so strong a need as to make a shoddy relationship seem beautiful. I wondered sometimes if loneliness had led me to dream dreams that had no basis in reality. I knew that I had a keen desire to give life to the procession of characters who walked with me through the woods or galloped beside me when I rode Peter the Great along the quiet countryside; still I didn't know whether my attempts to give them life held promise or were only ridiculous.

"Your head is in the clouds tonight, Julie," Danny would say to me sometimes, and I wanted to tell him all about my secret efforts and hopes. But might it not give Danny pause if he thought I was a female counterpart of my uncle? I would put my dreams aside against the day when Danny would read my work and be ever so proud of me.

We noticed a change in Uncle Haskell during the autumn of my last year in high school. The signs of age, so long apparently held in abeyance, seemed to appear suddenly in many little ways. Lines of fatigue or possibly, pain, showed up around his mouth; his eyes looked tired, and what was most unusual, he was given to long periods of silence. He still made an occasional trip to the banks of the creek with the old golf bag over his shoulder, but they were less frequent. For some reason his intake of *Le Vieux Corbeau* had diminished; so too, it seemed, had his gourmet's taste for his own cookery. There was a trace of wistfulness in the way he asked Aunt Cordelia if he might eat with us for a while, and there was a suggestion of humility in his appreciation for the plain but excellent meals she prepared for us.

166

He sought me out often during these early autumn days, and we would walk arm in arm through the bright woods, saying little, yet consciously fonder of one another, I believe, than we had ever been before. I noticed on these walks that the old buoyancy of his step was gone, that he walked slowly and deliberately; I noticed too, how his bright hair had become dulled by gray. He had always seemed at least ten years younger than Aunt Cordelia, but that fall he looked older.

One evening as we walked, I remember that he spoke quite suddenly and irrelevantly. "The old piper is clamoring for his pay these days, Julie."

I was perplexed. "I don't understand, Uncle Haskell," I answered.

He laughed, but less lightly than in other years. "Do you remember how we once discussed the state of my liver when you were little? You were entranced by a new word, and you asked me very directly if my liver was impeccable." He chuckled at the memory. "Well, it's no longer impeccable, Julie. As a matter of fact, the doctor tells me that my luck has run out. Cirrhosis."

I stopped in the path and looked at him. "Surely the doctors can do something, can't they, Uncle Haskell?"

"Apparently not. You see, I didn't aspire to just a *slight* touch of cirrhosis; I did a magnificent buildup."

To say that I was sorry seemed so trite, so inane. I was more than sorry; I don't think that even Uncle Haskell knew how desolate I felt at that moment.

Neither of us spoke for a long time. Then, when the silence became too much for me to bear, I told him of my wish to write.

It seemed callous when I thought of it later, a self-centered remark worthy of Uncle Haskell himself as it came in the face of what he had just told me. But any words of sympathy that I had were too empty, too inadequate; this was a little something I had to offer him for the grim days ahead, a something that I instinctively felt he would love.

"I've been trying for a long time to write a little, Uncle Haskell. I've never told anyone, and I'm telling you in confidence. I've wondered if you would read some of my stuff and criticize it for me? I warn you, it isn't very good, but I'd like to know if there is *any* good in it, and what I can do about what's bad in it."

There it was. I hadn't wanted to tell anyone — certainly not Uncle Haskell — about my ambition, but it seemed to have been drawn from me by an urgent necessity.

The obvious delight that came into his eyes was worth relinquishing my secret. He cut our walk short and asked me to bring him one of my manuscripts immediately. Later that evening when Danny and I walked past the carriage-house apartment on our way to saddle our horses for a ride, we saw Uncle Haskell sitting at his table, his glasses astride his nose, a sheaf of papers in his hand.

The manuscript I gave him was not my first, but I considered it at all odds to be my best. I had an old German musician telling the story of his youth, his sufferings in a cold, rat-infested attic where he composed his music. His one solace, other than his work in this desolate environment, was the beautiful daughter of his landlord. This girl, who listened enraptured to the young

man's music and poured out a chaste and gentle passion
for the young musician himself, was unfortunately the
child of a most brutal and sadistic father who, in a story
of four thousand words, wrecked the lives of all the characters involved. The musician, old and feeble, at the end
of the story, had apparently had very few satisfactions
in life since his criminally insane landlord went on that
last rampage so many years before.

When I came home that night I found my manuscript
encased in a neat manila folder and propped against my
door. The outside of the folder was covered with Uncle
Haskell's beautifully flowing handwriting; at the bottom of his comments he had given me a B minus.

Seated at my desk, I read his criticism:

Dear Julie:

If I didn't feel that there is some good in your
story, I wouldn't take the time to write a criticism
of it. But there *is* some good in it, some points that
make me feel that if you expend the effort (Look,
who's talking about expending effort, I couldn't help
thinking) you may well achieve your very worthy
ambition.

First of all, you have an ear for cadence. Your
sentences flow rather smoothly, and the continuity of
your paragraphs is quite good.

Secondly, your imagery is sharp and clear-cut. I
could *smell* that dank, rat-infested attic, and I was
more than a little in love with your pretty heroine
by the time she emerged from her third paragraph.
Furthermore, you occasionally achieve poetic effects

which are pleasing.

But, my darling niece, your villains have nothing but venom in their souls, and your sympathetic characters are ready to step right off into Paradise without one spot to tarnish their purity. People aren't like that, Julie. Take a look around you.

Again, all your colors, your moods, your nuances, are essentially feminine, and it just doesn't ring true to be told that a man is responsible for them. No, Julie, it will be a long time before you speak and think and feel like an anguished old German musician of eighty! And, after all, what do you know about the problems of musical composition, or the life of an impoverished German laborer such as the landlord in his nineteenth century environment? And how much do you know about sadism and brutality?

I must talk to you about any number of points. When you get home from school tomorrow, I shall have some recommendations to make; also some assignments. I am quite excited. It well may be that I have the making of a future writer in my hands.

Uncle Haskell.

I laid the manila folder aside thoughtfully. If I hadn't done anything else, I had given him something to get excited about. I felt very tender toward Uncle Haskell that night.

We had long talks about my writing in the days that followed. "Write of things you know about, Julie; familiar, simple things that you have experienced; things that have touched you deeply."

"But nothing's ever happened to me. I've just lived here with Aunt Cordelia and you most of my life, I've gone to school, visited Father — oh, sure, I'm in love with Danny, but that's something we've grown into — very wonderful for us, but not very exciting for the rest of the world. How can a person who has lived as quiet a life as I have find anything to write about?"

"Then you do have a problem. If you haven't lived long enough to have felt anything deeply, then you are in the same position I — as many would-be writers are. You've nothing to say. So take up crocheting."

I thought about that business of remembering an experience which had caused me to feel deeply, and finally as I thought, there emerged in my mind, three little figures standing at a gate in the bright October sunlight; I heard a small girl saying, "You aren't going to live here anymore, are you?" I saw a picture of sheets on the line being wrinkled into malicious faces as the wind blew them about; I heard Laura's voice begging me to stop crying, and I heard Mrs. Peters saying, ". . . and now our pretty petticoat . . ." As I remembered these things, the old feeling of desperation seemed to climb into my throat, and I saw the closet under the stairs, felt Aunt Cordelia's arms drawing me into her lap.

That evening I went to my room and wrote for many hours, neglecting some of my schoolwork because this paper for Uncle Haskell seemed to demand precedence.

I left it with him before I went to school the next morning, and when I came home in the evening I hurried out to discuss it with him. His face was grave as he turned the paper in his hands. "Is this the way it was,

Julie? Did you really experience all this?"

I nodded, and he reread a paragraph thoughtfully. "I never knew," he said after a while. "I didn't know that children felt that deeply."

He said no more about the story, but he did not hand it back to me. "I'd like to look this over a little more," he said without explanation, and laid it aside on a pile of papers.

He was as hard a taskmaster as if he had known only long hours of toil himself, and was unable to understand others who could not live up to his rigid standards. He would make me do a paper over, pointing out a hackneyed phrase, a contrived situation, a paragraph of strained dialogue. He wanted more and more copy, and he was very stern about my failure to turn it in as he demanded it.

"But I have my schoolwork to do, Uncle Haskell. I can't take a chance of getting low grades. High marks are very important to me this year."

"Any writer who really has the fire within him will *find* time to write, Julie," said Uncle Haskell with the air of a man who knew that fire well. "What about Coleridge and Stevenson, what about dozens of others, sick in body and mind, suffering acute pain, but still finding the energy and time to write?"

"They weren't finishing high school," I muttered. But I worked as hard as I was able, and Uncle Haskell went over each of my offerings with meticulous care. He would strike out clichés with impatient little crosses, brand paragraphs with such words as "Awkward," "Illogical," "Saccharine"; now and then he would reward me with a benevolent "Good!" or "Big Improvement!" My spelling

172

annoyed him occasionally. "Good Heavens, Julie, didn't Cordelia teach you *anything?*" he would inquire via his blue pencil. And at the end of the paper, he would spell out the major faults of my work and the qualities he found commendable. He usually placed a letter grade below his criticism; I received several C's; nothing ever higher than a B.

"Young writers get false ideas from indiscreet praise," he explained. "When I tell you that your work is good, I'm not suggesting that you're Madame de Sévigné."

Uncle Haskell must often have been in pain during those months; his face showed the effects of suffering, but he never mentioned it. Aunt Cordelia and Father talked with the doctors, and all that could be done for him was done. It was not much; temporary relief from pain, Aunt Cordelia's devotion.

"Your writing is helping him more than any medicine, Julia," Aunt Cordelia told me, for we had found it necessary to include her in our secret. "In all the years, he has had no more than a flash of satisfaction out of his strange, twisted thinking. Now, I believe he feels that finally he is making some small contribution to a society he has always ignored." She watched him as he waved to us and walked away for his evening stroll. "He might have been a very good teacher — a fine man if something terribly wrong hadn't distorted him."

Uncle Haskell suggested once or twice that I send out one or two of my best things. "See how they're received, Julie. The experience can't hurt you. Anyway, every young author must commence collecting his pile of rejection slips. You had just as well make a beginning."

173

But I couldn't bring myself to do it. It seemed too audacious on my part; I had a feeling that I might not only receive a rejection slip but that some outraged editor might give me a sound scolding for presuming to take up his time.

Then one week in April I had a telephone call from Father. "Julie, your story is in the *College Quarterly,*" he said in an excited voice. "Darling, why didn't you tell us?"

It was a day of considerable rejoicing by those who loved me most. Father called Laura and Chris; within a few hours Chris responded with a silly but very proud telegram, while Laura and Bill put through a long distance telephone call which was still considered an extravagance, and their congratulations extended for a period far beyond the three minutes to which Aunt Cordelia and I carefully restricted ourselves when making such calls. Jonathan Eltwing felt that I had created and sustained a mood in a way that showed promise; Aunt Cordelia and Alicia were pleased. Father, who should have known better, being familiar with the best in literature, rather lost control of his enthusiasm that day. He kept finding another point in my work to praise until I became uncomfortable; I feared that it sounded a little like Grandmother Bishop praising something Uncle Haskell had written. Everyone laughed indulgently, and I felt much relieved when Father finally achieved insight into his over-reaction and said quietly, "Well, after all, I remember her from a little vegetable on up. If what she writes gets into print, it seems great stuff to me."

Only Uncle Haskell remained aloof that day. I ran

over to his place early that morning, sure that he was responsible for submitting my manuscript, and anxious to talk about it. There was, however, no response to my knock, and all during the day we saw nothing of him. It was not until late evening when I was getting ready to drive into town with Danny that I saw Uncle Haskell turning into the path that led to the creek, his beret perched jauntily on his head, the golf bag without clubs slung across his shoulder.

I ran down the lane to overtake him. "When did you send my story to the *Quarterly*, Uncle Haskell? Why didn't you tell me?" I asked breathlessly.

"My dear child," he said with mock loftiness, "I had completely forgotten your little yarn. Did they publish it, really?"

"You know very well that they published it. Oh, Uncle Haskell, I've been walking on clouds today. And how I've missed you; why didn't you answer my knock?"

"I felt no desire to join the throng. I'd sooner discuss your work when we're alone." He smiled at me, but I noticed that his face looked ashen in the twilight. "Yes, I'll admit that I submitted your story. It was the right thing to do, wasn't it? You see, my judgment of work was accurate."

"I never could have done it without your help. Never."

"I like to think that, but I'm not fully convinced." He looked out toward the misty woods and sighed. "We'll talk about it — sometime later. You run along. You're going out with young Trevort, aren't you?"

"Yes, but I'll have time to walk down to the creek with you." The look of suffering on his face hurt me. "Don't you want me to come along just this once?"

He made an effort to regain his old gayety. "I do not. I reserve the right to invite guests to accompany me on my evening strolls. Tonight, you are not invited." He kissed me lightly on the forehead. "Congratulations, my sweet; your name looked very fine in print. I have felt quite proud of you all day." I stood watching him as he went down the winding path through the woods. He turned and waved just before he disappeared among the trees.

It was rather late when I came in that night. I had thought that if Uncle Haskell's light were still on, I might run over and see him for a few minutes. But his place was dark and so I prepared for the night, setting my alarm a few minutes early so that I would have time to see him before I went to school the next morning. The white suffering in his face had bothered me from time to time all evening.

My bed felt warm and safe that night as I listened to the rain falling steadily on the roof and splashing in little puddles below my window. It had been a beautiful day, full of love and encouragement. I smiled as I thought of Dr. Adam Trelling, behaving like any foolish father over a very simple little story; I thought again of Danny's good-night kiss and his whisper of how happy he was at my success. Just before I slept I thought of Uncle Haskell.

Our telephone rang very early the next morning. There are people who say that what I am about to tell must be in error; that I have imagined it this way. But I know. I know very well that when the ringing of the telephone awakened me, I lay stiffly in my bed and thought: "Aunt Cordelia will answer that ring. Then there will be a time of silence. After that, she will come up the stairs, knock at my door, and she will say, "Julia, Uncle Haskell is dead."

And it happened almost that way. Aunt Cordelia knocked at my door after the short silence, and she said, "Julia, wake up, dear. Some men have found Uncle Haskell's body in the creek. They think he fell from the old bridge last night."

For several days I wouldn't go near the old carriage house apartment, but there finally came an afternoon when Aunt Cordelia and I had to face the task of going through Uncle Haskell's few possessions, discarding what we must, putting away for no particular reason the things we could not bear to discard.

I folded the old velvet smoking jacket and the white silk shirt which he had worn the afternoon that he became the "good golden-haired man" for little Katy Eltwing. We packed his books and with them two unopened packages containing bottles such as the one that had once reminded me of bowling pins. We found a few papers with the opening paragraphs of a story or an article neatly typed, but never completed. The *College Quarterly* was lying on his desk, opened at the page where my story began. In the margin I read, "Sharp imagery; good plot; some tendency toward overwriting. B+."

We worked in silence for a long time, but at last I sat down at the desk and turned toward my aunt. "What happened, Aunt Cordelia? What distorted him?"

She pressed both hands against her temples for a minute; then she sat down at the desk and looked at me without seeming to see me.

"I'm not sure, Julia; no one can ever be sure of the forces that have shaped a character. I think, though, that our parents —" she paused, frowning, and then went on. "I'm not one of the school that holds parents responsible for all the weaknesses of their children, but I must say this: we had an odd pair of parents. I loved one of them, but not the other; Haskell loved neither of them."

"I thought that Grandmother Bishop adored him."

"She did. She smothered him with adoration and turned his father against him. Haskell resented her bitterly."

"You loved your father?"

"Yes. Father always seemed old to me. He was nearly twenty years older than Mama, a stern, undemonstrative man, but kind. Kind, that is, to most people, not to Haskell, nor to Mama in his later years. I think he felt that she had robbed him of his first child, his only boy. When he saw Haskell overindulged and spoiled by Mama, he rejected him completely. He loved your mother and me; he had no use whatever for his son. With Mama, it was the reverse.

"There are plenty of children who could have risen above such a situation. Not Haskell. Whether there was some basic weakness of character or whether he was, as you say, distorted, we can't know. In my heart I hold my parents responsible."

We sat there thinking. I ran my hand across the smooth velvet of Uncle Haskell's jacket; I remembered

178

his hair. There was, indeed, something of velvet and gold about him, something that Katy Eltwing's troubled mind had glimpsed. It was shoddy velvet and tarnished gold, and there lay the tragedy, for the shoddiness and the tarnish might have been prevented.

We set things to rights and packed and stored all that had value; the rest, we burned. Before we left, we drew the shades; then Aunt Cordelia locked the door and for a long time we tried to avoid looking at the place.

II

"I think, Julia," Aunt Cordelia said one morning as we stood at the kitchen table cleaning silver, "that it's time you were pushed out of the nest. I think you had better plan to attend the State University next winter."

"But I don't want to leave here, Aunt Cordelia. I want to stay with you for the next four years. Danny and I have it all planned. I don't think that I could bear to leave."

"Four more years with me and you'll be as dogmatic and opinionated as I am." She actually grinned at me. I was amazed; Aunt Cordelia often smiled primly, but I couldn't remember ever seeing her grin as though she

180

were sharing a joke with me. "Spinster aunts serve a need, but they should know when the time comes to push young nieces out on their own."

"But you would be all alone if I left you; anyway, this is my home."

She shook her head. "You must have new experiences, be exposed to new ideas, Julia. You've fallen into a pattern here; if you stay on, you'll be another Cordelia Bishop. I won't have it."

"I don't want to leave Danny," I said, near tears.

"It would be a good thing if Danny were pushed out of his comfortable little niche too. Jonathan agrees with me. I may even speak to Helen and Charles Trevort about it."

It seemed to me that she was disposing of other people on a grand scale that morning. "I thought that you were happy about Danny and me. Now, it seems you really want to see us separated."

"I *am* happy, Julia. However," she stressed the word strongly, "both you and Danny need to get out into life and give your love a test."

I felt weak inside. "If Danny would 'get out into life' as you put it, and find that he loved someone else, I would die. I know it. I would just give up and die."

"No, you wouldn't, dear. You'd go on living. It would be hard, but if your interests were wide and your life full, you would get over the pain and find a new life." She laid her hand on my arm. "Don't look so tragic. I have great confidence that four years from now I'll be getting this old place ready for your wedding — yours and Danny's."

"It's beginning to sound like an awful gamble." We finished the silver without saying anything more; when we were through I went away to walk in the woods. It was a cool day, and Aunt Cordelia made me wear a woolen stole that Jonathan had given her for Christmas; it was the color of ripe strawberries, and I couldn't help but be cheered by its beauty.

I was still reeling from Aunt Cordelia's firm line when word came that Danny had received a scholarship from the eastern university that Chris was attending. The professors in Danny's department were pleased; so were both our fathers and Aunt Cordelia. They seemed pretty callous to us during those first weeks; then we pulled ourselves together and commenced making our plans all over again.

It had been so simple before the new developments. I would stay with Aunt Cordelia in my familiar old room; Danny would continue living at home; we would drive into college together, home together, to all the college activities together. Everything together. Just Danny and Julie for at least three years; then there would have to be one year of separation while Danny did graduate work and I finished college, but when that year was finished we would be married. Now the plans called for four long years apart, both of us among strangers, a whole new way of life. It was frightening.

"Don't fall in love with someone else, Danny," I said. I tried to make it sound gay, but I was terribly in earnest.

"I'm not worried about *me;* it's you losing your head if some poet barges in on my territory," Danny said glumly.

Little by little, however, we became less fearful of the change, more aware of the fact that we *were* living in a narrow, comfortable world, and like some little old couple of eighty or so, highly apprehensive about branching off the beaten track. By the time Chris got home for summer vacation, Danny and I were ready to join him in plans for the coming year, plans that involved several trips back and forth across half the continent for holidays and special occasions together.

I wondered sometimes when I was alone what Aunt Cordelia had meant about my becoming another Cordelia Bishop. I knew that I must look a little like the girl in the picture, at least Jonathan Eltwing thought so, but I believed the resemblance ended there. I was quite sure of it until one evening when Chris and I were talking with Father and Alicia and the subject of Jane Austen came up. Father was telling us about a paper written by a girl in one of his classes, a paper bitterly critical of any and all of Austen's writings.

"I certainly think such an attitude indicates immaturity," I said severely. I had once been intensely bored by Jane Austen myself, but I supposed that all people who had lived seventeen years had progressed in their powers of discrimination.

I saw Alicia's lips twitch when she glanced at Father; neither of them would probably have said anything, but Chris never missed an opportunity to tease.

"And, by Jove, we just don't hold with the anti-Austen clique, do we, Aunt Cordelia?"

I laughed with them that evening, but the incident set me to thinking. And when, a few days later, I was caught again in an unconscious mimicry of Aunt Cordelia, I began to agree that it was time that I got out into a wider world.

It happened when Mrs. Peters brought her two small grandchildren over to visit us. They were a beautiful, winsome little pair, a girl of five and a little boy of about three. I was delighted with their large solemn eyes and their baby voices.

When I asked them their names, the little girl answered for both. "I am Peggy, and my little brother is Bobby," she told me.

I amused them with a few old toys for a time; then when they grew restless, I suggested that perhaps they would like to go out to the stable and watch me feed a lump of sugar to old Peter the Great. I lifted the small boy into his wagon, and offered my hand to the little girl.

"We'll let Robert ride, and you and I can pull him, can't we, Margaret?"

The little girl smiled at me, almost as if she understood that here was a young woman who was showing the effects of living ten years with an aunt of decided opinions.

"You didn't listen to our names," she said in gentle reproach. "I am Peggy, and my little brother is Bobby."

I glanced at Aunt Cordelia and Mrs. Peters, who sat watching us. "Another four years, Julia, and you wouldn't be able to leave unwashed dishes in the sink overnight," Aunt Cordelia remarked.

"Worse things could happen to her, Cordelia," Mrs. Peters said.

"Much worse," Aunt Cordelia agreed, "but Laura's

184

young Julie might feel some day that her aunt was a highly inflexible person. We don't want another generation of inflexibility," she added.

She was laughing at herself as well as at me, I thought. Perhaps Aunt Cordelia was not quite so inflexible as I had once believed her to be.

Whether or not they approved of the attitudes and opinions I had picked up from Aunt Cordelia, all the members of my family were pleased that I was named valedictorian of my class that year. Laura and Bill and young Julie would be coming a few days before graduation; Father and Alicia would stay at the old house too, in order to be close to all of us. Aunt Cordelia and I planned a supper to be served after the graduation exercises; besides the family there would be Jonathan, Danny's parents and Mr. and Mrs. Peters. Chris and Danny and I took over the task of getting things ready.

There were no half-measures with Aunt Cordelia. Long stored bedding had to be taken out and aired, curtains had to be laundered, walls must be wiped down, windows washed and floors waxed. The house was in a state of cheerful hubbub for several days as the boys and I carried out Aunt Cordelia's orders and were refreshed by the most appetizing meals she could dream up for us. We were reminded of the days when we had swept and dusted the schoolhouse for her, but we agreed that times were happier now; let people who have forgotten their childhood say that the early years are the happiest, I thought. For me, it was good to be over that stretch of the road which was beset by half-formed anxieties and resentments. I could now watch Aunt Cordelia glow over the two young men whom she loved devotedly, and I could catch her eye and know with complete confidence that I was just as close to her. No Grandmother Bishop denied the girl of my generation.

One bright afternoon Jonathan Eltwing came in, ostensibly for only a brief call in order to return one of Aunt Cordelia's books, but his face glowed with pleasure when we insisted that he stay. I tied an apron around his generous middle, and the boys led our venerable professor into the living room and pointed out the windows that had not yet been washed. He must have been the Jonathan of other years that afternoon, for he laughed and teased as lightly as did Chris or Danny, and in the evening when we had eaten the fried chicken and fresh cornbread Aunt Cordelia prepared for us, he led the singing that continued for over an hour as the five of us sat around the table. That afternoon and evening would be a picture to remember, I thought; something precious to hold when I would be out in the world viewing the new horizons and wider vistas that Aunt Cordelia felt that I must experience.

The spotlessly clean old house was filled with family on the day before my graduation. In the library we had a few small logs blazing in the fireplace; we didn't really need a fire, but I persuaded the boys that the wind drifting in from the woods still carried a slight chill that was sure to grow sharper by evening. So they built the fire for me, knowing very well that I wanted it for beauty rather than for comfort, calling me Emily Dickinson and asking me if I'd heard of people in some far-off places freezing for want of the fuel that I was wasting. Actu-

186

ally, the added warmth was not unpleasant, and the glow of the flames did much to soften the aging shabbiness of Aunt Cordelia's library. We had waxed the floor and washed the windows, but the faded paper on the walls and the rows of worn book bindings could not be brightened by either soapsuds or wax.

Jonathan approved of my fire. We stood before it, hand in hand, as we watched the play of the flames. "Firelight does for an old room like this what wisdom does for an old face, Julie. It softens the grimmer aspects and compensates for the drained color."

"Doesn't goodness do the same thing, Jonathan?" I asked, looking across the hall at good Mr. Peters, who stood talking to Chris.

"That's the kind of wisdom I am talking about. Learning isn't always enough, you know. I've seen some very unlovely old faces that belonged with very well-stocked brains. These were the ones that lacked the other elements of wisdom — kindness, compassion, a sense of humor."

Alicia came in through the open door, hand in hand with my little niece. "What are you talking about?" she asked, smiling. "You have something of a high school commencement look about you. You weren't, by chance, telling Julie that it is her generation that must carry the torch that is being thrown to them tonight, were you, Jonathan?"

"No, I realize that the torch passes from one set of hands to another almost before you get the state records settled, Alicia."

Alicia nodded agreement. She looked at me, and I

could see her quick eyes taking in every detail of my dress, my hairdo, even the color of my lipstick. She seemed to approve of me.

"I'd better go up and find Laura," I said. "Aunt Cordelia made her promise to hear my speech so I won't fumble it."

I noticed Father standing alone at one of the living room windows as I started to go up to my room. It struck me that he looked a little wistful that evening, a little less youngish, less animated. I noticed that the flags of gray above his temples were becoming wider and whiter lately; it didn't seem right. I went over and linked my arm in his and I noticed that his face lighted as if he were pleased.

"What were you thinking about over here by yourself, Professor Trelling?" I asked.

"About my littlest one. Forgive a cliché, Julie?"

"I'll work on it."

"Well, then it seems only yesterday—" he laughed a little and left the sentence unfinished. "I'm torn between gratitude to Cordelia and envy of her. I've never known you well enough, Julie."

"Why, we've had wonderful times together, Father. Remember how I used to love going out to dinner with you? Remember the fun we had when you and Alicia took the boys and me to New York?"

He nodded. "That's what I was thinking about, Julie. I've been a source of entertainment; I've been a father who was with you when everything was going smoothly. But I haven't been with you when you were troubled — when the crises came up. It's been Cordelia who has

188

stood by you in those times."

Once I had said the gist of that to Aunt Cordelia. I had called Father and Alicia "holiday parents." I tried to make light of the idea now.

"The next crisis that I stumble into, I'll come running to you, Father; depend upon it." I pressed my cheek against his. "Don't be a dope, darling, you have no idea how proud I am of you," I whispered.

He smiled. "You've grown up too fast to suit me, Julie," he said. He kissed me before I ran off to join Laura.

I didn't need to practice the speech, and Laura didn't insist. We just sat together at my window, and talked of little things. We were two young women, both of us in love, and it was a time of quiet happiness and relaxation. I wished that I could marry Danny the next day and move into a cottage next to Laura and Bill and live happily the rest of our lives.

"Do you agree with Aunt Cordelia that Danny and I should be separated — that we should get out into life and have new experiences?" I asked her.

"Yes, Julie, I do. I know it isn't what you want to hear, but I think Aunt Cordelia is right, dear."

"I've worked so hard getting up to this plateau; now it seems I have to start out on another climb."

"One never stops climbing, Julie, unless he wants to stop and vegetate. There's always something just ahead."

Then there was a knock at the door. "Girls," Aunt Cordelia's firm voice called, "we must get ready to drive into town. You and William and little Julie will go with Adam and Alicia, Laura. I suppose you will want to go

189

with Danny, Julia."

Graduation exercises are always much alike, dreadfully routine, really, except for the members of that long processional, each one trembling a little beneath his academic robe when the first sound of the organ announces that "This is It." For those trembling ones and for the bright-faced relatives in the audience, each commencement is unique and wonderful. Alicia was jaded with many such ceremonies, but even she admitted to a special thrill that night when the long line of us walked solemnly down the middle aisle of the auditorium, and when Ned Lawrence as salutatorian and I as valedictorian took our places on the stage beside Dean Evans and my dear old Jonathan Eltwing, who was to deliver the commencement address. I remember looking down from the platform into their faces: Laura with her great blue eyes suspiciously bright as if a film of tears might be in them; Bill whispering to small Julie, both of them looking at me while she nodded to what he was whispering and clasped and unclasped her hand in a surreptitious wave. Then there were Father and Alicia, holding hands and smiling up at me; there was Christopher with his arms folded, trying to look very serene and detached, while Danny nervously and quite openly chewed at a thumbnail, a gesture which I knew would continue until he was convinced that I wouldn't collapse when it was time for me to speak.

Finally, there at the end of the row was Aunt Cordelia, stiffly erect, poised, confident that no niece of hers could do other than well in this maiden speech. "Oh, Aunt Cordelia, how funny you are. And how I love you!"

I said to myself. She wouldn't have approved of such a childish thought; she would have expected me to be high-minded, reaching for the stars — that sort of thing.

I had dreaded the first few seconds of my speech just a little, that brief interval between the final words of the introduction and the sound of my own voice going out to several hundred people in the silent auditorium. But once on my feet and accustomed after a few seconds to the sound of my voice, I stood relaxed and confident, my notes at hand in case of panic, perhaps a trace of something inherited from Uncle Haskell helping to give me a sense of pleasure and well-being.

It was not a speech that was going to shake the world, but it was direct and earnest. I saw Father nod once or twice at an idea I brought out, and Danny was able to clasp his hands around one crossed knee and to give the impression of a young man entirely confident that his girl was doing all right. When I was through I had the pleasure of hearing applause ringing throughout the auditorium and of seeing Jonathan smiling at me as if I were someone very special to him.

Beautiful hours move so quickly. The speeches were applauded, the diplomas handed out, the triumphant recessional march completed, and then it was over except for the extended hands, the pleasant words of many kindly people. I walked through the crowded lobby of the auditorium, my left hand clasped tightly with Danny's, happiness in every fiber of my being.

We were almost to the exit when we stopped to stand for a minute with Aunt Cordelia, and as we stood there I saw Jonathan Eltwing making his way toward us.

191

He took my hand in both his own.

"You did beautifully, Julie; it was a good speech." Then he turned to my aunt and offered his arm to her. "Cordelia, you have every reason to be proud."

Aunt Cordelia was never one to lose her poise. She laid her hand on the arm of this man she had once loved, one whom I rather guessed that she still loved, and her voice was coolly proper and matter of fact.

"I am, Jonathan," she said, "within certain limits, I am quite proud of her."

PETS AND PEOPLE

JUV
SF
416.2
.S5
Cop.1

OTHER BOOKS BY
DOROTHY E. SHUTTLESWORTH

Animals That Frighten People
Gerbils and Other Small Pets

PETS AND
PEOPLE
how to understand
and live with animals

Dorothy E. Shuttlesworth

illustrated with photographs

E. P. DUTTON & CO., INC.   NEW YORK

Copyright © 1975 by Dorothy E. Shuttlesworth

All rights reserved. No part of this publication may be
reproduced or transmitted in any form or by any means,
electronic or mechanical, including photocopy, recording,
or any information storage and retrieval system now
known or to be invented, without permission in writing
from the publisher, except by a reviewer who wishes to
quote brief passages in connection with a review written
for inclusion in a magazine, newspaper, or broadcast.

LIBRARY OF CONGRESS CATALOGING IN PUBLICATION DATA

Shuttlesworth, Dorothy Edwards   Pets and people

SUMMARY: Discusses the history and characteristics of
a variety of animals, including dogs, horses, birds,
pigs, gerbils, rabbits, snakes, crickets, and goldfish,
and the advantages and disadvantages of keeping them
as pets.

1. Pets—Juvenile literature. [1. Pets] I. Title.
SF416.2.S5   636.08′87   74-26904   ISBN 0-525-36975-9

Published simultaneously in Canada by Clarke,
Irwin & Company Limited, Toronto and Vancouver

Designed by Meri Shardin
Printed in the U.S.A.   First Edition
10 9 8 7 6 5 4 3 2 1

FOR MAY PANTINA

who loves her own pets
and cares about all animals
of the Earth

acknowledgments

A very special "thank you" to all my friends who have shared with me their experiences with a variety of pets, particularly: Mark Gibson, Margaret Hennessy (Trustee, Dog Orphans, Inc.), Robert J. Pinkerton, Marion and Steven Rapp, Dorothy and Hermann Shaw, Lee Ann Williams.

CONTENTS

FOREWORD

Often we find it is hard to understand people. Why does someone do things we would not think of doing? Or carry out the same activities as ours but do them in a very different way?

Such questions can remain puzzling even though these people—friends, relatives, or strangers—speak our own language and may try to explain their behavior and feelings.

How, then, can we hope to understand our animal friends? With them, communication by speech is impossible.

There are some obvious ways: A dog's happy bark indicates one thing, an angry growl another. A cat's cry of hunger is very different from a contented purr. A horse's ears lying back show anger, but when pricked forward, they indicate friendly interest.

However, even with animals that have their own special "talking" abilities, using sound or body language, a real understanding of them requires more than interpreting feelings of the moment such as anger, hunger, and contentment. The pets that share our lives have varied backgrounds and instincts which influence their behavior. And anyone who is willing to accept the responsibility of having them join the family will find it rewarding to know as much as possible about their origins.

It is helpful, too, for families to know what they can offer pets. Is there room and exercise space for a big dog? Or should they adopt a small one? Or a cat? Or a hamster? Or some interesting insects?

One important consideration about a pet is its life-span. It can create a sad situation when a puppy is chosen by young people only a short time before they will be leaving home, if their parents are not "dog people." Dogs may live fifteen or twenty or more years. It could be that guinea pigs—friendly and easy to care for— would be a better choice. Their life expectancy is only four or five years.

Pet shop owners report that often a customer comes looking for one kind of pet—perhaps tropical fish—and suddenly is charmed by another, such as a kitten or puppy. Soon a cat or dog is in a home where no one is anxious to handle the responsibilities that are involved.

When a family decides to have a pet, a planning session is in order. If it is to be a dog, who will take it for a daily walk where dogs are not allowed to run freely? (An adult may welcome this activity because of the regular exercise it provides.) Who will brush and occasionally bathe the dog? Who will remember its food? (A puppy requires several feedings a day.) Who will be in charge of housebreaking a puppy and, later, be responsible for cleaning up after the dog's toilet functions in public places? (Many local laws now insist on this being done.)

Cats do not require all these same attentions. They can be trained to use a litter box, so daily walks are not a necessity. They rarely, if ever, need a bath. But they should be brushed, and they do need fresh water and food every day.

More than any other kind of pet, cats and dogs may create a heartbreaking problem when, after one has become a much-loved member of the family, it can no longer share the home. For example, the family may be forced to move some place where the landlord decrees: no pets allowed.

What to do?

Of course the best solution is to find another family willing to adopt the pet. If this is impossible, there are a number of animal shelters and humane societies which, unless overcrowded, will take a cat or dog and try to find it a new home. To simply abandon the animal, thinking

3

someone will rescue it, is both stupid and cruel.
More often than not, no rescue takes place, and
the unfortunate creature may endure weeks or
months of suffering before its life is ended by an
accident or starvation. Better, by far, to have the
pet "put to sleep" by a veterinarian.

Sometimes a veterinarian's waiting room is the
setting for a rescue. I know of one to which a
beautiful five-year-old cat was brought because
its owner had died and no new home could be
found for her. (On the whole people want to take
kittens rather than adult cats.) In the waiting
room another pet owner felt an instant attraction
to the stately long-haired beauty, and asked if he
might have her. So this "happy ending" was
quickly arranged.

Veterinarians are important from the time a
pet—particularly a cat or dog—is adopted. They
can check out its general health and, at the
proper times, give shots to prevent such diseases
as distemper and rabies.

Yes, people with pets have responsibilities
and chores that do not concern those who live
without them. But most pet owners accept the
responsibilities willingly. They feel a house or
apartment is not a true home unless it shelters an
interesting animal, to be cared for and loved. In
Pets and People we explore a variety of choices,
hoping the explorations will be of interest to all
who have, or dream of having, a pet to share
their lives.

4

MYSTERIOUS CATS
from tiger to tabby

1

A poem called "The Mysterious Cat" by Vachel Lindsay is not entirely responsible for this popular description of one of our favorite pets. But it did add to the reputation cats already had for being creatures of mystery.

Where does the mystery lie?

Actually in several directions, including their origin. Despite many years of research, scientists still do not feel sure about the first domestication of cats. The backgrounds of other pets are well known by contrast.

Legends that include tame cats have been handed down over many generations in such widespread areas as the Orient and South America. However, the first definite proof of people-cat relationships was found in Egypt, where the animals were clearly pictured as part of the adornment of temples. This dates the relationship back about five thousand years—a short time compared with people-dog association, which began when humans were still using caves as their homes.

Looking at evidence of a few thousand years ago, we must be convinced that the earliest use for cats was in protecting stored grain from rats. The great silos were invented in Egypt. Two or three African wildcats—the best known being the Kaffir—are believed to have been important ancestors of domestic breeds that were to follow.

Later, when trade developed between African ports and Europe, some tame cats were taken to Italy, Greece, and Palestine. As they were moved here and there in their new surroundings, they often would breed with wildcats of those vicinities, and before long there was a remarkable variety of wild, semi-wild, and tame felines.

Today all such cats, along with the lynx, bobcat, ocelot, and our own home-loving pets are classified as the genus *Felis*. Their larger relatives—lion, tiger, leopard, and jaguar—belong to the genus *Panthera*. True domestic cats have the pleasantly simple scientific name of *Felis catus*. In Latin *felis* means cat; *catus* is clever. All cats may be called felines.

Domestic cats have become increasingly complicated to identify because long ago cat enthusiasts began to develop a variety of individual

6

WIDE WORLD PHOTOS

Though they are true wildcats, ocelots are sometimes kept as house pets. They present problems that domestic cats do not, but owners prize them highly.

breeds: short-haired such as the Abyssinian, Manx, Burmese, and Persian blue, and the long-haired Persians. When the first large-scale cat show was held in London about a hundred years ago, dozens of varieties were displayed, each judged in its own special class. Since then still more pedigreed, pure-blooded, exotic types have appeared.

It seems, however, that highly bred, elegant breeds are really not far removed from the most ordinary of tabby cats, or even from some wild cats. If an individual of a special breed—perhaps having long white hair and blue eyes—mates with a common "short-hair" and their offspring also mate with ordinary cats, after two generations all trace of special breeding will disappear. The kittens revert to the characteristics of their early ancestors, before their appearance was altered by the whims of people.

Even experts in feline judging can be confused in identification. There was an instance when four judges were asked to identify several cats. Two decided the cats were African Kaffirs; the other two said they were European wildcats. Actually they were looking at domesticated tabby cats!

Nevertheless, we do not have to be experts or scientists to know one popular breed from another. Among the domestic short-hairs, most people recognize the Siamese, with its almond-shaped eyes, long tapering head, and distinctive markings, and the Manx, with its short back that slants upward from the shoulders to the haunches, and back legs longer than the front. Strangely, although the Manx is most noted for its lack of a tail, members of this breed do sometimes have tails. In a single litter some kittens may be tailless, others have a stub of a tail, and still others have a tail that is the proper length for other cats.

Almost all domestic long-hairs are properly called Persian. For many years another long-hair known as the Angora held a place of its own among recognized breeds. Angoras were brought to New England by traders from the Orient. They were named for the capital of Turkey, which at that time was called Angora.

There were obvious differences between the Angora and Persian cats which, several hundred years earlier, had been smuggled out of their native land and taken to Europe and then to the United States. Angoras regularly showed body, tail, and legs longer than those of the Persians, and their hair was longer and more silky and crinkly.

For some years Angoras and Persians were bred together, and in the course of this interbreeding, Angora characteristics faded while those of the Persians remained outstanding. Finally cat clubs and associations in the United States recognized almost all long-hairs as Persians. (The term Angora is still frequently used—but for rabbits, goats, and guinea pigs that have long, crinkly hair.)

With few exceptions, variety among long-hair cats lies in the color of their coats. Breeders rec-

9

ognize at least twenty distinctive Persians, from pure white to tortoiseshells with bright patches of black, orange, and cream. Exceptional long-hairs are the Himalayan and Peke-faced cats with the head resembling that of a Pekingese dog.

As interesting as the differences in breeds may be, the ways in which all cats—from leopards and lions to house pets—resemble each other are even more intriguing.

One trait they share is enjoyment of rest and relaxation; they seem born to take it easy. This is one reason a domestic cat makes a good house pet; it can be content even though idle for long periods of time.

Dr. Bernhard Grzimek, director of the world-famed zoo of Frankfurt, Germany, who has done tremendous work in saving wild animals of Africa, writes in his book *Serengeti Shall Not Die* of the sleeping habits of lions. In the zoo the big cats sleep from ten to fifteen hours out of twenty-four, and for several more they lie quiet, perhaps dozing. Lions who live free on the Serengeti plains show the same taste for inactivity. They hunt when necessary, but usually catch their prey quickly, then, after eating, are ready to rest again.

Yet although a cat may be thoroughly relaxed, at an unfamiliar sound—slight though it may be—it will explode into action, leaping away from supposed danger or possibly attacking if the "danger" proves to be another animal. From being curled into a tight sleeping ball, tabby can spring into the air in a straight line and arch its back in one quick move.

We see also how a cat can turn its head around far enough to be able to lick almost any part of its body. Its contortions cause human acrobats to admire and ponder.

This great agility is explained by the cat's anatomy. Its skeleton has more bones (about two hundred and thirty, not counting ear and certain other small bones) than that of a human skeleton, with two hundred and six. And the bones are distributed differently. Cats have more of some kinds of vertebrae, humans have more of other

Although it is a small animal, a cat has more skeletal bones than a human. The body is therefore very flexible. In this bone structure, you can see the large socket which accommodates a cat's big eye.

COURTESY OF
THE AMERICAN MUSEUM OF NATURAL HISTORY

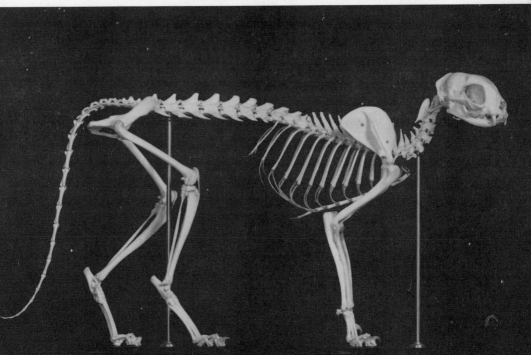

kinds. A cat's shoulder joint, by comparison with a human's, is free and open. Its collarbone (the clavicle) is very small or may be missing completely. Cats have more than five hundred muscles to manipulate their bones.

A fascinating mystery about cats is the source of their purr. They are the only creatures with this ability, and it has been studied by many experts in animal behavior. Such scientists have noted certain facts: Cats have two kinds of vocal cords, and these are called the inferior, or true, and the superior, or false. Apparently the false produce purring while the true are used for various kinds of calls. But exactly how they operate is still in question.

There are many varieties of purrs. A kitten begins to have its own "song" when about a week old. Some develop a loud, strong purr. With others it is so soft it scarcely can be heard. But we can feel a vibration revealing that an inward purr is going on.

One cat I know owes her life to her purr. She was rescued from the streets as a sickly, starving kitten. The friend-of-animals who discovered her, already having a household full of pets, and being unable to find any other adoptive home, took her to a veterinarian with the idea of having her painlessly put to a final sleep. However, whenever the little one was touched, she burst into such a happy purr her thin body seemed ready to burst. It could not be resisted! Her new friend asked the doctor instead to prescribe medication, and Miss Purr went home to be added to a menagerie of several other cats and two dogs. Soon she became "just another beautiful cat," but her purr remains remarkable.

A cat expresses emotion with its purr, but its calls and meows are its real speech. A meow of hunger, of welcome, or defiance to another cat are just a few types that can easily be understood. Then there are growls, hisses, and screams. Probably no other animal can express itself vocally as well as a cat.

It has a body language also. The tail, gently waving, speaks of quiet pleasure. When whipped from side to side, annoyance and anger are shown. When the front paws are used as if kneading dough, the cat is supremely happy.

No one can mistake a cat's emotion when its hairs "stand on end." It is frightened and defiant. But *how* is a sleek, soft coat suddenly turned into a mass of bristling hairs? It can happen because the hairs grow out of little sacs buried in the skin, and attached to the sacs are tiny muscles. If a cat is seriously alarmed, the muscles automatically react, pushing the sacs so that the hair stands straight out.

Some of the equipment for survival that all members of the cat family possess may seem wasted on those that live in homes where they are given food and shelter. But these features add to the fascination of our pets.

13

JAMES M. STAPLES PHOTO

Cats' eyes have always fascinated people, as they shine in the dark with a peculiar green glare. Cats have the largest eyes of all carnivores.

Look at the eyes that shine brightly in the dark. They are so impressive that long ago people began to associate cats with supernatural powers. However, we now know what causes the shine. There is an iridescent layer of cells on the eye's retina, and when the slightest trace of light reaches the cells, they brighten any picture that may be focused on the retina. Furthermore, the pupils dilate in the dark, allowing all possible light to enter. As a result, cats see much better in dim light than people do, but they cannot see in total darkness.

Cats are equipped with the sharpest canine teeth of all flesh-eating animals, and have the sharpest claws of all the mammals. Their sense of smell is keen—a fact that is apt to surprise people because a cat's nose is relatively small. Yet we have evidence of their interest in odors as we watch a pet enjoy the fragrance of roses and other flowers, as well as detecting favorite foods—and going into weird contortions when smelling catnip.

Just why catnip (a strong-scented herb) has this effect is still a cause for study. Wildcats are drawn to it also. The United States Fish and Wildlife Service has used it to lure bobcats and cougars in National Parks.

Extremely sensitive ears also aid a cat in dealing with its surroundings, and so do whiskers with acute nerves at their roots that carry messages to the brain.

Though it is interesting to understand the anatomy of a cat, most people are more concerned with its disposition and intelligence. And cat owners are apt to argue with dog owners over which kind of animal is more intelligent, more devoted, or more affectionate.

For years cats were given a low intelligence rating. It was admitted that "strays" must be quite smart because of the way they manage to survive under difficult conditions, but pedigreed aristocrats were thought to be "beautiful but dumb." Gradually this opinion was changed and

15

many accounts have been written, some by people of scientific standing, indicating that the exotic breeds can be as bright, active, and playful as their short-hair relatives.

We have only to remember that curiosity is a sign of intelligence to understand that cats *must* be smart because no creature is more noted for this trait. What moved outside the window? What is behind that door? Is anything in that box? Cats wonder about everything they see, hear, or smell, and usually find a way to investigate.

They can be taught important things, such as places in a home that are "off bounds" for them. However, trying to teach them to perform tricks is often unsatisfactory; they seem to feel this is beneath their dignity!

Not surprisingly, anyone who owns a variety of cats will find differences in the intelligence and disposition of individuals. And we know that certain breeds have qualities that are especially outstanding. The Manx, for example, is noted for being lively, affectionate, and extremely brave, often refusing to be intimidated by a dog or other possible enemy. Siamese cats are known for their intelligence and desire to "talk" in a clear, high, and strident voice.

One trait for which all cats, wild or domestic, are famed, is their devotion to their young. Not only do they give them good care, but fight fiercely to defend them. Once when I was walk-

WIDE WORLD PHOTOS

Curiosity—a sure sign of intelligence—is an out-standing trait in cats. This pet spent hours studying the "whats and whys" of a new aquarium.

17

ing my German shepherd dog on a leash, we were suddenly attacked (the only word for it) by a small black-and-white cat that charged from behind a wire fence. With difficulty I drove her off—my dog apparently being in a state of shock—then saw her return to her quarters. There was the explanation: a box in which lay several small kittens.

Delightful as kittens are, today they must be recognized as a real problem—simply because of their overabundance.

If a cat is not going to be used for breeding, it should be neutered or spayed. For many years people who care about the welfare of animals have been trying to interest everyone in the plight of the unwanted, homeless creatures that continue to multiply. But pet owners, though they love their own, often do not bother, or spend the money for a veterinarian's fee, to have their cat (or dog) altered in this way.

False notions also make some people hesitate to have a pet spayed. They think a spayed cat is certain to become overweight, and may become discontented and less satisfactory as a pet. On the contrary, there is no reason for a neutered cat to grow fat if it is altered after eight months of age (allowing it to first have full normal growth) and if it is fed a proper diet. As for being a satisfactory pet, a neutered cat or dog is more content to stay at home with its human family. And it is likely to enjoy health as good, or even better, than those which are not altered.

The situation of more animals existing than can be cared for has become serious enough for the United States government to give attention to it. Some Congressmen are asking that federal funds be used to help set up low-cost, non-profit spaying clinics. Church leaders are adding their pleas that animals be spayed unless their young are assured of homes. And certain organizations, such as Friends of Animals, Inc., with headquarters in New York City, are providing money for inexpensive spaying programs.

Fortunately for families who live in cities but vacation in the country, cats readily adjust to an outdoor life and back again to the indoors. And "home" changes instantly for them to wherever their people-family is located; they do not become confused and run away because the place is strange.

However, a city-country cat may have a problem or two. If one has been leading a strictly indoor life and had its claws cut far back (or removed) it cannot climb trees or even jump efficiently. And both these activities may be needed for self-protection in a country place.

Indoors, long claws must be avoided. They are uncomfortable for the cat and are likely to be destructive to furniture. (A pet usually prefers this to a specially constructed scratching post!) But, using a good clipper, the trimming of claws is a simple operation. They can be kept in reasonable shape for indoor seasons and allowed to grow when outdoor time is approaching.

A city cat finds country life exciting. There are usually chipmunks and birds to stalk, and perhaps to kill. However, leading a quiet, indoor life much of the year does not make it the best of hunters. I have seen a city cat held well in check by birds; some of them, especially cardinals and blue jays, will "gang up" to scream so fiercely at a stalking cat that it stays at a safe distance from all birds. Chipmunks are perplexing as they whisk out of sight into a hole in the ground or a stone wall; a cat may sit waiting endlessly for one to reappear before giving up.

If a hunt *is* successful, and the cat proudly brings home a small rodent or bird, there is nothing much to be done. A stouthearted member of the family should take the victim away for a quick burial, and the pet should be made to realize by unfriendly voices that no one is happy about the whole thing. Of course the feline hunting instinct cannot be changed overnight! Fortunately cats enjoy chasing an insect or a blowing leaf almost as much as larger game.

The travel between city and country usually is no hardship if a cat becomes accustomed to riding in a car from the time it is a kitten. However, when the only travel experience has been short trips to a vet, an adult cat may be frightened and upset when put in a car. But after several enjoyable visits in the country, tabby usually settles down to being a good passenger. Some people feel that a cat-carrying case is necessary for car travel. Others prefer that their pet not be caged, but condition it to enjoy the ride by soothing talk and petting.

Somehow cats have earned a reputation for hating water. Perhaps it was started because many people tried to bathe their pets, and did it without taking care of such important matters as the water's temperature and keeping soap out of the eyes. But even with good handling, most cats dislike being given baths, and actually are better off without them.

However, *water* is something else. They are fascinated by its flow from a faucet and try to play with it. If they live near a lake, they may enjoy splashing in the shallow parts, particularly if there are fish to chase. Many enjoy swimming. A friend who lives on a lake frequently sets out in her canoe with one or two of her cats going along for the ride. But if she stops to talk with other canoeists and the cats become bored, they jump overboard and swim back to their dock.

Some of the great cats, including lions, tigers, and cougars, are expert swimmers. Leopards are more noted for climbing ability; they can run up a tree with surprising speed and leap more than ten feet into the air.

Altogether we can see a number of similarities in our own pet cats and their jungle-living relatives. The wonder is that an animal still possessing so many wild instincts and abilities is able to settle down contentedly to a life with people.

THE WONDER OF DOGS
still people's best friends

2

When we look at a mighty Saint Bernard that weighs more than a hundred and fifty pounds and at a tiny Mexican hairless, weighing perhaps ten pounds, with hair limited to a tuft on the head and tail, we may wonder: Can both of these animals be *dogs*?

In spite of the tremendous contrast, they are. A careful study of dog anatomy shows that the basic structure of all the varied breeds is very similar. It is similar, also, to that of their wild relatives such as the wolf and coyote, and to certain ancestors known to us only by their fossil remains. All belong to the genus *Canis* (the Latin word for dog). The name draws attention to the well-known family trademark—the sharp canine teeth that are used to tear and shred food. The

MARY E. BROWNING
FROM NATIONAL AUDUBON SOCIETY

A bloodhound weighs about a hundred pounds and its skin is so loose it can be grasped by the handful. The weight of a full-grown Boston terrier is about fifteen pounds, and its skin fits without a wrinkle.

dog's popular name is canine. Our dog pets have the species name of *familiaris* (the Latin for "belonging to a household").

The beginnings of *Canis familiaris* go back to long before the time of recorded history. From fossils we learn that more than ten thousand years ago people in such widespread areas as Denmark, Austria, and the Middle East had added canines to the family circles. In fact, fossils take us back more than 40 million years to the original dog ancestor. This was Miacis, a tree-climbing, furry mammal, slim in body with a heavy tail. (Cats also came from this ancestry, but canines and felines developed along their own individual lines.) Gradually wolves, wild dogs, jackals, wolf-type dogs, and jackal-type dogs came into existence.

From very early times it appears that dogs had a remarkable ability to adapt to a variety of conditions. This must have made it easy for primitive people to breed them for special purposes such as hunting or herding or guarding. By the time history began to be written, most of the breeds we know today were in existence.

There were two kinds of hunting dogs—the sight hunters, which used eyes to find prey and pursue it, and the scent hunters, which depended on the nose for finding quarry.

Sight hounds were developed in Egypt where dry desert land made scenting difficult. (Greyhounds, Afghans, and the Saluki originated there.) Scent hounds were valued in areas where thick vegetation prevented game from being seen, and only a keen sense of smell would make it possible to track game. (Beagles and foxhounds came from these backgrounds.)

In such dogs we can easily see the results of special breeding. A greyhound, for example, has a long, reaching neck, with head carried high— just right for looking over obstacles on the ground. Its body is powerful and streamlined for speed. A beagle, as a scent hound, is stocky with short legs carrying the body close to the ground, and has a short neck. Long ear flaps, too, had a purpose; they stirred up scents from the grass as the dog "nosed" along after its prey.

A type that came after the hounds was the terrier, bred especially to dig into the earth. Terriers were not fitted for long-distance running, but huntsmen carried them and set them down when they knew wild animal burrows were nearby. Then the dogs lost no time rooting out prey, perhaps a badger or fox. This is an interesting picture to remember when your pet terrier, or one belonging to a neighbor, digs enthusiastically into your lawn.

Large dogs were bred for a number of purposes, including the protection of herds and homes and for use with armies. Very small types became popular also, most of them being miniature reproductions of larger ancestors.

The method used for producing a new breed, or altering one already established, is fairly simple. A breeder watches for dogs that have the special characteristics he wants, such as a fierce nature or a gentle one. He watches also for dogs with certain physical features such as great or small size, length of legs, and shape of nose.

When individuals which have the desired qualities to a noticeable degree are allowed to mate, their offspring show those qualities still more strongly. Selective breeding continues until dogs very different from their great, great, and still greater, grandparents are established.

Over a long period of time, as animals are domesticated, certain changes in the bone structure result. In dogs, the head and face are especially affected, the front part of the face becoming much shorter than in the wild animal. With some kinds, such as the collie, breeders have concentrated on reversing this face-shortening tendency. However, no dog has jaws that, in proportion to the body, are longer than the jaws of a wolf.

A dog's skeleton is much like that of a human. Therefore it is not surprising that many dogs can be taught to stand, and even to dance, on their hind legs. The modern dog is not especially sure-footed, however—certainly not when compared with a cat's built-in agility.

A new breed is considered established when it is recognized and registered by certain organizations and kennel clubs. In the United States well over a hundred breeds are recognized. Most listings divide these into six groups: sporting dogs, hounds, working dogs, terriers, toy dogs, and non-sporting dogs.

Each of these names gives a good description

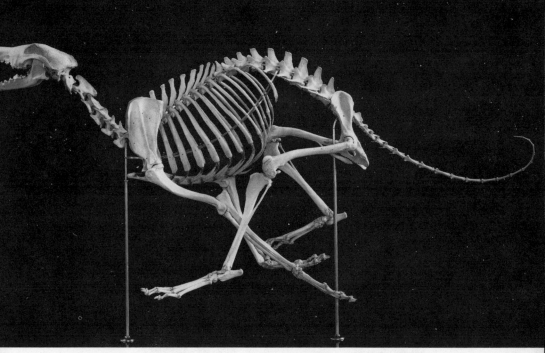

COURTESY OF
THE AMERICAN MUSEUM OF NATURAL HISTORY

A dog's skeleton is similar to that of a human's in many ways, and a comparison helps explain why many dogs can learn to stand on their hind legs. This skeleton of a Russian wolfhound has the long legs of breeds developed for speed in hunting.

of the type of dog included, except for non-sporting. This class was set up for some breeds which did not exactly fit into any of the other groups. Included in it are the beautiful, talented Dalmatians, the tremendously popular poodle, and the aristocratic Lhasa Apso.

As selective breeding goes on, unfortunate results as well as desirable ones may result. This happens when closely related males and females mate and unwanted characteristics and physical weaknesses of the family become increasingly

27

MARY E. BROWNING
FROM NATIONAL AUDUBON SOCIETY

The learning ability of dogs is proven by a variety of activities. This German shepherd enjoys acting as an assistant postman.

strong. The history of German shepherds is an illustration.

Long ago this breed was developed in Europe from several herding types, and the dogs were of great value to farmers. By the beginning of the

28

twentieth century, changes in farming styles ended such usefulness, but certain breeders felt their great qualities should not be lost, and they worked to standardize the breed. Its popularity grew rapidly, especially after two German shepherds named Strongheart and Rin-Tin-Tin became notable motion picture actors.

The sudden demand for shepherds brought about pitiable results. Greedy and ignorant breeders mated individuals that were physically and emotionally unfit—and suddenly German shepherds, as a breed, were considered nervous, unreliable, and "snappy." But determined efforts again changed the animal's fate; the breed was restored to its reputation for being devoted to its owners, easy to train, capable of doing many kinds of work, and handsome besides.

From time to time other breeds—from the tiny Chihuahua to the giant Saint Bernard—have been affected in this same unfortunate way as a result of sudden popularity.

When you buy a dog, it is important to know the backgrounds and potentialities of the different breeds. If you live in the country and want a dog to walk and run with, it would be foolish to get a terrier. Attractive as the puppies are, those short legs will not lengthen, as the pup grows, to make it a companion for long hikes. You would find this in a breed such as the Irish setter. If you live in an apartment, or in any built-up area, small and quiet breeds obviously are the most

WIDE WORLD PHOTOS

The size of a dog is important to consider when adopting one. The smaller breeds are more adaptable to city life. This Pomeranian, contentedly traveling in a homemade carrier, weighs five pounds; the average height is seven inches.

practical and best for the pet which can benefit even from limited indoor exercise.

In spite of all the facts known about backgrounds, no puppy can be guaranteed to live up to every trait for which a breed is known. In a single litter some of the pups will be friendlier, livelier, and smarter than others. The one you choose to be a watchdog may prove to be hopelessly friendly to all humans; a cute toy dog may snap at the heels of everyone who comes near. However, if you decide on a suitable breed, and then spend a while watching a litter of pups before adopting one, the chances are you will have a pet that is exactly right.

Along with differences in dogs are interesting similarities. Probably their most noted ability is the way they can detect odors. In some breeds, such as the bloodhound, this has been very much sharpened, but any dog is likely to display an extraordinary sense of smell. It is not to be wondered at: The inside of the nose and air passages leading back to the throat are lined with millions of special scent cells.

Dogs have keen memory where smells are concerned. They do not remember things they know by sight so well.

This memory is revealed in a historic story about Ulysses, a citizen of ancient Greece. When he returned to his home after ten years of wandering, he was so greatly aged neither his wife nor children knew him. But his dog, Argos, did, immediately jumping up on him, wildly barking a greeting.

A modern illustration concerns a young man who was drafted into military service and his dog, Tecumseh. This pet had been trained to carry letters in his mouth back to the porch. Since the family lived in a mild climate, the house was raised enough off the ground so that Tecumseh could have comfortable quarters underneath.

After the soldier had gone overseas, the letters he wrote home were never received. Many explanations were guessed at, but none came near the truth. This was revealed when he returned home after a year—and found all his letters stacked under the house by the dog's bed. Obviously Tecumseh had sniffed his master on the envelopes and quickly taken them to his own special retreat.

Something we might like to change about a dog's sniffing ability is its liking for decaying food. Even the most elegant canine, accustomed to fine meals from the family dinner table, will delight in a chance to raid a smelly garbage pail. This must be a throwback to wild ancestors which, of course, lived on raw flesh.

Some of our domestic dogs will kill and immediately eat a variety of animals—particularly certain rodents and rabbits. Others will not eat a freshly killed victim but will let it "ripen" for a few days, perhaps covering it with dirt.

Besides their smell-power, dogs have a great sense of hearing on which to depend. It is far superior to the hearing ability of people.

There is such a variety in dog ear flaps—large, small, those that stand up, those that turn

32

down—that we might expect hearing ability to differ. But the visible part of the ear has little effect on the actual hearing. The hole it surrounds leads into the head and to a delicate mechanism in the heavy bone at the base of the skull.

The extraordinary hearing ability probably accounts for certain happenings which people felt showed a supernatural power. Saint Bernards, for example, dedicated to rescuing mountain climbers in the Swiss Alps, were said to have mysterious foreknowledge of avalanches. On occasion they would lead a rescue party to the safety of their monastery by an unusual route— just as a great slide of ice and rock descended on their usual trail. But this behavior could be the result of the dog's having heard a slight earth tremor (which no human ear could detect) that was about to start the avalanche.

Dogs may howl just before such disasters as bombing raids and earthquakes. Again, they could have heard approaching airplanes or rumbles deep in the earth.

Its sense of smell has brought many a dog home after being lost, although pets that are closely confined to a house or apartment may be completely helpless if they find themselves alone only a short distance away. But there are happenings more difficult to understand, as when a dog has been taken to a strange place, in a closed car, and still finds its way home over many miles.

A dog that belonged to a family in Minnesota

was left with friends in the state of Washington. He broke loose and, after some months, appeared at his own home, eighteen hundred miles away. No wonder some scientists claim dogs have extrasensory perception! ESP—something beyond the usually recognized "senses"— seems the only explanation for certain behavior.

Dogs react differently to different kinds of noise. Many are frightened by gunfire. My own collie, with absolutely no unhappy experience with guns, was terrified even by the click of a toy pistol. But frequently they can be conditioned to the sound of guns. Hunting dogs and those involved with armies are inspired by the sound which, to them, is a call to action.

With thunder it is a different story. Often brave dogs seem to be trembling cowards when they hear rumbles from the sky, and no amount of reassurance from their human friends comforts them.

Why do some dogs chase cars and bicycles? Either the instinct to run after anything that moves or an instinct to protect its own territory may be the cause. Shepherd dogs and collies are among the worst offenders. There are several ways to break this dangerous habit which can be found in books on dog-training.

Barking and other vocal expressions can be something dog owners appreciate or consider a nuisance. Wolves, coyotes, jackals, and wild dogs howl. Occasionally wolves give a kind of bark,

COURTESY OF
THE AMERICAN MUSEUM OF NATURAL HISTORY

Coyotes, sometimes called wild dogs, occasionally mate with domestic dogs. They are about half the size of timber wolves. A single coyote can sound like a whole pack as it howls, barks, and whines.

and some wild dogs bark at the end of a howling session. But no one has decided whether barking as a regular habit was purposely bred in certain domestic dogs or whether it results from an ancestral trait that continued to develop naturally.

Today there are hunting dogs that bark and bay as they hunt, and dogs that hunt in silence. There are pets that bark only when strangers approach their home, and others that bark at anything and everything—often, it seems, for the pleasure of hearing themselves. The Basenji is one breed that does not bark at all. Its only "talk" is a growl or chortling noise to express pleasure.

With proper training pets can learn to restrain a tendency to be noisy. However, training is much easier if you work with a breed with the right background. For example, the larger sporting breeds and the Newfoundland and Saint Bernard are quiet by nature. Most terriers, toy breeds, and miniature poodles are excitable and like to make themselves heard.

Home-training of various sorts can be accomplished quite easily if the pet is adopted as a pup, and is never allowed to "master" its master or mistress.

My favorite example of how this can happen concerns a neighbor whose son was given a Great Dane puppy. Robert, the boy, begged to have King, the dog, sleep in his room. His parents agreed, and some months passed with

King happily growing up in his suburban home.

Then one morning Robert did not appear for breakfast at the usual time, and his mother opened his bedroom door. There she saw Robert asleep on a blanket on the floor and King, also sound asleep, stretched out on the bed. Robert explained that for a while it had been great having King sleep with him, but as the dog grew and shoved him around during the night, it became impossible to sleep. He hadn't been able to persuade King to move to the floor, so he did—and it had "worked out fine."

The family quickly thought of another solution: King was shut out from his master's room at bedtime. And after a stormy period of readjustment, sleeping arrangements really were "fine."

This had been a case of too-kindly treatment of a pet. At the other extreme are boys and girls who do not understand how to win the confidence of a dog, or how delicate a puppy is. Rough handling, even in play, can cripple or otherwise injure the small body, as it can with cats.

Unlike a cat, a dog is quite easily trained to obey simple commands. *Sit! Stay! Quiet!* These are helpful words for it to learn. However, even such training must not be started at too young an age; its nerves may be upset. Only the most elementary behavior should be taught during its first four months. Its hearing, so keen later on, does not function at all until after the first ten days of life.

Even though dogs have been well-conditioned to fit into our own way of life, and to guard and otherwise work for people, they still show signs of their wild ancestry. On the defensive or ready to attack, they bare those alarming canine teeth, or fangs. If a dog is about to lie down, we may see it first turn around a number of times. This apparently is still following an instinct inherited from ancestors which trampled and smoothed vegetation to make a comfortable bed.

Wild dogs, tame dogs—all are interesting. And through the years *Canis familiaris* many times over has proved to be a true friend to people.

HORSES
as friends and servants

3

Horses are probably the most satisfactory of part-time pets. Millions of girls and boys would delight in having one on a full-time basis, but if that is out of the question, they may still find it possible to have a horse in their lives.

I knew a ten-year-old who, it was suddenly noticed, went along the street with a peculiar kind of trot rather than walking. Her parents asked for an explanation and were simply told, "I'm riding my horse."

Fortunately her family was sympathetic and managed for her to take riding lessons.

Large cities often have riding stables and trails through their parks. Suburban riding stables make it possible to ride in more open country. Farther out, a farmer may be found with a few

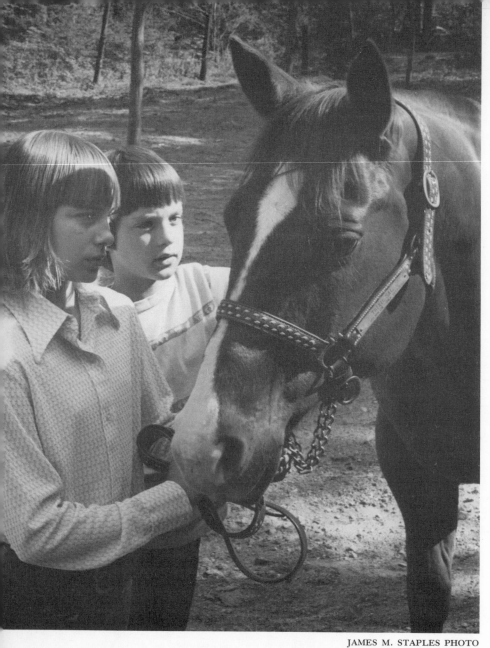

JAMES M. STAPLES PHOTO

A pet horse loves attention and enjoys the companionship of its riders if they understand how a horse should be handled.

riding horses for hire. And anyone who is able to ride quite regularly from one stable will soon feel a kinship with one particular mount.

A step closer to having your very own pet is to buy a horse and board it at a riding stable where the manager allows others to ride it, with the money received going toward the cost of boarding.

Surprisingly, a number of people who are anxious to ride, and are able to buy a horse of their own, know almost nothing about these wonderful animals. They believe that horses are horses, with little difference between them. Or they may think that all high-quality horses are thoroughbreds.

Both these ideas are false. Thoroughbred is the name of one particular breed of horse. There are a number of other breeds with known and recorded ancestry, and these are called purebreds. Among them are the Arabian, American saddle horse, Clydesdale, Morgan, and quarter horse.

Though each breed is noted for certain abilities and characteristics, personalities within each breed will vary somewhat; some will be smarter, more stubborn, or more docile than their stablemates.

If you are looking for a horse of your own, you will first want to decide what it will mean to you. Is it to be a show horse? Is it to be for riding pleasure? A farm worker? Do you want a hunter?

A jumper? If your purpose is clear, you will be able to make a wise decision about what breed to look for. Many horse farms specialize in certain breeds, and this is helpful to would-be buyers.

Of course there are also just plain horses— mixed breeds whose ancestry is anybody's guess. These are the kind usually found at auctions, and many a good and lovable character may be discovered there. But amateurs in the horse field should be cautious before investing. What looks like a bargain could be a bad investment because an attractive horse may have faults that only an expert would recognize.

It is generally known that its teeth reveal something about a horse's age. But just what is that "something"?

As the big front teeth—the incisors—grow, each develops small cups in its structure. As the teeth wear down, the "cups" show up as rings, and from studying them, an experienced judge can estimate the horse's age.

Back of the incisors, in a male horse, are canine teeth—four in all. These do not appear until the horse is about three years old; until then there are bare spaces. In a female horse canine teeth may never grow. If they do, they usually remain small. In back of the canines are big, flat teeth that crush and grind tough grasses, hay, and grain.

If you watch a horse grazing, you will notice how closely the grass is cropped—more closely

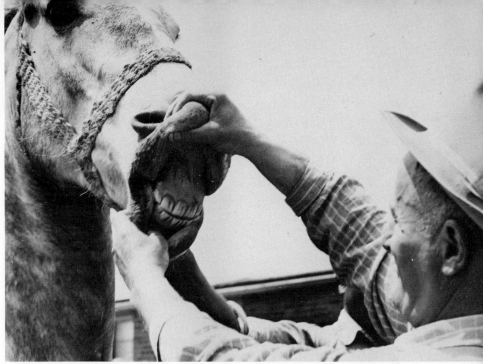

WIDE WORLD PHOTOS

When grazing, a horse crops grass very close to the earth with its big front teeth—the incisors. As these teeth wear down, an expert judge can estimate an animal's age by examining them.

than when cows graze. This serves as a warning about feeding a snack such as a lump of sugar from your hand: It should always be offered on an open palm. If held in the fingers, those incisors might give a bad nip, quite unintentionally on the horse's part.

When judging a horse for disposition and health, you will find the eyes an important guide. They should be clear and bright, with no discharge and no bluish tinge. And large eyes, with a friendly expression, indicate the makings of a good pet.

43

Horses do not have especially keen vision, but because the eyes are at the side of the head, any sort of action to the left or right catches their attention and causes them to shy. For this reason blinders are used on racehorses, and some others, to prevent their being startled by sudden movements.

Ears as well as eyes may give some indication of character. Especially large ones often are found on a horse with a quiet, placid nature while short, sharp ears, set close together, are likely to belong to an individual of unpredictable temper.

A good horse judge will check a number of features such as how an animal's head sets on the neck, the condition of its knees, and the bone structure of the shoulder.

Naturally hoofs are of great importance. For walking, running, and jumping, the feet must be in first-rate condition.

Actually, what appears to be the entire foot is one greatly enlarged toe. During millions of years of evolution, ancestors of the horse family depended on speed for safety, as they had neither claws nor horns with which to fight. Small Eohippus (the "dawn horse") had four toes on each forefoot and three on each hind foot. As the animals developed into swift runners, the center toes bore most of the body weight, and the outside toes became smaller. Finally a greatly enlarged center toe carried all the burden.

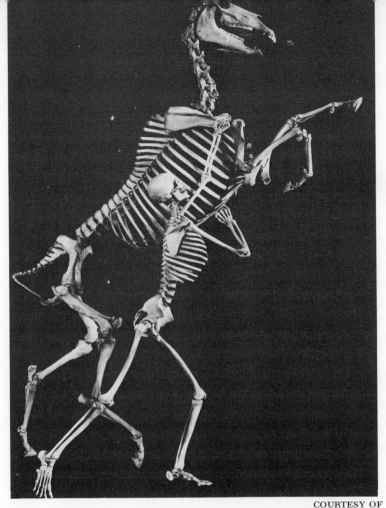

COURTESY OF
THE AMERICAN MUSEUM OF NATURAL HISTORY

*This museum exhibit shows the skeletons of a man
and a horse. There are interesting comparisons to be
made, especially with the feet. What seems to be the
foot of a horse actually is only one toe.*

In museums we may see fossil skeletons of
Eohippus and of Mesohippus (the "midway
horse"). Mesohippus had only three toes on each
forefoot. The first "true" horse, *Equus* (Latin for
"horse"), had a single toe, or hoof, on each foot.

45

Good, protecting shoes are of great importance for these valuable hoofs. Unfortunately, blacksmiths who do fine work are scarce; many shortcuts are used to save time and money, even though poor shoes can cause a horse considerable pain, and ruin it for riding.

A modern pet has a number of habits that relate back to its early ancestors. As it drinks from a trough, it is likely to look up once in a while to see if an enemy is approaching the "water hole." If anything should attack it from the front, it rears up on the hind legs and strikes out with the forelegs. Attacked from the rear, it shifts its weight to the front quarters and kicks out to the back.

Colts and older horses that have not yet learned to carry riders will at first react to training by kicking, bucking, and pawing. But as a trainer talks to his trainee in a friendly though firm voice, and the horse realizes no harm is intended, it begins to quiet down.

More often than not people who want to own a riding horse look for one already trained. It is wise for the buyer also to have some riding instruction before making such a purchase.

The best way to begin is to take lessons at a reputable riding school or from a qualified friend. Then it is possible to mount, sit, ride, and "talk" to a horse by means of aids such as reins and pressures with your knees and legs, as well as with your voice.

A horse loves to be talked to, and will often answer its human friends with a whinny as their voices are heard near its stable. It does not enjoy loud noises, however, and may become very upset by shouting. If one shies because it has been startled, its rider should immediately speak in a confident and encouraging way. Never a scolding voice!

In her book *Horses of Today*, Margaret Cabell Self, a noted authority, says that she reached the conclusion that colts are never born vicious or mean. She adds, however, "Many become untrustworthy from ignorant or brutal handling."

As with dogs, we can clearly trace the development of various breeds and understand in what ways they became especially suited to certain uses. Over thousands of years they influenced the history of the world. In warfare, men with horses fighting against those without, were certain to conquer. Horses made possible travel to new frontiers. Then they could pull plows and otherwise help pioneers become established.

The oldest and purest breed in the world is the Arabian. We are not sure from which area horses first came to Arabia (possibly from India), but it is known that for several thousand years horsemen of the Arabian desert have been jealously guarding the purity of their horses' bloodline.

Long ago the Arabs had a special need for alert and intelligent mounts—horses that would de-

47

tect the approach of an enemy and, by their behavior, give warning. They wanted horses that could get off to a quick start and run swiftly for long distances. And although they needed horses with a back strong enough to carry a man, they also wanted the animals to be small because forage is never plentiful in the desert.

Horses were raised almost like members of the family by these desert people, with affection and careful training. Today we find Arabian horses excel in looks, intelligence, and ability. But because their reactions are extraordinarily quick, they usually are not advised for beginning riders.

Not only is Arabian blood remarkable in its own breed, it has been used the world over to improve other breeds. This horse has a specially potent ability to pass its fine traits on to its descendants.

Probably the breed best known for being indebted to the Arabian is that outstanding racehorse, the thoroughbred.

During the time of the Crusades some crossbreeding between Arabian stallions and European mares was achieved. Then about three hundred years ago, three especially fine stallions were taken from Arabia to England—and they became the foundation sires of the thoroughbred line. Its members have the speed, intelligence, and spirit of their great ancestors of the desert, but they are larger and have longer legs.

As with Arabian horses, thoroughbreds are

most suitable for experienced riders. And they are not right for someone who wants only to wander along trails or in fields and woodlands. Nevertheless, some thoroughbreds have such beautiful dispositions they become delightful pets even for young or inexperienced riders.

The American saddle horse, the quarter horse, and the Morgan are a few of our other popular breeds.

Perhaps the most dramatic story in horse history concerns the Morgan. All individuals of this breed trace back to one animal, a small but muscular stallion that lived nearly two hundred years ago in New England. He not only worked with the strength of a giant, he was speedy, he could jump, and he had a friendly nature. And, for the most part, his offspring showed his outstanding qualities as well as resembling him physically. He was named Justin Morgan (after one of his many owners) and his descendants bear that name.

There are now three types of Morgan which have been specialized in certain ways. One of these, the trail Morgan, is ideal for young people.

Girls and boys are likely to be enthused over ponies, and these "small horses" can be wonderful pets. But let us understand just what a pony is, and what the problems may be in keeping one.

In general, any member of the *Equus* genus that is no higher than fifty-eight inches at the highest point of the shoulder (the withers) is properly called a pony. However, the so-called polo pony and cow pony are somewhat taller than this.

Also, some fine breeds of horses such as Arabian and quarter horse include individuals that come under the fifty-eight-inch measurement, and therefore may properly be called ponies.

Besides this variety, there are breeds whose ancestors were especially noted for their small size, and their bloodlines were kept pure. Today the most famed of purebreds are the Welsh, Shetland, Hackney, and Connemara. There are also miniature ponies with a height at the withers of no more than thirty-six inches. These are attractive pets but obviously too small for riding.

It might seem that, because of their small size, ponies would be easier to care for and handle than full-size horses. But this is not exactly the case.

If a pony is kept in a stable and fed grain, it is likely to develop an inflammation in the feet—called foundering—from the rich food. And because the grain is stimulating, the pony may kick and bite to relieve its frustrations. Turned loose in fresh green pastures, it may overeat and, if not sufficiently exercised, develop the same inflammation. And while a well-trained pony is a joy to own, finding one is not easy. There is a scarcity of qualified trainers who are small enough to ride the little animals!

Besides proper exercise, good grooming is important for ponies and horses. Frequent rubdowns help the circulation and keep an animal looking its best.

For a daily beauty treatment a currycomb should be used with a firm circular motion over the body. This loosens any dirt which should then be removed by a brisk brushing. Hoofs should be examined and any stones or clumps of dirt lodged in them removed with a hoof pick.

Special vacuum cleaners are now available for more occasional grooming. Though the horse may be startled the first time such a machine goes over its coat, it quickly learns to appreciate the good feeling of such a powerful rubdown, and stretches out its body to the fullest extent to enjoy the massage.

TALKING BIRDS AND A SINGER
parrakeet, parrot, mynah, canary

4

"A pet that can talk to me!" This is the happy boast of someone who has become the owner of a parrakeet or mynah.

And it is true these birds can produce sounds that are perfect copies of human language. However, they are not really communicating; they are simply repeating words they have heard. They might, instead, imitate a dog's bark, the squeak of a door, or another bird's song.

Still, this fact need not spoil the fun of hearing a perky feathered friend ask, "How are you?" Or say, "Good morning!" or other phrases it has learned. And the wonder is always there: How is it that certain birds can and do manage to talk?

We might think that an understanding of a bird's vocal equipment would give a ready answer, but it doesn't. Parrakeets, parrots, and mynahs have the same vocal apparatus as other birds that do not talk. There is a windpipe (the trachea) with a voice box (the syrinx) at its lower end. A larynx (which serves humans in producing sounds) is at the upper end, but it is very little developed.

Since all birds have a syrinx, yet only some kinds imitate human speech, we still do not have an explanation.

At one time it was noted that in members of the parrot family, the upper and lower parts of the bill (the mandibles) are hinged and are able to move independently of each other. With most birds the mandibles are fixed; they cannot act separately.

This might seem like a good clue—until we find that the mynahs, which can talk very well indeed, have fixed mandibles just as sparrows have. And crows and ravens which, when tamed, may learn human speech, also have fixed mandibles. Therefore the answer cannot lie in the bill.

An example of how misled people can be about bird talk is an old superstition concerning crows. The belief was that splitting the tongue of one of these birds would enable it to speak. Only after such a cruel operation had been performed was the truth learned: A split tongue is no aid in producing sound.

Aside from dividing birds into talkers and non-

WIDE WORLD PHOTOS

Parrots can be taught to do tricks and they like to copy human behavior. This six-year-old, Skipper, prefers to eat from a spoon firmly held in his claw.

talkers, we can divide those which may be expected to have this ability into those which learn rather quickly to use our words and others that keep strictly to their own bird chatterings.

We can easily find guidance about teaching methods in books, and from owners of other birds that talk. But while certain fundamental rules usually work, there are some birds that stubbornly refuse to be converted to people-talk.

A friend once obtained a young mynah bird, and after a few months of training, Major was able to speak clearly and loudly in his raucous voice. Major met with a freak accident which ended his life at the age of ten, so my friend immediately bought another mynah. She repeated the same speech lessons, under the same conditions she had used before, but Major the Second was not impressed. He mimicked many other sounds but never her words.

Our family had a parrakeet that showed the same resistance to human speech, even though all teaching rules were carefully followed. On one occasion we took Buddy to board at a pet shop while we were to be away. When we called for him a week later, the pet shop owner said, "Your Buddy is a great talker!"

My children were delighted. So was I. "What has he said?" we asked in chorus.

The woman laughed. "Oh, he only used his own language, but he was chattering all the time."

Buddy became expert at singing and whistling, but he never did talk. Most parrakeets do respond to careful teaching. Some begin to "talk back" in a few weeks; others, not for a year.

Even without people-talk, parrakeets are interesting and amusing pets. They were discovered more than a hundred years ago in Australia, living in large flocks, and were recognized as members of the parrot family. The Australian name for them was budgerigar, from the aboriginal word meaning "pretty bird." Today this often is shortened to budgie.

WIDE WORLD PHOTOS

If carefully handled, a parrakeet may make friends with all members of the family—including the cat.

There are other species of parrakeet, some of them also found as cage birds, but the budgie is by far the most popular. The name parrakeet indicates their relationship to the parrot family which includes lovebirds, cockatiels, and macaws.

When it was found that budgerigars could easily be tamed, a number of them were taken from Australia to Europe and America, where they flourished in captivity. Though the original imports had lovely green coloring, striped with black, it was decided that variety would make them still more interesting. Through selective breeding, blue, violet, gray, and other colors in plumage gradually were produced.

Caged birds have a problem that does not trouble their relatives in the wilds: They have little opportunity to wear down their claws, which never stop growing. In time overgrown claws will prevent a bird from standing on a flat surface, or even grasping its perch properly. They can be clipped with small nail scissors, but great care must be taken not to cut into the blood vessels. By holding the foot in front of a strong light, you can see where the blood vessels end.

Some people prefer "real" parrots as pets— usually the African gray, with a bright red tail. It is handsome, and the best of all talkers. However, caring for parrots requires much more work, in cage-cleaning and providing proper food. Also, they can give a serious wound if provoked into biting. There are a number of dwarf species, some as small as eight inches in length.

Mynahs are not members of the parrot family. They are closely related to starlings—birds brought from Europe to America and allowed to go free.

WIDE WORLD PHOTOS

Mynah birds can be entertaining companions. This one, Mahatma, became an expert ball player. He catches paper balls in his beak while in flight or on a perch.

The hill mynahs, a variety from India, are the ones usually found in pet shops. Their shiny black feathers set off by yellow beaks and patches of yellow around the eyes and back of the neck give them a well-groomed, attractive appearance.

Mynahs belong to the "soft-bill" group of birds; that is, they live on soft foods such as fruit. In a wild state they eat mostly fruit and insects. In captivity they enjoy a great variety of foods, both cooked and raw, but a well-balanced diet is assured by giving them a good commercial

58

mynah bird-food mixture and plenty of fruit.

Parrakeets and canaries are among the "hard-bills," whose diet is mainly seeds. But these two kinds of birds are not closely related.

Canaries belong to the finch family, which includes more than four hundred species, and is the largest of all bird families in the world. Our native bird, the goldfinch, with its yellow and black coloring and lovely flight song, rather closely resembles its "cousin," the canary.

Pet canaries originally came from the Canary Islands off the west coast of Africa, and from the Azores and Madeira. But long ago, as a great breeding program began to flourish in Europe and America, the importing of wild canaries stopped.

Canary breeding became big business as well as a hobby for amateurs. And two types of singers became recognized—the "roller," best known for its long trills and a variety of low, soft notes, and the "chopper," which has a strong, loud song and staccato notes.

With either kind (and with some wild birds such as purple finches) the wonder is how they can sustain their tremendously long songs without pausing for breath.

In addition to lungs, a bird has five or more air sacs connected with the lungs and extending into the large bones of the body. It is believed that in some birds, including canaries, the air reserves can be used for prolonged singing. Such air sacs contribute to the light weight of a bird, and they help to keep its body cool. Birds do not sweat, and they have a hot, rapid metabolism.

As with the wild birds, pet male canaries are more inclined to sing than the females. Some females do have a song of their own, but it is the males that give these birds their reputation as outstanding songsters.

If you are buying a canary, you will want to choose one that already sings. While the bird's general singing ability is inherited, a breeder usually trains young ones by arranging for them to have a "tutor" bird. Under the tutor's influence, in about three months they should establish a good song of their own. A well-trained roller may sing from ten to fourteen different notes in connected phrases.

Sometimes a pet which has been a cheerful singer becomes silent. Reasons vary. The bird may be in poor health, due to improper cage conditions or food, or it may have become overweight. But, on the whole, canaries thrive in captivity.

As you watch a bird pet, you may become curious about things that would escape notice with wild birds.

How can it sleep soundly on its perch without falling off? How can it turn its head so far it appears to be on backward?

A bird may relax, but its feet never do. As it sleeps, it tilts its head backward so that the body is in perfect balance and exerts a pull on tendons in the feet. The threadlike tendons—two in each foot—cause the toes to turn inward, anchoring the bird securely to its perch. This is effective for wild birds, even when a high wind is blowing tree branches on which they are resting.

The flexible neck which turns so readily is explained by the skeleton. In its little neck a bird has twice as many vertebrae as are found in the long, long neck of a giraffe, which has only seven.

Years ago there was great concern about keeping pet birds because of a common disease called "parrot fever," or psittacosis. Happily, antibiotics now do away with worry about contagion, not only from members of the parrot family, but from other birds as well. Seeds or other foods treated with the correct antibiotics keep birds disease-free.

BIRDS FOR OUTDOORS
pigeon, duck, goose

5

Many people cannot understand why anyone would want to have pigeons as pets. "Nuisance birds," they call them. But others admire and enjoy them immensely.

Of course it is the wild, not domesticated, pigeons that are unpopular. However, even these wild birds have their admirers who feed them in parks or in front of gargoyled old buildings where the birds can find convenient roosts. If only they didn't make such a mess of things! There are never just a few pigeons. Their numbers increase endlessly, and their droppings create tremendous cleaning problems.

Pigeon pets are a different matter. Their numbers are controlled. And after being freed for daily exercise flights, they return to their own roosts, content to be back home again. They are interesting, beautiful, and often financially rewarding birds to own. They have been domesticated for thousands of years.

Today there are more than two hundred different varieties of pigeons, of many shapes, sizes, and colors. The "fancy" are valued for their beauty. Some are "fliers," valued for the ability to fly swiftly and directly to their home loft from far distances; pigeon racing, in fact, is a popular sport. Still others are "utility" pigeons, valued because they produce nest after nest of young which serve people as an excellent food.

It is believed that all these varieties are descendants of the rock pigeon, found in Europe, Central Asia, and China. Many of the popular breeds of today were developed in the Old World, but all were brought to America, where they flourished.

Sometimes people ask, "What is the difference between pigeons and doves?"

Really there is no difference; both belong to the same bird family. All the members have a sleek, rather small, rounded head, and a full-breasted body densely covered with feathers. Doves, for the most part, are smaller and gentler.

Strutting and cooing by the males is typical behavior. Their courtship ritual is a performance that fascinates even the most casual birdwatcher. A male fluffs the feathers around his throat to form a large collar, spreads his tail

63

WIDE WORLD PHOTOS
A pet pigeon, devoted to its owner, waits on the young lady's head for the school bus. After the bus comes, the bird flies along beside it, perching on the roof at every stop. When school is reached, the pigeon flies home.

feathers, and dances in front of a female that attracts him. His dancing, walking beside her, and cooing continues until she touches his bill with hers. Then the contented pair go off to mate, and they are likely to remain partners for life. Mated pigeons form a deep attachment for each other.

More than cage birds, pigeons are likely to become an important hobby to their owners. Usually it is not a case of having "a" pigeon. Most people who are at all interested want at least a pair, and this may well grow into a whole flock, and their owner may look for a Pigeon Fanciers' Club to join.

Before investing in pigeons, therefore, it is important to know just why you want them, and what kind of housing you can offer.

The fantail is a fine choice if you want really beautiful birds. Members of this breed are distinctive in shape, with a small, rounded body, small head, and a fine tapering neck. The "fan" tail is almost flat and circular; the coloring may be one of a number of hues, including yellow, silver, black, or white. The bird seems almost to dance on tiptoe as it walks, and it stands like a peacock with its head pulled backward.

Fantails quickly become tame if handled properly. They are home-loving birds and are awkward fliers. They need a roomy loft—one that protects them from wind, rain, and snow.

The pouter pigeon is another breed that can safely be given the freedom of a backyard. It is sometimes called the clown of the pigeon world because it performs endless funny antics.

Pigeons that excel in flying are known as homing or carrier pigeons. Before modern communication systems were invented, they were trained by army signal corps to carry messages to battle stations that otherwise could not be reached. They flew at about sixty miles an hour and could find their way across a thousand or more miles.

Such use for pigeons with a strong homing instinct was discovered many centuries ago. During the Crusades they carried messages for soldiers, and in ancient Rome, Nero sent the results of sporting events to his friends by means of his pet pigeons.

Racing-homer pigeons provide a challenge to breeders who want birds that can fly fast and continuously for hours, returning without fail to their own lofts. Year after year birds of great ability are mated to produce talented "homers." Their training starts when they are about four months old. At first they are released from a box only a mile from home. In a few months they may manage a hundred miles, but it takes a few years to achieve their full-distance ability.

A worry of any owner of pet pigeons must be wild pigeons. These bold ones are not at all shy about pushing their way into a loft meant for pets, crowding the tame birds and possibly bringing with them parasites and other germs. Antibiotics put into the birds' drinking water is helpful in preventing the spread of disease.

As with pigeons, ducks have been useful domesticated birds for many centuries. And wherever we find a domesticated animal, we find the makings of a pet. In recent years ducklings have been high on the list of animals bought most frequently for this reason.

But this was not a happy development, either for the baby ducks or their owners. The little birds often were sold to people who had no proper place to keep them, and no knowledge of their needs. Today many states forbid, by law, the sale of ducklings (and chicks) as pets. However, if you live in the country and can fence off a bit of property on which there is water, you have a good setup for some interesting "barnyard friends."

At first a single duckling must have special care because it has been taken from the comfort of huddling with its own family. Even though it is thickly covered with down when it hatches, the body temperature control is only partially developed.

One or two ducklings can live comfortably indoors for some weeks. A box or carton with high sides, kept in a warm place, and large enough for the babies to run around, provides a comfortable home. When they are old enough to be moved outdoors, a low shed gives sufficient shelter, and a wide basin filled with water and sunk in the ground makes a suitable swimming pool. Without a mother to guide them, they may be a little slow to realize they are birds of the water even more than of the land.

On land, a duck's body seems overbalanced. With its short legs set wide apart, far back on the

An ideal place for duckling pets is a yard with good shelter. A large basin of water, set in the ground, is sufficient for the beginners' swimming pool.

C. P. FOX
FROM NATIONAL AUDUBON SOCIETY

body, its steps must be taken with great care. In water the widespread legs and webbed feet serve as efficient paddles.

There are many varieties of domestic ducks, as there are of wild breeds. Some have been bred so that they cannot fly. Other domestic ducks (especially the Muscovy) fly very well, and it is customary to clip their wings.

One of the best known of wild ducks is the mallard—the male being outstanding with his head a rich, glossy green, set off by a white collar. All varieties of domestic ducks, except the Muscovy, are descended from mallards.

If you watch a variety of wild ducks, you may be puzzled by their behavior in the water. Some dive deeply to find food, others merely dabble along the shore, probing the mud that lies under shallow water. This difference is understandable because there are two distinct groups—one belongs to rivers and ponds, the other to bays and the open sea. It is the river-pond group that browse in shallow water.

Ducks may be kept successfully without a pond but, because they are really in their element in water, it is best if they have one. With geese it's a different matter; they can thrive in a field or backyard, though a supply of fresh water must always be available. On a goose the legs are not set so far back on the body as on a duck. As a result, this bird can walk and run more freely. The beak is harder and not as flat, so that

69

WIDE WORLD PHOTOS

The owner of this gaggle of pet geese, anxious about their safety, put up a warning sign for motorists.

it can feed more easily on land vegetation. The neck of a goose is usually noticeably longer than that of a duck.

As a backyard resident, a goose presents one problem: Its loud *honk* carries far and wide, and may be disturbing to neighbors, as well as to its own human family. However, this is part of its value as a "watchdog." A goose is ever alert to an unusual noise, and immediately sounds an alarm when it senses danger. If a suspected enemy is reachable, it doesn't hesitate to attack. A goose is considered the most intelligent of domesticated birds, and among the smartest of all animals.

Wild geese mate for life, and once a pet gander

is paired with a goose, the two will live together "happily ever after." If one dies, the survivor may never accept another partner. Without a mate, one of these birds is likely to give its complete devotion to a member of its human family.

The first day of school causes an unhappy parting for a boy and the pet goose which he raised from a gosling. The big bird likes to follow his young master everywhere.

WIDE WORLD PHOTOS

FOR A COUNTRY LIFE
pigs and some wild pets

6

Who would think that a pet pig could be as much fun as a dog? As an enthusiastic lover of dogs, I was not easily convinced that the two even rated a comparison. However, a number of pet pigs that were brought to my attention gradually changed my mind. This one is my favorite story:

Tom, a boy who lives far enough out in the country so that he not only must take a school bus, but has a long walk to the bus stop, was given a young pig. The pig, named Sow-Sow, quickly made herself at home, playing ball with Tom and his dog, Pal, and joining in other activities.

When school days began in the fall, Pal, as he had done the year before, accompanied Tom to the bus. Sow-Sow trotted along, too, and went

WIDE WORLD PHOTOS

A special saddle is all the equipment this nine-year-old uses to ride her pet pig. No bit is needed.

back home with Pal after the bus had gone. This routine was followed every morning for a few days. Then came the surprise: When the bus returned in the afternoon, Sow-Sow was waiting for it. Somehow she was able to sense the time for Tom's return and had set off to meet him. This continued for the rest of the school year.

A piglet as a pet presents a problem. It grows to maturity in a year, and unless there is plenty of room to give the adult comfortable quarters, it probably would have to be turned into an ordinary farm pig.

Pigs have been friends to people for something like seven thousand years—though not as pets. Of course they were used as food, but they had other uses as well. In ancient Egypt they trod seeds into the earth after a rain; their pointed feet made holes of just the right depth. Sometimes they furnished the power for threshing. During the Middle Ages, when hunting dogs were forbidden in Europe, they were trained to point and retrieve game. Even today in southwest France they are used as hunting aids. The hunt is not for other animals but for fungi called truffles (much enjoyed as a food) that grow underground. Though the truffles are hidden in the earth, a pig can smell them and leads its owner to the right places to dig.

Zoologists give pigs a high rating in intelligence. On a rating scale, it is just below that of the apes!

A pig learns tricks quickly, and has a good memory. It "talks" with a variety of grunts and squeals that show such emotions as pleasure, disappointment, and anger. Though a pet can be trained to walk on a leash, if it really doesn't want to go in the direction it is being taken, it protests with squeals that will weaken the spirit of a strong-minded leader.

Through the years pigs have been the objects of many insults. To call a person a "pig" suggests he is dirty, greedy, or a glutton. This is most unfair; the reputation developed only because of the way pigs were treated by people.

74

A pig really likes to be clean; if given a choice between clean and dirty water in which to bathe, it chooses the clean. It likes to wade in mud because the soft, wet earth feels comfortable against its legs (as with its cousin, the hippopotamus), but it prefers *clean* mud.

Because pigs are able to eat, digest, and benefit from a great variety of foods, some farmers tend to treat them like living garbage disposals. In a natural state these animals eat no more than they need to stay alive and well.

Piglets can begin to eat soft mashes and cereals from a bowl or trough when about three weeks old. The feeding vessel must be kept very clean, for the digestion of a young one is easily upset.

Another unusual pet, also high on the intelligence scale, is the raccoon. Unlike pigs, raccoons have never been domesticated. Yet a young one, perhaps rescued when its mother was killed, will adjust to life with people in a remarkable way.

In a book called *Rascal,* Sterling North tells the story of his pet, adopted when the little raccoon weighed less than a pound. Rascal was the most exciting and lovable of pets, but after he became adult, he found joy in using his natural talents for food-finding. Occasionally he raided a neighbor's cornfield, a grape arbor, or a chicken run.

75

Sterling knew he had to make a decision: Keep Rascal confined at all times or release him to a natural life. He decided on freedom for his adored pet, and one day took Rascal in a canoe to a wilderness area, giving him the opportunity to leave to join others of his kind. The raccoon obviously was excited by the possibilities, and suddenly he plunged from the canoe and swam to shore.

The boy was sad, but not worried. He knew his pet would find plenty of his natural food, such as fish, frogs, insects, and mice; would find a mate; and would enjoy the freedom of the woods and river. All this would make up for the love and companionship of the boy whose home and life he had been sharing.

A unique feature of a raccoon is the long, agile toes on the front feet which are used like fingers. These are very fine for the raccoon, but disturbing for anyone who has a raccoon as a house guest. The animal can open drawers, doors, boxes, and jars, and its sense of curiosity prompts it to investigate all such things. It can also turn faucets, but once water is flowing, it usually will not worry about turning it off again.

Raccoons are noted for their habit of dunking food in water before eating it, and for a long time people believed their purpose was to clean it. In fact they were given the species name of *lotor*, which in Latin means "washer." But this explanation is no longer accepted by many students of

LEONARD LEE RUE III
FROM NATIONAL AUDUBON SOCIETY

The beautiful, intelligent raccoon makes a fascinating pet. Since raccoons have not been domesticated, adopting one from wild life can present problems.

animal behavior. One theory now suggests that wet food slips into the throat more easily. But like the earlier theory, this is not proven.

A raccoon pet should always have a pan of water available, but if it is being given dog food, the water should be put out of reach during feeding time.

An interesting relative of raccoons is the giant panda. Long ago pandas were thought to be a kind of bear. However, studies proved that many basic features of pandas were like those of raccoons, and they were grouped in the same family.

If you were to tell someone you had a pet skunk, it is likely the "someone" would hold his nose or make a face. But if you said you had a wood pussy, the news would probably be greeted with a smile and the question, "What's a wood pussy?"

The answer is, "A skunk with another name." And it is a good one, because skunks can be as affectionate and clean as pussy cats.

Skunks are often bought in pet shops rather than being captured or rescued in their natural surroundings. Nearly always these captive ones have had their scent glands removed. This is a simple operation, but it should be performed by a veterinarian when the animal is young, perhaps at only five weeks, and surely before two months of age.

JAMES M. STAPLES PHOTO

The great claws of a skunk are not used for fighting, but for digging. Skunks are closely related to badgers, which are world-famed as diggers.

79

The sickening odor that is a skunk's trademark comes from a fluid in two musk glands located at the base of the tail. When the skunk is frightened, it raises its tail, contracts muscles that surround the glands, and forces the fluid out in a fine spray. This could hit a target as far away as ten feet! But a skunk is not anxious to use such ammunition; it is saved for a time when defense really seems needed. After it has been spent, the glands take some hours to recharge.

The trouble with descenting a baby skunk is that if you later want to give the adult its freedom, it would have to be released into the wilds without any means of discouraging enemies. The best solution is to find a zoo for native animals where it could continue a safe and interesting life.

A skunk can be a fun pet, for these animals are playful and, if kept indoors, can be trained to use a cat's litter box. But a roomy outdoor wire cage, with some straw as furnishing, makes a good romping room. The wire must be dug well into the ground, however, for skunks are expert diggers. They belong to the same family as the badger—famed for its digging ability.

Using all four feet, a badger can get its entire body underground in a few seconds. Badgers also are playful. They have been seen, living in a wild state, turning somersaults and enjoying what looks very much like the children's game of leapfrog.

Another lively acrobat often enjoyed as a pet is the flying squirrel. This is a beautiful little creature—one that will breed in captivity and accept the friendship of people. There are flying-squirrel ranches where the animals are raised and then sold to pet shops or individual customers.

It is said that their ability to fly makes these squirrels different from most mammals. Actually they glide rather than fly; a fur-covered membrane that extends from the front paws to the back legs acts as a sail. Outdoors, especially traveling with a strong breeze, one can cover a hundred feet or more in a single swoop. And even in a room, by taking off from a tall piece of furniture, one can glide very well indeed. It moves in complete silence so that it may land on someone's head without the slightest warning.

But a flying squirrel will be content much of the time in a large, properly equipped cage. It will be especially happy if it has a mate and, eventually, a whole family.

Anyone who has a flying squirrel must remember it requires gentle treatment. Unlike the sturdy tree squirrels, its body is delicate, and it may die of shock if roughly handled. It should also be remembered that flying squirrels are nocturnal. The best schedule for pets is to let them out of their cage, or otherwise encourage their play, in the evening. Hopefully, then, they will quiet down by the family's bedtime.

Tree squirrels, especially the gray, can be

81

tamed so easily without their being confined, it seems this is the best way to have them as pets. You may come to know certain individuals in a park, or close to your home, by giving them bits of food. In this way the squirrels enjoy a free life, yet come to know you as a friend.

THE LOVABLE RODENTS
guinea pig, gerbil, hamster, mouse

7

Someone who wants a pet that will not fly, glide, climb, jump, or be noisy, but is attractive, cuddly, and affectionate often is happy to discover the guinea pig.

Like squirrels, guinea pigs are rodents—far removed in relationship from true pigs. Why, then, do they have this name? The accepted explanation is still based on guesswork.

One of the sounds a guinea pig makes is a soft grunt—usually of pleasure, such as when it is especially happy with its food. Pigs also grunt. This is a slight connection, but apparently it was seized upon long ago when people wanted a name for the little creature that, in ancient times, was of great importance to the Inca Indians of South America.

Before Spaniards conquered the Inca Empire, these animals flourished from high in the Andes Mountains to low river valleys. They were an important food, and sometimes were used in ceremonies as a sacrifice to the gods. Obviously they were highly regarded, for their bodies often were mummified and placed in a tomb with their owner at his death.

After Europeans invaded South America, sailors found pleasure in making pets of the animals and taking some of the little "pigs" back home. Because the ships often stopped at Guinea on the west coast of Africa en route to Europe, the sailors became known as "guinea-men" and the name guinea pigs was coined for

A guinea pig is easy to care for and fun to play with; it is an ideal pet in many ways.

JEANNE WHITE
FROM NATIONAL AUDUBON SOCIETY

their pets. Now that scientists have placed them in the genus *Cavia*, they sometimes are called cavies. But guinea pig is an older, and surely more colorful, name.

As pets, guinea pigs ask for little except affection and food. They can provide their own exercise, indoors or out, simply by running around on their short legs. They are hardy and enjoy people to such an extent that a single individual can be content without the company of others of its own kind.

A friend who bought a guinea pig, named Penny, for her son, finds she has also acquired a new friend for herself. Penny enjoys playing with young Steve, hiding in paper bags, then suddenly running out at him and doing a variety of cute stunts. But in the evening when Steve's mother is watching television, Penny likes to sit on her lap, and seems to pay attention to the screen, especially during sports events.

Penny is a mixed breed. Her bright copper-color hair is rough, indicating one ancestor was Abyssinian. The short, rough hair of pure Abyssinians grows in swirls or rosettes. The English breed—probably the most popular as a pet—has smooth short hair. The Angora (also called Peruvian) has hair so long it completely hides the animal's legs. Such a guinea pig is impressive to exhibit, but its coat requires a great deal of care to prevent matting.

If lawn-cutting is part of the upkeep of your

85

home, guinea pigs can serve as reliable assistants. A wire mesh pen—about four feet square—should be constructed. If it is eighteen inches or more high, it will not need a covering. Guinea pigs placed within this will neatly clip the grass; then it can be moved to an adjoining area.

As with any defenseless pets taken outdoors, guinea pigs must be watched to see that no roaming animal bothers them.

While guinea pigs are among the oldest of rodent pets, gerbils are the newest. We even know the exact year they were first shown in pet shops. It was 1964.

Ten years before that, some gerbils had been brought to the United States from Asia for research in medical laboratories. Other gerbils were known to live in Africa and southern Russia. They are typical of small mammals found in desert regions of these parts of the world. Seeds, grasses, and roots are their food. They live in colonies, making one long tunnel with several branch tunnels and small burrows opening from it. Here they store food and make nests.

There are about forty different species, and they resemble other jumping rodents such as the jerboa. Those we have as pets are called Mongolian gerbils because they are descendants of those imported from Mongolia.

I have known many gerbil enthusiasts during the past few years, but the most enthused of all is Mark Gibson.

THOMAS CERVASIO PHOTOS

Proud parents: Mr. and Mrs. Gerbil (standing upright) have been caring for their babies for several weeks; all are in fine condition.

Proud owner: Mark Gibson beams as one of his gerbil pets shows how expertly it can jump up stairs.

Mark first learned about gerbils from a pair in the nature room of his school. Soon he managed to buy a pair of his own. He was so devoted to them that when the school decided against keeping its gerbils (many girls and boys insisted on handling them roughly), they were offered to him.

This gave Mark an opportunity to observe two different pairs with differing backgrounds. For a while those that came from the school were nervous and inclined to bite. But gradually they became calm and really enjoyed being picked up and gently stroked. Mark finds pleasure in making toys for them, and has tested their intelligence by constructing a large maze to discover how successful each one is in finding the right way to get out.

Both for his own convenience and for the sake of his pets, Mark keeps a day-by-day record on a desk calendar, noting when each of the cages is cleaned and when the animals have been fed. He recorded their actions when in the maze and—in the course of time—was able to note the birth of babies. It remains a puzzle that one couple produces young while the other does not.

Just before Christmas, Mark decided to make small wreaths to hang on each gerbil cage. As he was working, he found he had some unexpected presents for his pets, for they took fir branches from his hands and had a wonderful time snipping the needles off the twigs with their teeth.

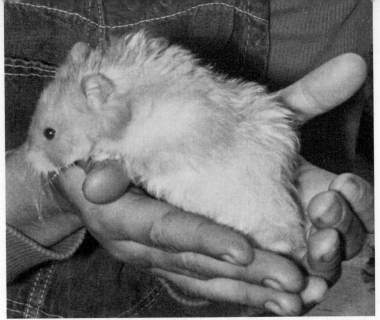

JAMES M. STAPLES PHOTO

Pet hamsters have a history very similar to that of gerbils. They graduated from laboratory animals to become household favorites.

Mark tried several different diets for the gerbils. The one that seemed the most satisfactory was a mixture of bird seed and sunflower seeds. He then made a good business arrangement with a pet shop that supplied him with seeds and, in exchange, he gave them young gerbils when they were old enough to be separated from their parents.

Compared with gerbils, hamsters are old-timers in the pet world. As with gerbils, they were first brought to the United States as laboratory animals. However, this was nearly thirty years earlier—in 1938. And it was not long before they were accepted as pets.

Today, despite the tremendous interest in gerbils, the hamster still holds its own in popularity. It, too, is hardy in captivity. It is companionable, playful, and charming with its broad, pixie face topped by rounded ears, and brightened by shiny black eyes. Often it is called the golden hamster, for its velvety coat is reddish gold.

Gerbils leading a normal life are active during the day, and pet gerbils are inclined to follow the same pattern of wakeful days and nights of rest. Hamsters, on the other hand, are nocturnal; their activities begin after sunset.

This program can be awkward for someone who wants to play with his pet. However, nocturnal animals that live with people can be persuaded to alter their habits. If they are coaxed out of a daytime sleep with bits of food, and find they are being given special attention, they are likely to be sociable. In time this alters their inherited pattern of activity and rest.

Anyone who undertakes the raising of hamsters or gerbils should be aware of a startling fact: There are times when a mother will eat one or more of her babies. We are not sure why this happens. One theory is that her diet before giving birth was not adequate, and was especially lacking in minerals. Another suggests there has been too much disturbance, perhaps from handling, and she is upset. Or there may be too many babies in a litter for her to nurse. No matter what the cause, this may happen sometimes with a female who, with other litters, is a normal and protective mother.

There is a prejudice against mice and rats as pets that some people cannot overcome. And this is understandable, since these same rodents are dreaded pests in our society. Rats not only thrive in garbage, they make their way into warehouses and granaries; the house mouse manages to invade homes in city and country alike. Both are a menace to health.

How, then, can they even be thought of as pet material?

The fact is, rats or mice that have been specially bred for life in a home or laboratory are a

Tame mice are not always white. They have been bred to show many colors or combinations of colors. Here a black-and-white pet is being admired.

JAMES M. STAPLES PHOTO

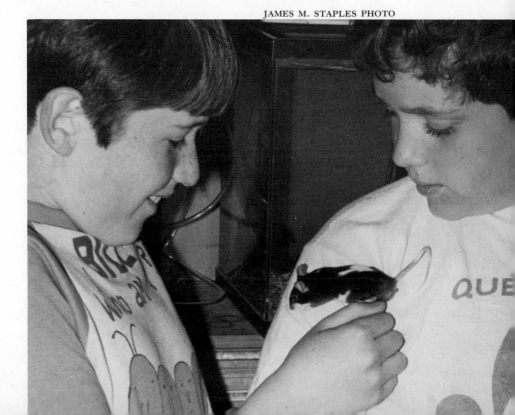

great contrast to the unwanted pests that bear the same names. In captivity, when well cared for, they are clean to the point of constantly grooming themselves, and smart enough to learn tricks and to play with the same kinds of toys that gerbils and hamsters enjoy.

Tame mice and rats are often white, but breeders have produced a wide variety of colored coats—everything from silver, pink, and orange to blue and dark brown, and some with a combination of colors. More than a hundred varieties of "fancy" mice have been bred. Some have curly tails, others have no tails at all. Some have long, wavy hair, others have short-haired, shiny coats.

The development of many different varieties in a short time is made possible by the amazing reproductive ability of these rodents. They will begin to mate when only two or three months old, and there is no breeding "season"; a pair will produce one litter after another. If not separated, they may be responsible for well over a hundred babies in a single year.

This, we can see, is one way tame mice and rats resemble their wild relatives, whose amazing fertility makes the rodent population so difficult to control. Of course, a pet owner can regulate the number of offspring simply by using separate cages for the males and females.

RABBITS AND HARES
which are which?

8

You may wonder why rabbits and hares are not included in the chapter about rodents. It is for the very good reason that they are not rodents.

This seems rather surprising, because their prominent chisel-like front teeth are outstanding features also of rodents. However, members of the two groups are different in many ways, and they are placed in different orders in the animal kingdom. If you watch the way a rabbit hops and then watch a mouse or guinea pig scamper, you will have an idea where some of the differences lie.

Large hind limbs and feet, which make hopping possible, are outstanding in rabbits and hares, which always move in a series of leaps.

Their tracks never can be confused with those of any other animal. The general pattern is, two large imprints side by side in front; behind them, two smaller footprints, one behind the other.

There is plenty of variety in the rabbit-hare family alone, and we also find a confusing variety of names. For example, the so-called Belgian "hare" is really a rabbit, and a snowshoe "rabbit" is really a hare.

True rabbits—the animals to which the name was first given—are native to central and southern Europe. Many hundreds of years ago some were taken to England, probably by Roman invaders. The wild rabbits served people as an important food. Then it was possible to tame them, and the domestic rabbits proved, like their wild relatives, to be hardy and fast-breeding. Fossils show that this great family began to develop some 30 million years ago.

Because rabbits are so attractive and gentle, it is easy to understand why and how some were turned into pets. Originally their coat color had been grayish brown, but this was lightened until a snow-white fur, such as we see on many pet rabbits, was achieved.

But changes did not stop with the coloring. Breeders worked to develop many variations, and today rabbits come close to rivaling dogs in the variety of breeds. Some are bred especially for commercial purposes. Some are known as particularly fine pets.

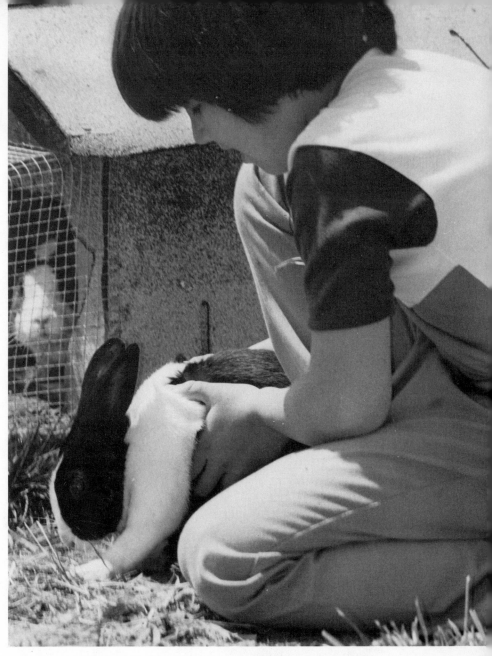

JAMES M. STAPLES PHOTO

Domestic rabbits make fine pets. There is a wide choice of breeds with varying sizes. Adults can weigh less than three pounds or more than twelve.

Albinos, Dutch, English, New Zealand white, and Himalayan are considered top choices as pets. Among these you will find colors ranging between white, gray, black, blue, tan, red, and brown. The size may be as small as the Himalayan (white, with black nose, ears, and feet), which may weigh only two and a half pounds, to the big Belgian hare (reddish tan with black ticking), which could be well over twelve pounds.

With pets that live in conditions not natural to them, the difference between rabbits and hares is of no great concern. The same kind of care serves for both. But in a natural state, there is an important contrast in their way of life. True hares give birth to young that are well-covered with soft fur and have their eyes wide open. Newborn rabbits are naked, blind, and helpless. Hares nest on the surface of the ground. Rabbits make their home in underground burrows. Hares are larger than rabbits.

But despite the differences between them, the general pattern of life for both rabbits and hares is much the same. All are vegetarians and all live on land.

In making friends with any breed, as with other pets, your approach should be slow and gentle. If you give a rabbit comfortable quarters, quietly stroke its back from time and time, and offer it food from your fingers, in several days it will be anxious to follow you and be willing to be picked up.

Here is where a serious mistake often is made. The long ears give the impression of being made-to-order handles with which to lift the animal into your arms. The truth is, the ears are delicate; the cartilage can easily be hurt or even broken. A rabbit should be lifted by pushing one hand under its rump while the other hand grasps the loose skin over the shoulders.

Wild rabbits and hares are said not to be successful pets. If they are rescued as orphaned babies, they may become tame and friendly, but often they do not thrive in captivity.

An exceptional case was a wild rabbit owned by Beatrix Potter who, many years ago, wrote and illustrated the famous story about Peter Rabbit's adventures in Mr. McGregor's vegetable garden. Her model for the pictures was the rabbit she had been enjoying as a pet for nine years. He died just before *The Tale of Peter Rabbit* was completed.

COLD-BLOODED PETS
snake, turtle, lizard, salamander

9

There are people who feel that any pet must be an animal that is furred, warm, and cuddly. They cannot understand how anyone would want the companionship of a reptile or any other cold-blooded creature.

Nevertheless, countless girls and boys do want to adopt such animals.

Not surprisingly, we find the care of cold-blooded pets is somewhat different from that for warm-blooded. Warm-blooded animals have an internal heating system that keeps the body at a high, constant temperature. Cold-blooded animals, such as reptiles and amphibians, do not have this internal heat, and their bodies become hot or cold according to the temperature surrounding them.

This difference is important to remember. Sun shining directly on you may feel quite comfortable, but it can be uncomfortable and even dangerous to a reptile or amphibian whose body will continually absorb the heat, becoming hotter and hotter. A snake or lizard enjoys sunshine for limited periods, but there must always be a shady area to which it can retreat. A salamander or frog should always be able to get to water, or at least to a damp, cool place.

Many cold-blooded animals do not need to be fed daily. A snake, for example, may thrive on one good meal a week. (Some need food more frequently, or less, depending on their size.) But providing their meals is not a simple matter of opening cans or using leftovers from the family table, as with many mammal pets.

Where living under natural conditions, snakes eat live food such as rodents, insects, worms, and other snakes. You may be able to capture such supplies, but it probably will not be easy. Or you may buy them at a pet shop. You may even buy some frozen, defrosting as needed. Some snakes learn to accept dead animal food quite easily, especially if you move it around slowly. Some will even eat chopped raw meat.

Many contrasts are found between different kinds of snakes, not only in appearance and their natural way of life, but in their dispositions. Some are nervous and quick-moving; others are placid and gentle. But one factor overshadows all

99

JAMES M. STAPLES PHOTO

The owner of a reptile sometimes finds it hard to convince friends that it is a desirable pet. However, explanations about the anatomy and habits of snakes usually create interest.

100

others in deciding on a pet. Is it poisonous or non-poisonous?

This is an easy decision to make, for no dangerous animal should be kept in captivity unless for professional reasons. A venomous snake presents a very definite danger. Even zoologists who have poisonous reptiles for study purposes, and who are expert at snake-handling, sometimes meet with disaster. An unguarded second—an unexpected move by the snake—and fangs can sink into flesh with serious, if not fatal, results.

Fortunately there are plenty of interesting choices among non-poisonous species. Possibly the most popular as pets are garter snakes, found all over North America near streams and ponds and in woodlands and damp meadows. They adapt well to captivity and are likely to become gentle and friendly enough to take food from their owner's fingers.

Hognose snakes also are popular favorites. They are found in many areas of the United States, usually in sandy localities, but sometimes in woodlands. This snake was named for its unusual upturned nose which suggests the shovel-like snout of a hog. It is an expert actor, playing out one or two dramatic scenes to bluff a suspected enemy. First it will flatten its neck and head (much as a cobra does) and hiss. If this isn't frightening enough to banish the threat, the snake flops on its back, imitating death (a bluf-

101

fing act for which opossums also are noted). In captivity a hognose becomes very gentle, and does not object to being handled.

Green snakes make pretty pets, and the eastern rough green species is rather spectacular. It is slender but may reach a length of nearly four feet. The smooth green species attains only about half that length. All are good pets if given a large enough cage and some branches on which to climb.

Some non-poisonous species, such as milk snakes and racers, do not thrive in captivity. They should not be captured because in natural surroundings they help to keep rodent pests under control.

A snake has an enormous number of ribs—sometimes as many as three hundred pairs—loosely attached to the backbone. Each free end is attached to a small shield on the outside of the skin, beneath the body. The ribs can move forward, a pair at a time, thrusting forward the shields to which they are fastened. At each movement the shield grips a rough spot on the ground below and, by this action, the snake is able to crawl.

The length of the body in proportion to the tail length varies with different species. But in any case a snake should be well supported when it is picked up. It is hard on the animal to be dangled as if it were a piece of rope.

We might say that snakes need understanding more than any other kind of animal, simply because they have been so constantly misunderstood through many centuries. When certain things are explained, even people who might never want one for a pet find them interesting and not repulsive.

For instance, a snake is not trying to hypnotize a victim with its unblinking, staring eyes; it simply has no eyelids to close. Nor is it being threatening when it sticks out its forked tongue; this is done to bring tiny particles into the mouth where a sense organ can detect what lies close by. Snakes are not slimy; the body is covered with scales (their colors combine to form various patterns) and over the scales is a delicate skin.

Snakes grow at varying rates, largely depending on the amount of food one eats in a season. As the body grows, the skin does not. Therefore it must be cast off whenever it has stretched to its limit.

If a pet snake begins to look dull in color and its eyes have a milky appearance, you will know that molting is about to take place. After a week or two, the skin breaks loose around the jaws. Then the snake rubs against rocks or other objects to help pull the skin back over its head.

A snake that lives indoors sometimes has trouble molting, especially if the air is very dry. Setting a shallow pan of water in the cage helps—if the snake will crawl through it. However, if the snake is slow to "catch on," you may cover it with a wet cloth once or twice.

During a shedding period the eyesight becomes dulled as the old eye caps—actually a part of the skin—are pushed away from the new ones underneath and an oily fluid comes between the two. At such times even a docile pet is likely to strike at any moving object. It is confused because it cannot see as usual.

Snakes fit well into the part-time pet category. That is, they may be caught in the spring, enjoyed until late summer, then released. When this is done, they should be given their freedom very near the place where they were captured. In this way they readjust more quickly to their natural world.

Turtles are among the most popular of reptile pets. They are quite easy to capture and can be bought at many pet shops. There are a number of species, including water-loving turtles and the land-roving tortoise. Not all have the same needs, and it is important to know the habits of any kind you wish to care for.

Since turtles on the whole seem to be associated with water, new owners often put one or two into a bowl of water or an aquarium, and expect them to thrive there. They definitely will not, unless they happen to be marine turtles— and these are not good pet material. Islands on which they can enjoy sun and air are needed, and soil in which to dig.

On the other hand, some turtle owners think that desert turtles do not need any water, and

JAMES M. STAPLES PHOTO

A turtle's shell is its protection against many kinds of dangers. But a pet that feels safe will "stick its neck out" to be friendly.

that they will not become overheated, even in a blazing sun. As a matter of fact, they can die in a short time under such conditions. They must have plenty of shade, with drinking water always available.

Painted turtles—those that grow their own decorations—are most attractive with their bright-colored stripes or blotches. But often "fake" painted turtles are sold, the paint having been put on by human hands. This paint causes the shell to soften and prevents its growing normally. If you should acquire one of these, the

105

paint should be removed immediately by carefully scrapping or peeling it off the shell.

Unlike snakes, turtles have movable eyelids. Their sight is sharp and they can distinguish colors almost as well as we can.

One reason turtles often do not thrive as pets is because they are fed commercial "turtle food," which consists of ant eggs. This is a poor substitute for their natural diet of worms, grubs, insects, and fish. Small worms, mealworms, and finely cut meat should be made available to them.

Anyone who has a garden should be able to enjoy the companionship of a box turtle, a species that spends most of its time on land. Usually when they are found, box turtles are at least half grown, and too large to be comfortably kept indoors. However, if given a home in an enclosed garden, with a large, shallow pan of water, they will be active and content through the spring and summer. When cold weather is due, they must have an area—either outdoors or indoors— in which to dig for hibernation. Or they can be released into their natural surroundings. Some individuals have been known to live on a farm or in a suburban yard for a number of years.

Lizards are closely related to snakes. In fact, they resemble small snakes, except that most lizards have legs, while snakes never do. Many kinds become very tame if kept in a suitable terrarium.

106

Often people buy one of these little reptiles at a circus or fair, where it is called a chameleon. While true chameleons *are* lizards, they are not a kind that is native to the United States, and they are rare pet shop offerings. They belong to the Old World—especially to Africa.

The correct name of the lizard sold so commonly is the anole. There are certain resemblances between these two, but it is principally because the anole can change color much as the true chameleon does that the name chameleon has been borrowed for its American "cousin."

Fortunately the anole proves quite hardy in captivity if kept in a warm, sunny place and fed properly. When you watch one changing color, it is interesting to understand what is happening: Beneath the skin are a number of tiny cells containing pigments of various colors. Changing conditions, or emotions, cause the lizard to expand or contract these cells and the positions of the pigments are changed. Those that move toward the surface become responsible for the animal's color.

Salamanders often are mistaken for lizards because they have a similar form. But the salamander's skin is smooth, with no scales such as a lizard has. Its legs are quite small; there are no claws on its toes. And a big difference is that lizards are reptiles while salamanders are amphibians. Salamanders have more need of water and should never be handled with dry hands.

Small reptiles and amphibians furnish an interesting hobby if you house them in a terrarium or vivarium. By either of these names, such a home is an enclosure—perhaps no larger than $3' \times 2'$, perhaps much larger—where animals and plants live together in a well-balanced environment. It should be planted to reproduce a woodland, a desert, or a marsh, depending on the type of animal that will live there. Plants may be ordered from suppliers or at well-stocked florists.

There is much to be learned from life in a terrarium, but study must be done before starting one. How many animals can be supported? (Overcrowding must surely be avoided.) What kinds will live peacefully together? Which natural environment should be furnished?

Books are available which give detailed advice and make a terrarium workable right from the start.

AQUARIUM
PERSONALITIES
goldfish, tropical fish

10

Each year, in the United States alone, millions of goldfish are bought for home aquariums. This popularity is not surprising, for not only are they interesting, they decorate any room in which they are kept.

Goldfish come from a hardy stock, and taking care of them requires little effort. They belong to the carp family—fishes found commonly in many parts of the world. It was in China many generations ago that people first became interested in the golden tones that were noticeable on certain carp. They started to capture such individuals and encouraged their breeding, and this selective work continued until an overall gold color was achieved.

About a hundred years ago American sailors

brought home some of these "gold fish," and their popularity was immediately established in the United States.

Today there are many varieties, not only the solid gold, but gold marked with black, purple, or silver; or they may be solid black. The color is mainly the effect of pigments which, for the most part, are scattered in the surface layers of the skin and are visible through the scales. There is some color in the scales also.

Besides the simple streamlined form, there are fantails, fringetails, and other fancy models.

Young goldfish and young wild carp are much alike in looks, including their brownish color. But as they grow, the carp becomes black while the goldfish takes on its exotic hues.

Among the questions that occur to people watching goldfish are: How can they stay quietly in one place, neither sinking nor rising, with no apparent effort? Why do they seem to be drinking all the time? Don't they ever sleep? Their eyes are always wide open. How can they learn to come when called at feeding time? They don't appear to have ears.

The power to remain so easily suspended in the water is due to a swim bladder in the forward part of the body that holds a mixture of oxygen, nitrogen, and a trace of carbon dioxide. Most fish with skeletons made of true bone possess a swim bladder, but sharks and some others with skeletons of gristle do not. They must constantly exercise muscles to remain suspended in water.

When any fish with a swim bladder dies, the body rises to the water's surface. Without one, the body sinks.

A goldfish opening and closing its mouth as if in need of drinking water gives a wrong impression. It is the oxygen in the water that is needed. The water quickly goes out again, passing through two flaps on either side of the head. Beneath the flaps are the gills that extract the oxygen.

Goldfish do sleep (that is, their faculties become completely inactive) but this must happen with wide-open eyes because they have no eyelids to close.

Although fish do not have ears, other sense organs make it possible for them to gain some of the same impressions that we receive through our ears. Goldfish, and some others, can "feel" certain sounds through their skin.

It is true that giving goldfish proper care takes little effort, but it is necessary to understand their needs, simple though they are, and tend them regularly. An aquarium must not be overcrowded, either with fish or plants. Fish must not be overfed. They must not be chilled when water is being changed. Aquarium water taken from a faucet should be allowed to stand until any chlorine evaporates. The aquarium should have some sunlight, but not too much.

A pet store that handles fish can give detailed

information on setting up different styles of aquariums—a "balanced" aquarium, the balance being between fish and plants as in a natural pond, or one without plants. You may have a simple tank without equipment or one with water filters.

Sometimes there are unexplained failures with goldfish; they die in a short time, even though all rules have been followed. Our family had a perplexing experience some years ago when we stocked an aquarium with four goldfish and some plants. One after another, three fish soon died. The fourth lived on, and on, and on—for more than five years. We named him Stanley.

As his companions passed away, we had not replaced them, waiting to see if we were going to lose all. But after Stanley had been with us for a few months, friends asked us to take care of their fish pet while they were away, and we thought this would be a good chance to let Stanley associate with another goldfish.

Fortunately when we slid the visitor into Stanley's tank, we stayed to watch; it didn't take long for Stanley to attack. Quickly we scooped the newcomer into a net and put it back in the fish bowl in which it had arrived. Obviously Stanley was going to resent other fish in his aquarium.

After a while we did add a pond snail to his kingdom, and this was acceptable. The snail, too, flourished, and we named him Perry Mason after the fictional sleuth-lawyer. We had begun to

WIDE WORLD PHOTOS

The wonders of underwater life can be brought into the home with an aquarium and a variety of fish.

wonder if, in some mysterious way, Stanley had been responsible for the sad fate of his fellow-goldfish. Perhaps a Perry Mason stalking through water plants would solve The Case of the Disappearing Goldfish. Needless to say, we are still wondering.

Goldfish seldom breed in an aquarium, but it is not unusual for them to produce offspring in a pond. In a pond, also, the common goldfish grows quite large—perhaps to as much as a foot in length.

Though there is variety among goldfish, it is

nothing compared with the vast number of choices we find with tropical fish. Many species of many families have been brought from South America, Africa, and the waters of other tropical areas to the United States. Today their descendants are so numerous there is little need to import more, except for the rarer species.

Probably the most widely known of all tropical aquarium fish are guppies, which originally were brought from Trinidad. Although not especially attractive, they were interesting and were noted for the large families they produced, even in captivity. And thanks to selective breeding, today we have many beautiful color varieties and fin forms.

Tropical fish divide into two main groups—those which produce living young and those which lay eggs. Guppies belong to the first group.

Anyone interested in raising fish is happy with this type because the newborn fry are considerably larger than those hatched from eggs, and they are easier to raise. A female carries eggs within her body for about four weeks, then they hatch internally and are released. One thing must be watched: Some species will eat their young as fast as they can catch them.

Closely related to guppies are the mollies. There are a number of different species. Their popular names, such as lyre-tailed molly and sailfin molly, give a good idea of their appearance. Their markings vary, though black is predominant as a color.

Popular among the egg-layers are the killifish. Here again there are a number of attractive species, some of which are hardy and may be long-time aquarium pets. However, in spite of good care, certain species have a short life-span.

People who choose Siamese fighting fish enjoy them for their beauty rather than the activity they take their name from—fighting. Therefore males cannot be kept in the same tank or their gorgeous fins become torn and battered. In Thailand and other parts of Southeast Asia, where these fish originated, their fighting is a popular sport, with much money being bet on fish fights.

The Siamese fighter is one of a family of "labyrinth" fish, so named because of their unique breathing apparatus. Instead of taking oxygen from the water in the usual manner, they gulp in air at the water's surface, using a branching structure of gills (the labyrinth) to extract the oxygen. As a result they can better survive in polluted water, be it in an aquarium or in their natural habitat.

Among the most colorful of tropical fish are the barbs. Besides having attractive color normally, at spawning time they take on new, striking hues. With the rosy barb, for example, the males become bright red with dusty black fins.

It is important to remember that most tropical fish are jumpers, and they can leap quite easily

115

out of an average-size aquarium. As a prevention, a glass cover may be placed over the top, loosely fitted so that air can get in.

Another overall necessity is to provide warmth. Some fish can survive a considerable variation in temperature, but tropical species do not. Their average water temperature should be from 70° to 80°, with as little variation as possible.

Tropical fish very often become more than pets; they furnish a major hobby for many families. Advice and news concerning them may be found in magazines, pamphlets, newspapers, and books.

INTERESTING INSECTS
butterfly, ant, cricket, praying mantis

11

Insects are "something else" in the world of pets, being quite different from mammals, reptiles, amphibians, and fish. All these animals are vertebrates, that is, they have backbones. Insects are part of the second great division of the animal kingdom, the invertebrates—creatures without a backbone.

Some insects, such as those that pollinate plants, are extremely valuable to us. Others, such as disease-spreading flies, do great harm. But until recently almost no kind of insect would have been considered as a pet.

Today, however, we can buy the materials to start producing our own butterflies, to study ants at home, and to house a cheerful cricket. Perhaps such interests are considered more as hobbies

A. W. AMBLER
FROM NATIONAL AUDUBON SOCIETY

A "painted lady" is one of the most colorful of butterflies, and this species is one of the best for raising in the home.

than pet care. Yet it is hard not to feel some affection for butterflies that you watch develop from tiny caterpillars, ants that you see working industriously in their colony, or a cricket that chirps so tunefully.

Butterfly-raising with a high degree of success has come about only recently. For many years people who enjoyed nature study sometimes brought caterpillars or cocoons into their homes, hoping to watch them develop. But because of many factors involved, the adult insects would only rarely materialize.

The work of two scientists, Carlos White and John Nickelsen, of Shafter, California, changed this. Their major work had been for farmers, controlling insect pests. Then a novel idea occurred to them: Why not create "butterfly gardens" in which people could watch the metamorphosis from larva to pupa to butterfly?

A number of important facts had to be considered. Only species could be used that were not considered pests in any parts of the country. This narrowed their choice to just a few, among them the handsome orange and black monarchs. However, these are long-lived butterflies and it takes about six months for them to go through the development stages.

Finally two satisfactory species were decided on, the painted lady and the buckeye.

The next big problem was: What kind of food could be furnished for quantities of growing caterpillars? In a natural state they would live on such plants as thistles, nettles, and sunflowers. It was not practical to package this diet for future use.

The "butterfly producers" worked out one formula that the caterpillars ate contentedly, and went on to become chrysalides which in turn became butterflies. But there was still a problem. They were butterflies that could not fly! They were not able to inflate their wings.

More experimenting went on, and finally a mixture of the malva plant, cooked and combined with vitamins and antibiotics, proved successful. When the furry caterpillars are fully grown and the chrysalides emerge, there is no more feeding concern; chrysalides do not eat. The adult butterflies need only sweetened water, comparable to flower nectar.

The caterpillars are sold when about half grown, and they are packaged with enough food to take care of their needs. There is also a container to serve as their first home, where they will attach themselves to the inside of its cover until they become chrysalides. Within the chrysalis, for a week or more (the time depending on the temperature), parts of the caterpillar body are changing into the different parts that form the butterfly.

The chrysalides are now ready to be put into their second home—the butterfly garden. In a few days the winged adults appear. Having been nourished with a proper diet in the beginning, they crawl up the side of the garden, pause, and pump their wings to full size by forcing blood through the veins.

In one or two hours the wings have hardened and the butterflies are ready for flight. Now they may be kept as "pets" for a few days and then, if the season is right, given their freedom. Kept indoors, they may live about two weeks.

Butterfly gardens may be bought at a number of hobby shops and toy stores. Scientists White and Nickelsen supply them by mail if ordered from Insect Lore Products, P.O. Box 1591, Shafter, California 93263.

The painted lady butterfly is well named. The upper sides of the wings are decorated with red, orange, blue, brown, and black markings and white spots. The underwings have still more patterns and colors.

We could not find more of a contrast in insect pets than butterflies—beautiful and apparently so carefree—and ants—dull in appearance and involved endlessly with work. Still, for insect-watchers, no kind gives more fascinating performances than the lowly ant.

Of course we would never understand much about these insects from watching one individual. Each life is so much a part of an entire colony that we need a whole group to observe. Their living quarters may be constructed as a do-it-yourself project, or they may be bought in hobby shops. Usually when an ant home is purchased, the ants come along with it. But if you are collecting your own, you must know what to look for.

A kind that does well in captive living is a small brown species, commonly known as the garden or cornfield ant. They are very numerous, and may be found in cities as well as countryside in many parts of North America.

Colonies are made up of three principal types—a queen, the males, and infertile females

121

(the workers). Colonies vary greatly in size. One that has been established only about a year will have about twenty-five workers. Older colonies have many more, and their nest covers a much larger area. For home observation, a small group is best.

If you capture a queen (recognizable because of her larger size) and secure a number of larvae and pupae, you should, in time, see the entire cycle of life, from egg to adult. But even without a queen, the workers put on quite a show. They

Three "garden" ants (the kind often kept in captivity) are exploring a slice of bread in this enlarged photo. Their true size may be estimated by comparing them with the breadcrumbs and the "spike," which actually is a common straight pin.

BERNARD L. GLUCK
FROM NATIONAL AUDUBON SOCIETY

excavate tunnels, lick themselves clean, feed on the food and water you provide, stretch, and lie down to sleep before getting back to work again.

A colony requires little care. Water inserted into the soil about once a week, and tiny bits of apple, banana, walnuts, lean cooked meat, and dry bread crumbs form a good basic diet. A drop of honey every few days satisfies their need for sweets.

Well-fed and sheltered from bright light (if their home has glass sides, these must be covered except when you are observing), the ants work diligently. You will be amazed at how much they accomplish with tiny claws and outer jaws as their only tools.

A single cricket may be kept through the winter with happy results. During summer and fall this insect is heard much more than it is seen; its chirping is one of nature's most cheerful sounds. Most crickets die with the arrival of cold weather but, kept in the warmth of a house, one may well live through the winter.

A cricket "cage" may be a terrarium, landscaped with grass, plants, and rocks, or it may be a large flowerpot filled with earth. A glass chimney (the kind used for kerosene lamps), sunk well into the soil and topped with mosquito netting held firm with a rubber band, keeps your insect guest confined. Bits of lettuce, apples, and other fruit, dry crackers and cake provide nourishment to make your cricket sing happily.

Although we speak of a cricket's "song," a more accurate description would be his "playing," because these insects have no larynx or lungs with which to produce sounds. Theirs are made by friction and vibration. There is a scraper and file on each front wing cover, and rubbing the files against the scrapers sets up a series of musical vibrations. Only the males give this performance.

To hear a cricket chorus on a summer evening, you gain the impression that this is a sociable group of insects. However, kept indoors, in one enclosure, they are inclined to fight, sometimes quite savagely. It is best to keep them in separate compartments if you have more than one.

Cricket pets really are not a new idea. In China they have been popular with children and adults for many years.

The praying mantis is another good tenant for a terrarium, and it is often enjoyed as an indoor pet. Some mail order houses ship mantid egg clusters to customers. The eggs hatch at the proper season for the young insects to be released outdoors.

Spooky in appearance, fascinating in actions, mantids are fun as well as being valuable. In the Orient they are sometimes tied near a bedroom window with a silk thread so they can trap mosquitoes and other flies.

Mantids are native to the United States, but

the most common species in this country was imported—brought here less than a hundred years
ago from the Far East. These Oriental mantids
are larger than any of our native species, and it
was thought they would be helpful because they
would destroy many garden pests such as aphids
and plant lice. They also eat lady beetles and
other valuable insects, however, so they cannot
be considered entirely beneficial. Their close
relatives, grasshoppers and katydids, often become their victims. And a female mantis is apt to

*A praying mantis can be an interesting creature to
have in a terrarium. Mantids also may be raised
from the egg stage and released as adults in a garden.*

DR. WILLIAM J. JAHODA
FROM NATIONAL AUDUBON SOCIETY

eat her slightly smaller mate once mating has taken place.

People sometimes wonder how to tell the difference between mantids and grasshoppers. There are a number of resemblances, but no grasshopper ever assumes the attitude of prayer, with forelegs upraised, that is typical of a mantis. Those front limbs are not used for walking; they are innocently folded until the insect is within snatching distance of its prey.

Another recognizable feature of the mantis is its long neck-like thorax. On this "neck" it can turn its head so that the great black eyes look to either side and even backward. This is something no other insect can do.

So many different animals—from insects to horses, from birds to cats and dogs—give us abundant variety from which to choose a pet or pets. But whichever creatures are chosen, it is always important to remember the definition of a pet: "An animal kept as a companion and treated with affection."

BOOKS ON PET CARE

Axelrod, Herbert R. *Axelrod's Tropical Fish Book.* New York: Arco, 1965.

Benson, B. A. *How to Live with a Parakeet.* New York: Julian Messner, 1959.

Carr, William H. A. *The Basic Book of the Cat.* New York: Charles Scribners Sons, 1963.

Clear, Val. *Common Cagebirds in America.* Indianapolis: Bobbs-Merrill, 1966.

Guthrie, Esther L. *The Home Book of Animal Care.* New York: Harper & Row, 1966.

Kramer, Jack. *Pets and Plants in Miniature Gardens.* Garden City, N.Y.: Doubleday, 1973.

Naether, Carl A. *The Book of the Pigeon and of Wild Foreign Doves.* New York: David McKay, 1964.

Pope, Clifford H. *Turtles of the United States and Canada.* New York: Alfred A. Knopf, 1967.

Rine, Josephine Z. *The World of Dogs.* Garden City, N.Y.: Doubleday, 1965.

Self, Margaret Cabell. *Horses: Their Selection, Care and Handling.* New York: A. S. Barnes, 1943.

INDEX